D0871507

new MAGICS

EDITED BY PATRICK NIELSEN HAYDEN

Starlight 1

Starlight 2

Starlight 3

New Skies:

An Anthology of Today's Science Fiction

New Magics:

An Anthology of Today's Fantasy

AN ANTHOLOGY OF TODAY'S FANTASY

EDITED BY

PATRICK NIELSEN HAYDEN

TOR

A TOM DOHERTY ASSOCIATES BOOK

NEW YORK

This is a work of fiction. All the characters and events portrayed in the stories in this collection are either fictitious or are used fictitiously.

NEW MAGICS: AN ANTHOLOGY OF TODAY'S FANTASY

This book is printed on acid-free paper.

Book design by Michael Collica

A Tor Book
Published by Tom Doherty Associates, LLC
175 Fifth Avenue
New York, NY 10010

www.tor.com

Tor® is a registered trademark of Tom Doherty Associates, LLC.

ISBN 0-765-30015-X

First Edition: January 2004

Printed in the United States of America

0 9 8 7 6 5 4 3 2 1

Copyright Acknowledgments

For Teresa,
who was looking for
this book

Contents

Introduction

It's hard to come up with a good definition of fantasy. It's easy to come up with a definition that includes fantasy, but most such definitions also take in a lot of other kinds of storytelling. For instance, it has been observed that, in a sense, all fiction is fantasy. This is true, but it isn't useful.

Here's another: *Fantasy is tales of things that never were and never could be.* That hardly narrows things down at all. Along with fantasy it scoops up folktales, fairy tales, allegories, utopias, and loosely imagined historical novels. Admittedly, many of those do have a strong family resemblance to fantasy literature. Unfortunately, that definition also takes in 95 percent of the dramas ever written, 96 percent of the political memoirs, 97 percent of the spy novels, 98 percent of the real-estate brochures, 99 percent of the comics, 99.5 percent of the operas, and a great many bad novels that were supposed to be realistic, only their authors got things wrong.

Another definition says that *fantasy is tales of marvels and wonders.* This, too, has some truth in it. But the unintended fish caught in this particular net include some religious literature, a lot of science fiction, "Ripley's Believe It or Not!" articles in *Popular Mechanics* magazine, and travel writers from Marco Polo to Richard Halliburton.

And so forth. We could go on this way for a long time, trying this definition and that; and at the end, all we'd know is that no definition of fantasy is perfect. We can skip that. If you already know that a road is a dead end, you don't have to drive all the way to the end of it. Instead, we can turn around and look at how fantasy works.

There's a rule for what makes good fantasy work, and it's as strange as any riddle ever asked in a fairy tale: *In fantasy, you can do anything; and therefore, the one thing you must not do is "just anything."* Why? Because in a story where anything can happen and anything can be true, nothing matters. You have no reason to care what happens. It's all arbitrary, and arbitrary isn't interesting.

Say there's a path through a forest, and a knight comes riding along. You, being the reader, are standing by the side of that path, maybe floating a few feet in the air so you can see better. You're invisible, as readers always are. And you can hear the hoofbeats of the horse on the path as the knight approaches.

He comes into view. The horse is tall. The knight is also tall, and wears armor. He carries a shield, painted green, that has a shining gold star on it. This is good. You watch the knight to see what will happen next.

But wait! Did I mention that he wears a heavily embroidered surcote over his armor? He does. It's embroidered all around with a dozen different knightly and heraldic emblems, one for each month in the year; and each symbolizes a different virtue. His horse isn't just any horse; it's a noble and fiery steed, with a curving neck, a flowing mane and tail, and an expressive eye that shows an almost human intelligence. The horse's trappings—that's the harness, the saddle, and all the bits of draped cloth—are made of fairest samite, richly ornamented, with deeply cut and scalloped edges; and from each pointy bit on the scalloping there hangs a tiny silver bell. Furthermore, it's a magic horse. And there's a noble hawk perched on the knight's shoulder, and it's a magic hawk. And the knight is magic; in fact, he's an elf from the planet Vulcan. And the knight's sword is magic too, and has twelve different jewels set in its handle, each with a different magical power—

I'll bet you're starting to roll your eyes. Somewhere in there it will have occurred to you that it's just as easy to type "magic horse" as "horse," and no more expensive to write "fairest samite" than "rough woolen fabric." It stopped being a story, and turned into nothing but words. Once you notice it's arbitrary, you stop believing and cease to care. This is the curse of the arbitrary, the too-much, the easily-had: it means nothing.

But say the man who comes riding down the path is just a tall knight on a tall horse. Winter has set in. The afternoon's already growing dark, and the forest is deep and wild. The knight should be at home, far from here, at the court of Camelot. There it's warm by the fire, and everyone he loves in this world will be bustling about, laughing and making old jokes, as they get ready for Christmas.

He should be there, but he isn't, because a year ago an extraordinary thing happened. On Christmas Day, a strange knight—a huge man, green from head to toe, holding a green ax, wearing green armor—rode a green horse straight in through the door of King Arthur's court at Camelot, and issued a challenge. That's a fancy way of saying, "I dare you." The Green Knight dared the knights of the Round Table to come forward and strike him one blow with his own ax. Twelve months and a day later, he'll return the blow.

Nobody wanted to do it. It was all too weird. But dares mean a lot to knights—it's one of their rules—so finally King Arthur said he'd accept the challenge. At that point our knight—his name is Gawain, by the way—jumped up and said no, he'd do it. He's one of the greatest knights of the Round Table, not that he'd mention it himself, and it's only proper that he should be the one to take up the challenge.

The Green Knight gave him the ax and knelt down, baring his neck. Gawain took a deep breath, hefted the ax (it's heavy), took one huge swing, and *wham!* He cut the Green Knight's head clean off. The head went rolling and skittering across the floor like a bowling ball, bumping into the guests' feet, getting blood all over everything. Then the Green Knight's body stood up from where it was kneeling, walked over to the head, picked it up by the hair, and got back on the horse, holding his head up like a lantern. The head's eyes opened. "See you in a year, Gawain," he said, and rode away.

It's been almost a year since then, getting close to Christmas. That's why Gawain is off in the wilderness, looking for the Green Knight's castle. He knows it wasn't a fair challenge. He figures he's going to die. But he's Sir Gawain, most honorable of knights, and he said he'd do it; so here he is.

This is not a story in which "just anything" can happen. It's a story in which very few things can happen, and so far only one of them has been magic. By the time Gawain comes riding down that forest path, the story's down to a handful of possible outcomes. Gawain may or may not find the castle. The Green Knight may or may not cut off his head. And Gawain may or may not continue to be the most honorable knight in the world, which for him is the really important part.

And how about us, the invisible readers, standing there watching him ride through the forest? It's time for a test. If I'm right about how fantasy works, you're going to feel a little bit ticked at me for not telling you how the story comes out.

There are a lot of different ways a story can mean something to us. Caring how it comes out is one of them.

(I'm not going to tell you. Sorry about that. It's a cool story. You'll have to read it for yourself.)

And a word here about what we mean when we talk about fantasy meaning something to the reader. What we *don't* mean is one of those dumb worksheet study-question systems where the knight symbolizes courage, and the Green Knight's challenge symbolizes the fine print at the bottom of contracts that you should always remember to read before signing, and the road symbolizes the writer's subconscious, and the wilderness symbolizes the wilderness only not the one you're thinking of, and the knight's horse symbolizes the oppression of the working class. No. When everything in a story means a specific something else, and it means that something else more than it means itself, what you have is *allegory*: a kind of writing almost no one does well. Allegory is frequently irritating, and seldom successful.

Fantasy can mean things in a lot of different ways. It doesn't always have to be black and white, good vs. evil, fate of the world hangs in the balance, et cetera. Sometimes it's just telling you something about how the world works, or making room in the understood universe for something that wasn't there before.

And it doesn't always take place in Europe during the Middle Ages. Check out the stories in this collection and see. Some of them take place in Appalachia during the Depression, or on the American frontier during the nineteenth century, or in New York City right now. Some are sad, some are funny. You'll see.

We won't tell you what to make of them. We know you can do that for yourself. Have a good time doing it.

—Patrick and Teresa Nielsen Hayden

new MAGICS

Neil Gaiman is the author of the enormously popular graphic novel series Sandman *and of several acclaimed fantasy novels, including* Neverwhere, Stardust, Coraline, *and the Hugo and Nebula Award–winning* American Gods.

Chivalry

NEIL GAIMAN

Mrs. Whitaker found the Holy Grail; it was under a fur coat. Every Thursday afternoon Mrs. Whitaker walked down to the post office to collect her pension, even though her legs were no longer what they were, and on the way back home she would stop in at the Oxfam Shop and buy herself a little something.

The Oxfam Shop sold old clothes, knickknacks, oddments, bits and bobs, and large quantities of old paperbacks, all of them donations: secondhand flotsam, often the house clearances of the dead. All the profits went to charity.

The shop was staffed by volunteers. The volunteer on duty this afternoon was Marie, seventeen, slightly overweight, and dressed in a baggy mauve jumper that looked like she had bought it from the shop.

Marie sat by the till with a copy of *Modern Woman* magazine, filling out a "Reveal Your Hidden Personality" questionnaire. Every now and then, she'd flip to the back of the magazine and check the relative points assigned to an A), B), or C) answer before making up her mind how she'd respond to the question.

Mrs. Whitaker puttered around the shop.

They still hadn't sold the stuffed cobra, she noted. It had been there for six months now, gathering dust, glass eyes gazing balefully at the clothes racks and the cabinet filled with chipped porcelain and chewed toys.

Mrs. Whitaker patted its head as she went past.

She picked out a couple of Mills & Boon novels from a bookshelf—*Her Thundering Soul* and *Her Turbulent Heart*, a shilling each—and gave careful consideration to the empty bottle of Mateus Rosé with a decorative lampshade on it before deciding she really didn't have anywhere to put it.

She moved a rather threadbare fur coat, which smelled badly of mothballs. Underneath it was a walking stick and a water-stained copy of *Romance and Legend of Chivalry* by A. R. Hope Moncrieff, priced at five pence. Next to the book, on its side, was the Holy Grail. It had a little round paper sticker on the base, and written on it, in felt pen, was the price: 30p.

Mrs. Whitaker picked up the dusty silver goblet and appraised it through her thick spectacles.

"This is nice," she called to Marie.

Marie shrugged.

"It'd look nice on the mantelpiece."

Marie shrugged again.

Mrs. Whitaker gave fifty pence to Marie, who gave her ten pence change and a brown paper bag to put the books and the Holy Grail in. Then she went next door to the butcher's and bought herself a nice piece of liver. Then she went home.

The inside of the goblet was thickly coated with a brownish-red dust. Mrs. Whitaker washed it out with great care, then left it to soak for an hour in warm water with a dash of vinegar added.

Then she polished it with metal polish until it gleamed, and she put it on the mantelpiece in her parlor, where it sat between a small soulful china basset hound and a photograph of her late husband, Henry, on the beach at Frinton in 1953.

She had been right: It did look nice.

For dinner that evening she had the liver fried in breadcrumbs with onions. It was very nice.

The next morning was Friday; on alternate Fridays Mrs. Whitaker and Mrs. Greenberg would visit each other. Today it was Mrs. Greenberg's turn to visit Mrs. Whitaker. They sat in the parlor and ate macaroons and drank tea. Mrs. Whitaker took one sugar in her tea, but Mrs. Greenberg took sweetener, which she always carried in her handbag in a small plastic container.

"That's nice," said Mrs. Greenberg, pointing to the Grail. "What is it?"

"It's the Holy Grail," said Mrs. Whitaker. "It's the cup that Jesus drunk out of at the Last Supper. Later, at the Crucifixion, it caught His precious blood when the centurion's spear pierced His side."

Mrs. Greenberg sniffed. She was small and Jewish and didn't hold with unsanitary things. "I wouldn't know about that," she said, "but it's very nice. Our Myron got one just like that when he won the swimming tournament, only it's got his name on the side."

"Is he still with that nice girl? The hairdresser?"

"Bernice? Oh yes. They're thinking of getting engaged," said Mrs. Greenberg.

"That's nice," said Mrs. Whitaker. She took another macaroon.

Mrs. Greenberg baked her own macaroons and brought them over every alternate Friday: small sweet light brown biscuits with almonds on top.

They talked about Myron and Bernice, and Mrs. Whitaker's

nephew Ronald (she had had no children), and about their friend Mrs. Perkins who was in hospital with her hip, poor dear.

At midday Mrs. Greenberg went home, and Mrs. Whitaker made herself cheese on toast for lunch, and after lunch Mrs. Whitaker took her pills; the white and the red and two little orange ones.

The doorbell rang.

Mrs. Whitaker answered the door. It was a young man with shoulder-length hair so fair it was almost white, wearing gleaming silver armor, with a white surcoat.

"Hello," he said.

"Hello," said Mrs. Whitaker.

"I'm on a quest," he said.

"That's nice," said Mrs. Whitaker, noncommittally.

"Can I come in?" he asked.

Mrs. Whitaker shook her head. "I'm sorry, I don't think so," she said.

"I'm on a quest for the Holy Grail," the young man said. "Is it here?"

"Have you got any identification?" Mrs. Whitaker asked. She knew that it was unwise to let unidentified strangers into your home when you were elderly and living on your own. Handbags get emptied, and worse than that.

The young man went back down the garden path. His horse, a huge gray charger, big as a shire-horse, its head high and its eyes intelligent, was tethered to Mrs. Whitaker's garden gate. The knight fumbled in the saddlebag and returned with a scroll.

It was signed by Arthur, King of All Britons, and charged all persons of whatever rank or station to know that here was Galaad, Knight of the Table Round, and that he was on a Right High and Noble Quest. There was a drawing of the young man below that. It wasn't a bad likeness.

Mrs. Whitaker nodded. She had been expecting a little card with a photograph on it, but this was far more impressive.

"I suppose you had better come in," she said.

They went into her kitchen. She made Galaad a cup of tea, then she took him into the parlor.

Galaad saw the Grail on her mantelpiece, and dropped to one knee. He put down the teacup carefully on the russet carpet. A shaft of light came through the net curtains and painted his awed face with golden sunlight and turned his hair into a silver halo.

"It is truly the Sangrail," he said, very quietly. He blinked his pale blue eyes three times, very fast, as if he were blinking back tears.

He lowered his head as if in silent prayer.

Galaad stood up again and turned to Mrs. Whitaker. "Gracious lady, keeper of the Holy of Holies, let me now depart this place with the Blessed Chalice, that my journeyings may be ended and my geas fulfilled."

"Sorry?" said Mrs. Whitaker.

Galaad walked over to her and took her old hands in his. "My quest is over," he told her. "The Sangrail is finally within my reach."

Mrs. Whitaker pursed her lips. "Can you pick your teacup and saucer up, please?" she said.

Galaad picked up his teacup apologetically.

"No. I don't think so," said Mrs. Whitaker. "I rather like it there. It's just right, between the dog and the photograph of my Henry."

"Is it gold you need? Is that it? Lady, I can bring you gold . . ."

"No," said Mrs. Whitaker. "I don't want any gold thank *you*. I'm simply not interested."

She ushered Galaad to the front door. "Nice to meet you," she said.

His horse was leaning its head over her garden fence, nibbling her gladioli. Several of the neighborhood children were standing on the pavement, watching it.

Galaad took some sugar lumps from the saddlebag and showed the braver of the children how to feed the horse, their hands held flat. The children giggled. One of the older girls stroked the horse's nose.

Galaad swung himself up onto the horse in one fluid movement. Then the horse and the knight trotted off down Hawthorne Crescent.

Mrs. Whitaker watched them until they were out of sight, then sighed and went back inside.

The weekend was quiet.

On Saturday Mrs. Whitaker took the bus into Maresfield to visit her nephew Ronald, his wife Euphonia, and their daughters, Clarissa and Dillian. She took them a currant cake she had baked herself.

On Sunday morning Mrs. Whitaker went to church. Her local church was St. James the Less, which was a little more "Don't think of this as a church, think of it as a place where like-minded friends hang out and are joyful" than Mrs. Whitaker felt entirely comfortable with, but she liked the vicar, the Reverend Bartholomew, when he wasn't actually playing the guitar.

After the service, she thought about mentioning to him that she had the Holy Grail in her front parlor, but decided against it.

On Monday morning Mrs. Whitaker was working in the back garden. She had a small herb garden she was extremely proud of: dill, vervain, mint, rosemary, thyme, and a wild expanse of parsley. She was down on her knees, wearing thick green gardening gloves, weeding, and picking out slugs and putting them in a plastic bag.

Mrs. Whitaker was very tenderhearted when it came to

slugs. She would take them down to the back of her garden, which bordered on the railway line, and throw them over the fence.

She cut some parsley for the salad. There was a cough behind her. Galaad stood there, tall and beautiful, his armor glinting in the morning sun. In his arms he held a long package, wrapped in oiled leather.

"I'm back," he said.

"Hello," said Mrs. Whitaker. She stood up, rather slowly, and took off her gardening gloves. "Well," she said, "now you're here, you might as well make yourself useful."

She gave him the plastic bag full of slugs and told him to tip the slugs out over the back of the fence.

He did.

Then they went into the kitchen.

"Tea? Or lemonade?" she asked.

"Whatever you're having," Galaad said.

Mrs. Whitaker took a jug of her homemade lemonade from the fridge and sent Galaad outside to pick a sprig of mint. She selected two tall glasses. She washed the mint carefully and put a few leaves in each glass, then poured the lemonade.

"Is your horse outside?" she asked.

"Oh yes. His name is Grizzel."

"And you've come a long way, I suppose."

"A very long way."

"I see," said Mrs. Whitaker. She took a blue plastic basin from under the sink and half-filled it with water. Galaad took it out to Grizzel. He waited while the horse drank and brought the empty basin back to Mrs. Whitaker.

"Now," she said, "I suppose you're still after the Grail."

"Aye, still do I seek the Sangrail," he said. He picked up the leather package from the floor, put it down on her tablecloth and unwrapped it. "For it, I offer you this."

It was a sword, its blade almost four feet long. There were

words and symbols traced elegantly along the length of the blade. The hilt was worked in silver and gold, and a large jewel was set in the pommel.

"It's very nice," said Mrs. Whitaker, doubtfully.

"This," said Galaad, "is the sword Balmung, forged by Wayland Smith in the dawn times. Its twin is Flamberge. Who wears it is unconquerable in war, and invincible in battle. Who wears it is incapable of a cowardly act or an ignoble one. Set in its pommel is the sardonyx Bircone, which protects its possessor from poison slipped into wine or ale, and from the treachery of friends."

Mrs. Whitaker peered at the sword. "It must be very sharp," she said, after a while.

"It can slice a falling hair in twain. Nay, it could slice a sunbeam," said Galaad proudly.

"Well, then, maybe you ought to put it away," said Mrs. Whitaker.

"Don't you want it?" Galaad seemed disappointed.

"No, thank you," said Mrs. Whitaker. It occurred to her that her late husband, Henry, would have quite liked it. He would have hung it on the wall in his study next to the stuffed carp he had caught in Scotland, and pointed it out to visitors.

Galaad rewrapped the oiled leather around the sword Balmung and tied it up with white cord.

He sat there, disconsolate.

Mrs. Whitaker made him some cream cheese and cucumber sandwiches for the journey back and wrapped them in greaseproof paper. She gave him an apple for Grizzel. He seemed very pleased with both gifts.

She waved them both good-bye.

That afternoon she took the bus down to the hospital to see Mrs. Perkins, who was still in with her hip, poor love. Mrs. Whitaker took her some homemade fruitcake, although she had left out the walnuts from the recipe, because Mrs. Perkins's teeth weren't what they used to be.

She watched a little television that evening, and had an early night.

On Tuesday the postman called. Mrs. Whitaker was up in the boxroom at the top of the house, doing a spot of tidying, and, taking each step slowly and carefully, she didn't make it downstairs in time. The postman had left her a message which said that he'd tried to deliver a packet, but no one was home.

Mrs. Whitaker sighed.

She put the message into her handbag and went down to the post office.

The package was from her niece Shirelle in Sydney, Australia. It contained photographs of her husband, Wallace, and her two daughters, Dixie and Violet, and a conch shell packed in cotton wool.

Mrs. Whitaker had a number of ornamental shells in her bedroom. Her favorite had a view of the Bahamas done on it in enamel. It had been a gift from her sister, Ethel, who had died in 1983.

She put the shell and the photographs in her shopping bag. Then, seeing that she was in the area, she stopped in at the Oxfam Shop on her way home.

"Hullo, Mrs. W.," said Marie.

Mrs. Whitaker stared at her. Marie was wearing lipstick (possibly not the best shade for her, nor particularly expertly applied, but, thought Mrs. Whitaker, that would come with time) and a rather smart skirt. It was a great improvement.

"Oh. Hello, dear," said Mrs. Whitaker.

"There was a man in here last week, asking about that thing you bought. The little metal cup thing. I told him where to find you. You don't mind, do you?"

"No, dear," said Mrs. Whitaker. "He found me."

"He was really dreamy. Really, really dreamy," sighed Marie wistfully. "I could of gone for him.

"And he had a big white horse and all," Marie concluded. She was standing up straighter as well, Mrs. Whitaker noted approvingly.

On the bookshelf Mrs. Whitaker found a new Mills & Boon novel—*Her Majestic Passion*—although she hadn't yet finished the two she had bought on her last visit.

She picked up the copy of *Romance and Legend of Chivalry* and opened it. It smelled musty. *EX LIBRIS FISHER* was neatly handwritten at the top of the first page in red ink.

She put it down where she had found it.

When she got home, Galaad was waiting for her. He was giving the neighborhood children rides on Grizzel's back, up and down the street.

"I'm glad you're here," she said, "I've got some cases that need moving."

She showed him up to the boxroom in the top of the house. He moved all the old suitcases for her, so she could get to the cupboard at the back.

It was very dusty up there.

She kept him up there most of the afternoon, moving things around while she dusted.

Galaad had a cut on his cheek, and he held one arm a little stiffly.

They talked a little while she dusted and tidied. Mrs. Whitaker told him about her late husband, Henry; and how the life insurance had paid the house off; and how she had all these things, but no one really to leave them to, no one but Ronald really and his wife only liked modern things. She told him how she had met Henry during the war, when he was in the ARP and she hadn't closed the kitchen blackout curtains all the way; and about the sixpenny dances they went to in the town; and how they'd gone to London when the war had ended, and she'd had her first drink of wine.

Galaad told Mrs. Whitaker about his mother Elaine, who was flighty and no better than she should have been and something of a witch to boot; and his grandfather, King Pelles, who was well-meaning although at best a little vague; and of his youth in the Castle of Bliant on the Joyous Isle; and his father, whom he knew as "Le Chevalier Mal Fet," who was more or less completely mad, and was in reality Lancelot du Lac, greatest of knights, in disguise and bereft of his wits; and of Galaad's days as a young squire in Camelot.

At five o'clock Mrs. Whitaker surveyed the boxroom and decided that it met with her approval; then she opened the window so the room could air, and they went downstairs to the kitchen, where she put on the kettle.

Galaad sat down at the kitchen table.

He opened the leather purse at his waist and took out a round white stone. It was about the size of a cricket ball.

"My lady," he said. "This is for you, an you give me the Sangrail."

Mrs. Whitaker picked up the stone, which was heavier than it looked, and held it up to the light. It was milkily translucent, and deep inside it flecks of silver glittered and glinted in the late-afternoon sunlight. It was warm to the touch.

Then, as she held it, a strange feeling crept over her: Deep inside she felt stillness and a sort of peace. *Serenity,* that was the word for it; she felt serene.

Reluctantly she put the stone back on the table.

"It's very nice," she said.

"That is the Philosopher's Stone, which our forefather Noah hung in the Ark to give light when there was no light; it can transform base metals into gold; and it has certain other properties," Galaad told her proudly. "And that isn't all. There's more. Here." From the leather bag he took an egg and handed it to her.

It was the size of a goose egg and was a shiny black color, mottled with scarlet and white. When Mrs. Whitaker touched it, the hairs on the back of her neck prickled. Her immediate impression was one of incredible heat and freedom. She heard the crackling of distant fires, and for a fraction of a second she seemed to feel herself far above the world, swooping and diving on wings of flame.

She put the egg down on the table, next to the Philosopher's Stone.

"That is the Egg of the Phoenix," said Galaad. "From far Araby it comes. One day it will hatch out into the Phoenix Bird itself; and when its time comes, the bird will build a nest of flame, lay its egg, and die, to be reborn in flame in a later age of the world."

"I thought that was what it was," said Mrs. Whitaker.

"And, last of all, lady," said Galaad, "I have brought you this."

He drew it from his pouch, and gave it to her. It was an apple, apparently carved from a single ruby, on an amber stem.

A little nervously, she picked it up. It was soft to the touch—deceptively so: Her fingers bruised it, and ruby-colored juice from the apple ran down Mrs. Whitaker's hand.

The kitchen filled—almost imperceptibly, magically—with the smell of summer fruit, of raspberries and peaches and strawberries and red currants. As if from a great way away she heard distant voices raised in song and far music on the air.

"It is one of the apples of the Hesperides," said Galaad, quietly. "One bite from it will heal any illness or wound, no matter how deep; a second bite restores youth and beauty; and a third bite is said to grant eternal life."

Mrs. Whitaker licked the sticky juice from her hand. It tasted like fine wine.

There was a moment, then, when it all came back to her—how it was to be young: to have a firm, slim body that would do whatever she wanted it to do; to run down a country lane for the simple unladylike joy of running; to have men smile at her just because she was herself and happy about it.

Mrs. Whitaker looked at Sir Galaad, most comely of all knights, sitting fair and noble in her small kitchen.

She caught her breath.

"And that's all I have brought for you," said Galaad. "They weren't easy to get, either."

Mrs. Whitaker put the ruby fruit down on her kitchen table. She looked at the Philosopher's Stone, and the Egg of the Phoenix, and the Apple of Life.

Then she walked into her parlor and looked at the mantelpiece: at the little china basset hound, and the Holy Grail, and the photograph of her late husband Henry, shirtless, smiling and eating an ice cream in black and white, almost forty years away.

She went back into the kitchen. The kettle had begun to whistle. She poured a little steaming water into the teapot, swirled it around, and poured it out. Then she added two spoonfuls of tea and one for the pot and poured in the rest of the water. All this she did in silence.

She turned to Galaad then, and she looked at him.

"Put that apple away," she told Galaad, firmly. "You shouldn't offer things like that to old ladies. It isn't proper."

She paused, then. "But I'll take the other two," she continued, after a moment's thought. "They'll look nice on the mantelpiece. And two for one's fair, or I don't know what is."

Galaad beamed. He put the ruby apple into his leather pouch. Then he went down on one knee, and kissed Mrs. Whitaker's hand.

"Stop that," said Mrs. Whitaker. She poured them both cups of tea, after getting out the very best china, which was only for special occasions.

They sat in silence, drinking their tea.

When they had finished their tea they went into the parlor.

Galaad crossed himself, and picked up the Grail.

Mrs. Whitaker arranged the Egg and the Stone where the Grail had been. The Egg kept tipping on one side, and she propped it up against the little china dog.

"They do look very nice," said Mrs. Whitaker.

"Yes," agreed Galaad. "They look very nice."

"Can I give you anything to eat before you go back?" she asked.

He shook his head.

"Some fruitcake," she said. "You may not think you want any now, but you'll be glad of it in a few hours' time. And you should probably use the facilities. Now, give me that, and I'll wrap it up for you."

She directed him to the small toilet at the end of the hall, and went into the kitchen, holding the Grail. She had some old Christmas wrapping paper in the pantry, and she wrapped the Grail in it, and tied the package with twine. Then she cut a large slice of fruitcake and put it in a brown paper bag, along with a banana and a slice of processed cheese in silver foil.

Galaad came back from the toilet. She gave him the paper bag, and the Holy Grail. Then she went up on tiptoes and kissed him on the cheek.

"You're a nice boy," she said. "You take care of yourself."

He hugged her, and she shooed him out of the kitchen, and out of the back door, and she shut the door behind him. She poured herself another cup of tea, and cried quietly into a Kleenex, while the sound of hoofbeats echoed down Hawthorne Crescent.

On Wednesday Mrs. Whitaker stayed in all day.

On Thursday she went down to the post office to collect her pension. Then she stopped in at the Oxfam Shop.

The woman on the till was new to her. "Where's Marie?" asked Mrs. Whitaker.

The woman on the till, who had blue-rinsed gray hair and blue spectacles that went up into diamante points, shook her head and shrugged her shoulders. "She went off with a young man," she said. "On a horse. Tch. I ask you. I'm meant to be down in the Heathfield shop this afternoon. I had to get my Johnny to run me up here, while we find someone else."

"Oh," said Mrs. Whitaker. "Well, it's nice that she's found herself a young man."

"Nice for her, maybe," said the lady on the till. "But some of us were meant to be in Heathfield this afternoon."

On a shelf near the back of the shop Mrs. Whitaker found a tarnished old silver container with a long spout. It had been priced at sixty pence, according to the little paper label stuck to the side. It looked a little like a flattened, elongated teapot.

She picked out a Mills & Boon novel she hadn't read before. It was called *Her Singular Love*. She took the book and the silver container up to the woman on the till.

"Sixty-five pee, dear," said the woman, picking up the silver object, staring at it. "Funny old thing, isn't it? Came in this morning." It had writing carved along the side in blocky old Chinese characters and an elegant arching handle. "Some kind of oil can, I suppose."

"No, it's not an oil can," said Mrs. Whitaker, who knew exactly what it was. "It's a lamp."

There was a small metal finger ring, unornamented, tied to the handle of the lamp with brown twine.

"Actually," said Mrs. Whitaker, "on second thoughts, I think I'll just have the book."

She paid her five pence for the novel, and put the lamp back where she had found it, in the back of the shop. After all, Mrs. Whitaker reflected, as she walked home, it wasn't as if she had anywhere to put it.

Ellen Kushner is the author of Swordspoint, *the World Fantasy Award–winning* Thomas the Rhymer, *and (with Delia Sherman)* The Fall of the Kings. *"Charis" is a story from the "shared world" of the Borderlands, which was created by Terri Windling and which has served as a basis for several anthologies and novels by a variety of writers.*

Charis

ELLEN KUSHNER

I

I have this very blond hair, see, almost white. About the most thrilling thing I've ever done in my life was to go to this elvin club called the Wheat Sheaf which is in Soho. It's not like the Border itself, I mean they can't actually keep you out if you're human, but it's understood you don't go there if you are. I put on a ton of makeup, made my face utterly white, painted on swirls which were the thing that year, covered my ears up, and left my hair just the way it is. I got in all right. The music was not bad, what I heard of it. And the lighting was truly weird, gorgeous colors swirling around in the air, almost *too* bright, too vivid for my eyes. And there were all these elves, dancing the way they do, as though they didn't have any joints in their bodies. Some of my friends spend hours after school trying to teach themselves to dance like that.

About the most thrilling thing I've ever done. That says it all. I stood against the wall and watched elves dance. I bought myself a drink, and drank half of it. Then I went home. Scullion trailed me all the way, to make sure I didn't get roughed up by any halfie kids.

Scullion never told on me, either. He knew my parents would skin me if they knew, but he told me once that wasn't his job: Lena and Randal hired him to protect me, not to spy on me.

Scullion's all right. He's half elf, half human, born and bred in B-town. He's very tall and very strong. What he doesn't know about the streets here isn't worth knowing. He has a Tree of Life tattooed all the way up his left arm. I loved looking at it when I was young. I don't know where he came from, but I suspect he was in some kind of trouble, and Lena got him out of it on the condition that he become my guard. Bordertown's a rough place, even if you live up with the other privileged folk on luxurious Dragon's Tooth Hill, like we do. And important High Council members are an easy target for unrest. You'd figure, in a city made up of poets, wizards, halfies, runaways, and folk trying to strike it rich, there'd be plenty of unrest. In the middle of this chaos, anything that needs ruling gets ruled on by the Council, or some branch of it, from regulating currency prices to deciding what crimes are punishable by banishment to the open Borderlands.

So now we're getting ready for the M-Bassy Ball, *the* social event of the year for little old B-town. I don't know what "M-Bassy" means; probably the name of the person who started it: M. Bassy—Michel, Maude, Milo, something like that. The M-Bassy Ball is held every year in one of the oldest buildings, all the way in the heart of decadent Soho. They cordon the whole area off for days beforehand, and clean up the building and decorate it. And you can only get in if you're carrying a special invitation. People will do anything to get an invitation. But unlike most big parties and private clubs where you can use your power, money, or contacts to get in, the

M-Bassy Ball is only for a select crew on a carefully picked guest list.

Invitations to the M-Bassy Ball can't be faked: they're hand-scribed and decorated by a different artist every year. If there's one thing Bordertown has, it's lot of artists looking for work. Whenever it's humans' turn to run the ball, Lena and Randal make a bit point of encouraging new talent. People (I use the term loosely) keep those invitations, have them framed and everything. I've got a terrific collection my parents gave me. But this is the first year I'm going to the ball myself.

I'm terrified.

I know I'm supposed to be this walking glamour: born and bred in exotic Bordertown, where every kid who hates his parents and can play three guitar chords runs away to be Artistic. I've known elves all my life, and every weird fashion that comes along I've worn. I heard Leaf and Winter's Sorrow play for one of my parents' dances when I was ten. Let me tell you something: it doesn't make a bit of difference. If you're born ordinary and clumsy and, let's face it, with a big nose and no cheekbones, you might as well come from East Succotash for all the good it does you.

Lena disagrees. She says every sixteen-year-old girl feels the same, that there's nothing wrong with my nose, and she wished she had legs like mine when she was my age. A lot she knows about it. She always had enormous eyes the color of poured chocolate. And she was brilliant. When my mother was nineteen, she was the go-between in a market fight between elves and humans. When she was twenty-one she was aide to Serif Boynton on the Bordertown High Council. The rest is history.

She even married a poet, when everybody told her not to. This was Randal, a Worlder who'd come to the Borderlands to learn enough magic to power the world's fastest motorcycle. Not the sort of guy you'd expect a rising young power to favor. But Lena says she's always been mad for red hair. And in fact, Randal's not as crazy as most poets. He spends most of his time now on Council stuff and prettying up his cycle. It still doesn't go very fast, but it looks real good.

So I know my mother means well, but I still want to kill her when she starts going on about my Good Qualities. It is a small, peevish comfort to me that, where her only child is concerned, my mother's famous diplomacy is a joke.

They want me to dye my hair. My very own silver hair, which looks bleached but isn't, which looks elvin but isn't. The thing is, the M-Bassy Ball guest list is very carefully made up to be half human, half elf. Just like the High Council. All the Council folk come, along with the seriously important ones they do business with. It's supposed to be this big party where we all rub shoulders and show how well we get along. In years where the political situation in the city is tricky, the least little thing can set off an Incident. Elves can be very touchy when it suits them. Lena doesn't want any elf getting the notion that her daughter is trying to look elvin.

It's not as though I couldn't dye it and get away with it. Dark purple is a big thing this year, because of that band, the Guttertramps. But I like my hair the way it is. Everyone in the city knows I was born with it. I don't see why, now that I'm sixteen and going to Council functions, I have to pretend to turn into someone else.

My best friend Lise says she'd shave her head if it meant getting a ball invite. But that doesn't mean much: she shaved her head last year, and painted rainbows on it. Lise is very artistic. I wish she could come with me, because I dance a lot better when I'm watching her, kind of following the steps. Two years ago we were going to run away together. Her father's wives were being a pain, and Lena and Randal were threatening to make me stay home at night unless my school papers got better. So we were going to get those grubby clothes and pretend to be boys and escape.

The dumb thing was, there wasn't anywhere to run away to. You can't get into Elfland (not that I'd want to!) and there are no other real towns in the Borderlands, just farming villages and stuff like that. Lise said if all the artists in the World really do come here, it meant there weren't any left down in the World, and if we went there, she could make a lot of money. But I said they all left because it was even more boring down there than here. Everyone knows the Worlders are totally without brains, music, or style. So in the end we stayed where we were. And Lise got picked to do the scenery for the Full Moon Festival at school. And my parents let me go with this boy to the Dancing Ferret in Soho. He kissed me after, but I didn't see the point, and I don't think he did, either. I think he only asked me out because his mother told him to: all the traders want to get in good with people on the Council.

I wonder sometimes if the elf kids have to put up with this kind of thing. Council elf kids and rich traders and such live on the Hill, too, but on the other side, nearer the river. They go to a different school, and they're always dressed really sharp. But you don't really hang out with them unless it's at one of those Soho clubs no one's parents really approve of. It used to be that only real Slummers went down there, trying to pretend they were some kind of gang; but things are different now. Slummers still slum, but the rest of us go for the music, when we get the chance. There are private clubs all over the Hill, but they're not too hot, and there's no mixing. A human could never get into an elf club on the Hill.

It would serve them right if I shaved my head.

II

I'm scared now, really scared. Too much depends on this. And I have to do it alone. Which means that, no matter what happens, if I fail, there's no one else to blame. But there's no one else he can turn to. I'm his only hope.

Silvan. The man in green.

Two days before the Ball, the word went round the inner circles of Bordertown: important elvin personages would be attending, from the Lands Beyond the Border. (Of course it threw the balance of the guest list off. They had to suddenly invite more humans.) In Council the elves were especially touchy all week, trying to gain points, to show their power. Old disputes about fishing rights resurfaced, and Windreed proposed a tax on ground corn, of all things! Dinner at our house—when we got to eat in private—was nothing but griping from Lena and Randal, how impossible the situation was, how they'd trusted Riverrun to take a moderate stance on the fishing issue but she'd got a bug up her pants like all the rest, must be acting on higher orders and blah blah blah. At least they forgot to nag me about my hair.

So the night of the M-Bassy Ball I did myself up right: tight-laced boots up to the thigh, that flashed out between layers of elvin glitter cloth when I walked, moved, danced. Bare arms with silver cuffs. And black glitter in my hair. Conservative, but striking. If I wasn't going to turn heads, at least I didn't have to be embarrassed either.

We hauled out the carriage for the occasion. Because the night was warm, we got to ride with the top down, which I always love. It's such a heavy old piece of junk that it doesn't go too fast, even with both horses pulling it. And you have to take the widest streets. Once you get past the Old Wall, of course, that isn't a problem: they built streets for two or three carriages, back in those days. Finally we pulled up at the

M-Bassy building. Behind the guards, Soho punks were hanging around watching to see who drove up next. We had to wait behind another carriage, a little number obviously made out of wood, with old machine parts tacked on to make it look more realistic. Then we passed our invitations by the gatemen and went on in.

I wasn't prepared to be so impressed. The M-Bassy Ball was like nothing I'd ever seen: more like the opening of Council than like going to a club or even a party. There was a giant staircase that curved, and you came down it with everyone watching from the bottom. Lena and Randal looked great, as always, but with all those eyes on them they seemed like stars. Like the best act in the hottest club in town. I had this stupid feeling like I was going to cry. Because there I was, their daughter, and even if I wasn't so great, like not brilliant or pretty or coordinated, we were all three of us a unit, we belonged together, and there was nothing anyone could do to change that.

At the bottom of the staircase was the crowd of people, the music, and the food. I mostly checked out what everyone was wearing. People were looking good. And everyone who'd been coming to my parents' house since I was a baby came up to me and told me how great I looked. Which was nice of them. I smiled until my face hurt.

This boy Johnsson who goes to my school and whose father is an important trader came up to me and rolled his eyes like, "Is this boring or what?" So I had to give the same look back like I agreed with him. He said, "You wanna dance later?" and I said, "Sure." *Later.* Maybe I'd better get drunk before then.

I wandered off in search of drinks. Then I realized nobody else was moving. The room was quiet. Everyone was looking up at the staircase.

Coming down it was the most beautiful woman I had ever seen. Elf or human. I mean it. Long silvery hair floated back from her face like a cloud or as if she were standing looking out to sea. She was slender and graceful. And her face was . . . well, it was perfect. I can't describe it any better without making it sound like I had a lech on her, which I definitely did not. It was just perfect.

Then something creepy happened. All the elves in the room got down on the knee. It made a rustling sound, like the wind on the hillside. Every human was left standing up, feeling awkward. We really showed, looming above their heads like that.

The band had stopped playing. In the perfect silence, there was the elf woman's glittery laughter.

Then everybody got up off their knees and began to move around again. It seemed that I was the only one still watching the stairs. Behind the woman came a man, elvin like her, all dressed in green, from boots to the tie that held back his long silver hair. There's a certain shade of green that only elves can look really good in. No B-town men were wearing long hair this year—everything about him said *Elfland.* The man in green was not perfect. He went beyond perfect to beautiful: nose not quite straight, eyes a little long. Not that anyone would find him ugly—certainly the gorgeous lady didn't. When he got to the bottom, she put her arm in his.

I'm not nuts about elves or anything. A lot of girls go through a phase when they get crushes on elves, especially musicians in bands, and they won't even look at human guys. The whole thing's pretty sick if you ask me. Nobody needs more halfies in the world.

So I turned away from the newcomers. I almost ran into Windreed. He bowed to me with that mocking half smile of his. "The daughter of the House of Flame looks splendid tonight."

"I thank you," I said correctly. There was a silence I was

obviously supposed to fill. "Uh . . . that was some entrance, just now."

He looked pleased. Either I'd just made a fool of myself, or it was the right thing to say. "The new Lady and her Lord honor us."

"Yes," I replied, trying to keep from fidgeting under his pale gaze, "very much." Go away, I thought fiercely at him. Everyone knows you're the coldest, meanest, toughest elf in Council. Go pick on someone your own size!

As if in answer to my plea, Shoshana Mizmag appeared behind him. "Windreed!" she said. The woman knows no fear. I hope I'm like that when I'm forty. "I'll forgive you insulting me in Council yesterday if you'll come dance with me now!"

His formal face thawed a bit. Elves love to tease. "Formidable lady! At home we have a Dance Challenge. How I would love to test you in it!"

"How you would love to give me a heart attack!" She chuckled. "But not tonight, sir. I know about those elvin contests. Nice if we could settle all city disputes over possessions by dancing, but somehow I don't think the town would go for it. And this is a civilized party. Tonight we dance away our troubles, but nothing more substantial."

"Certainly not, to this music." The old elf almost sniffed.

"What a traditionalist! Elvin folk music by all means, but not at the ball; here we must be stylish or perish! Shall we hurl ourselves into the fray?"

"And let others profit by our example?" he said. "Look!"

We looked.

It was the Lady, the silver-haired lady, dancing with my father. Randal looked like an amiable, shaggy red bear beside her. He also looked like he was having fun.

"An example has been set," said Windreed smugly. He offered Shoshana his hand.

When the band really got going, there wasn't much for me to do but watch and listen. They were fantastic, and it was wild to see all the Councillors and powers, human and elvin, enjoying themselves like normal club-goers. I didn't see Johnsson, which was good: there's nothing worse than having to dance with the only free person in the room. It gives new meaning to the phrase, "I wouldn't do it with you if you were the last human in the World."

The silver Lady was everywhere. I'd sell my soul for a pair of enchanted shoes that could make me dance the way she did. It's a good thing that that magic stuff doesn't work reliably in Bordertown, or I'd be minus one soul now. As for her escort, he was hard to spot. I noticed him once, leaning against a wall peeling a piece of fruit with his fingers. But I quickly looked away. He was doing it so carefully, so smoothly, with delicate concentration; it was as though I had come on him undressing someone. *Someone.* All right—it was as though I'd come on him undressing a woman. I didn't stick around to watch him take a bite.

When the Lady left the room, everyone pretended not to notice. She paused in the doorway, and for a moment her eyes seemed to stare into mine. The dancers closed ranks over the silver trail she left. I followed.

I just did. It was the same impulse that led me once to the Elvin Wheat Sheaf: wanting to get away with something I shouldn't. And a faint feeling that I could do it.

She didn't go far, just down a wide hallway, dimly lit and private. Her Lord was waiting there.

I didn't dare get close enough to hear what they were saying. I scrunched myself into the darkness of the window bay. Even just standing and talking they looked like they were dancing. It made my throat hurt, watching. Suddenly she turned sharply away from him, lovely as a swan wheeling over a lake. I heard myself make a small noise. He held out his arms to her. She pulled him to her, close, his green and her silver together. His mouth was against her ear, moving her hair. She stood back a pace, looking at him. Then she lifted her arm and slapped him, hard, across the face.

And he just stood there. He didn't even look angry. She took off a ring and gave it to him. And he put it on his finger.

I remember hearing the band playing a new hit, "Free Me," the music faint but followable if you already knew the words:

Used to gaze with my heart,
Follow my fingers home.
Did you want me or my need?
Then there was hope,
Now there's none—
Free me!
Once I burned for your touch
Now even one look is too much—
Free me!

Rope me to the wind and set me free,
Cuts like a knife,
Power scream,
Ten thousand volts is not enough
To free me . . .

She left him then and went back down the hall to the dancing. I could have reached out and touched her drifting silver tunic. She was smiling to herself as she went by.

Of course it was none of my business. Some weird elvin ritual. Or maybe what I'd just seen was only your basic lovers' spat. Just because Randal and Lena never slug each other doesn't mean I'm ignorant.

I didn't even know who they were. Even in B-town, surrounded by elves, there's a lot about the customs of Elfland we don't know. You get the feeling that if the elves in B-town had been so in love with their home, they wouldn't have settled in the Borderlands. So it's no wonder they don't talk about Elfland much. "The new Lady and her Lord," Windreed had said. Some kind of rulers or powers, then, come down past the Border to check out the ball, pick up some good food for cheap, or maybe get a kick out of having a roomful of elves bow to them. . . .

She'd passed me, but I didn't know where he'd gone. So, cautiously, I stuck my head out to look.

He was standing where she'd left him, turning the ring on his finger. I don't know why he looked up then. But my hair was very bright in the gloom of the half-lit hall, and he saw me.

"Maiden," he said.

I just froze. I literally couldn't move. I didn't want to.

"Don't come out," he said. "Wait there for me."

What could I do, jump out the window? I watched him come down the hall to me, until we were both standing in the tiny space of the window bay together, looking out over Soho.

He reeked of magic. I felt dizzy. He might have been trying to cast a spell, but if he was, it wasn't working. I had the feeling, though, that magic just clung to him as grace and beauty did to the Lady.

He was much taller than me, so he sat on the windowsill. I could barely see his face. His words came out of darkness.

"The Summons," he said. "And so soon. Maiden, I am afraid."

"Oh," I said, because saying anything, no matter how dumb, was better than letting *that* lie there. "I'm sorry."

I mean, nobody had ever talked to me that way before. Beautiful strangers out of nowhere don't start suddenly telling you how afraid they are. Not in real life. Maybe in stories.

"Can I help?" I said.

I thought he'd say, like; "Oh, no, thanks a lot, it's just really got me down," (only Elfland-y). But he said, "Yes."

"I can help?" I repeated, to be sure.

"If you will. Because you've offered. I am not allowed to ask for help; but if you offer it, I can take it."

This was beginning to sound a lot like magic. I hated to disappoint him, but I'm not real good at that stuff. I can't even put a few extra RPMs on Randal's bike. "Are you under a spell?" I asked.

I could hear his smile in the dark. "No, maiden. Not really. The Lady chose me last year at Dancing Night. It is my pleasure to serve her"—here I'll swear he blushed—"in all things. I could ask for no greater honor." Suddenly he pulled off the ring. The twisted silver caught the light. "But this honor is too much!" he said angrily. "I had no idea she would Summon me."

"Summon you where?"

"Forever," he whispered, staring at the ring. "Not from one Dancing Night to the next, but to stay by her side for the rest of her life."

"You don't love her?" I asked softly.

"Love the Lady?" he said bitterly. "One doesn't love the Lady; one serves her. Maybe I'll learn to love her, over the years . . ."

"Is it someone else?" I couldn't believe I was daring to ask a question like that. But something about the way he was trusting me, putting himself in my hands, made me feel it was all right.

"No," he said. "There's no one else I've loved. And now there never will be. I'm young, you know; she was the first. And I was so pleased when she said she'd take me to Bordertown. I've always wanted to see it. I've heard stories about the music, the dancing . . . It's different here. You get the feeling that anything could happen."

Anything can, I thought.

"I would stay here, I think, if I could," he went on. "But we must be back to Kingsmound by the New Moon. And then we'll go back. Under the Hill and that will be that. For our lifetime." He sounded so sad.

"I said I'd help. I will. Just tell me what to do."

"I'll tell you," he said, "but you must decide. If you are to save me, you must claim me before the Lady and all the company."

I gulped thinking of how much I hated speaking in public. "Sure," I said.

"But first, you must win the right to claim me. And that means Dancing the Challenge."

Then my heart froze. I'm just not a very good dancer. If it meant it was me against the Lady, there was no hope for him.

"Don't you dance?" he asked quickly.

"Oh, sure I dance, but . . ."

"I didn't see you dancing in the hall before."

"You . . . noticed me?" I couldn't believe it.

"I noticed you. You have beautiful hair."

I didn't know what to say. I've never, ever heard anyone tell me that before. Not anyone I wanted to hear it from.

"Let me tell you about the Challenge," he said. "It's not what you think. The Challenge is not a contest, it's a battle. A battle you win through your strength and your will. Style and grace don't mean anything there, you know. They never do, they're just the outer trappings of what's inside. In the Challenge Dance only one thing matters: that you outlast our opponent." He looked straight into my eyes. "You can do that, I think."

"I'll try," I managed to say. "Is my opponent you, or her?"

"Me, I hope. I have the right to Dance for myself. But if the Lady enters the Challenge, too, it will be hard. Hard but not impossible."

"I understand." I swallowed dryly. "Do I have to do it now?" In front of my parents? I wondered silently.

"No, not tonight. And not in this place. Three nights from tonight will mark the turn of one year from the night my Lady first chose me. While we are here, she wants to taste all the pleasures of Bordertown. So we are going to dance at a club called the Dancing Ferret that she's heard about, to hear a band called the New Blood Review. Can you be there then?"

"Oh, sure." I thought about ditching Scullion. And I thought about bringing Scullion; he's a halfie, he can go anywhere. If things get rough, he'll be good to have along. I'm still thinking about it. I want to do this myself. It's not through Scullion's strength and will that I can win him free.

"Thank you," he said. "When you claim me, remember: my name is . . . you won't be able to pronounce the elvin name. Here I would be called Silvan. Now listen." To my surprise, he began to sing quietly:

"Up she starts as white as the milk
Between the king and all his company.
His fifteen lords all cried aloud
For the bonny Lass of Engelsea.

"She's taken him all by the hand,
Saying, 'You'll rise up and dance with me,'
But ere the king has gone one step,
She's danced his gold and his lands away.

"She's danced high and she's danced low,
She's danced as light as the leaf on the broken sea.
And ere the moon began to set
She has gained the victory.

"Up then starts the fifteenth knight,
And O an angry man is he.
He says, 'My feet will be my death
Ere she gain the victory!'

"He says my feet will be my death
Ere this lass do gain the victory—
He's danced fast, but tired at last,
He gave it over shamefully.

"She's danced off all their buckles and shoes,
She's danced off all their gold and their bright money.
Then back to the mountains she's away
The bonny Lass of Engelsea!"

His voice was soft and low, but I heard the song perfectly. It was a pretty tune, cheerful and eerie at the same time.

"You see?" Silvan said. "It's been done before by a white-skinned maiden. An old, old song among us. The Challenge is not new."

"How can you dance against me," I asked, "when you want me to win? Won't people think you'll throw the match?"

"Not when the Challenge starts. I will not be truly free unless you've won me fairly."

"I will."

He leaned forward, and I thought he was going to kiss me. And I would have let him. Maybe to have the mouth that the silver Lady owned be pressed against mine; and maybe because he was alone and I could help him and for once kissing felt like a prize I deserved, instead of a present some boy felt obliged to give me even though I was ugly.

It still scares me to think how much I wanted that kiss.

But I didn't get it. He leaned back with a sigh. "You are gracious," he said. "May the Stars always guide you Home."

It was too late to explain his mistake, if it was one. Because that's what the elves in Bordertown say only to each other. Did he really think I was an elf the whole time? A halfie? Doesn't he know? Doesn't he care? Can't they tell their own kind, even in the dark?

I can't help my hair.

I don't care, I don't care, I don't care. I'm going to do it. I said I would help him, and I will. He needs me, and there's nobody else to do it.

III

I'm not going to die. I only think I am.

I went to the Dancing Ferret. That part wasn't hard. I even told Lena and Randal where I was going—just not who I was coming home with. Soho makes my parents nervous—too much weird stuff happens there—but they know you can't play it safe forever, and having a daughter who never went anywhere the other kids go would make the family look just as bad as having one who got into a Soho brawl.

Also, Scullion takes a lot of the risk out of it. Or so I thought. And I didn't see any way of giving him the slip. So I let him follow me to the Ferret.

I felt like I was going to war. I chose my clothing carefully, for wear and not for show: fitted tights that moved when I moved, soft boots, and a loose tunic without sleeves. Dancing for hours at the Ferret can really make you sweat, and tonight I meant to dance like I never had before. I tied my hair up off my neck with a twist of bright rag. My one really splashy accessory was a pair of earrings I'd just gotten the week before from one of the street people: miniature machine parts carved out of wood and painted silver to look like steel. I thought they were the greatest. I'm going to burn them.

Over the whole outfit went a giant wrap of elf cloth: black with silver spangles, like the night sky. My mother says it's too old for me, but I bought it with my own money, and Randal says it looks terrific.

Then I went out into the night. God, what a feeling! Autumn chill in the air and darkness beckoning. I found myself whistling, but for a second I didn't recognize the tune. Then I realized what it was: Silvan's "Bonny Lass of Engelsea." Pleased with myself, I whistled it louder.

I crossed the Mad River on the arched bridge they call the Dragon's Claw. Usually I like to pause at the crest of the Claw to take in a really good view of the city below; but tonight it was rush-rush-rush, my heart beating in my ears like the river rushing under the bridge pilings. Behind me Scullion's steady footsteps echoed the beat. I heard a strain of music, and realized he'd picked up my tune: "Up she starts as white as the milk . . . She's danced light as the leaf on the broken sea . . ."

Under the Old Wall, then, with a nod at the punk guarding it. Ahead of me people were rushing, too, kids with a sense of the night, the glitter, and the dancing ahead.

It felt good to be in Soho, where anything could happen, where gangs who were as tough as I was going to have to be, and as desperate, held their rule. It felt good to be going alone, to meet someone I wanted to see.

Then I got to the club, and all my nervousness came rushing back with the business of getting in, paying my fee, adjusting my eyes to the gloom, and finding someplace to stand among all the people already crowding in to hear the Review.

I looked around for Silvan and the Lady. There'd been a lot of talk about them the last few days. More than one girl at the elf school around the corner from ours had been going around dressed in silver. And one from ours had abruptly gotten over her crush on Eadric Vole, lead singer for Magical Madness, and was trying to find out what clubs the Lord and

Lady would be going to. It made me feel funny to hear other people talk about them. They didn't know. I think Lena must feel this way when she hears people in the market talking politics.

Politics had been rough lately, too. Ever since the ball, Lena and Randal had been complaining to anyone who would listen about how rotten things were in Council and out of it. The elves were making trouble, finding insults in everything from seating arrangements to old laws nobody's disputed for twenty years. The most annoying thing, Randal said, was how much they seemed to be enjoying it. On the streets elves are usually controlled and distant; there it's the hot-blooded humans who pick fights. There's even a saying, "Cold as elf blood." But when it comes to politics, elves seem to like it hot. It gives them a chance to be good and arrogant, I guess.

With Randal and Lena under pressure, and me almost jumping out of my skin with nerves over the upcoming Challenge, home had been tranquil as a pit of dragons. I could imagine what it would be like when I brought Silvan home.

It wasn't very exciting, but that was the best thing I could think of to do with him. My parents' house is very safe, and here he'd have time to think about what he wanted to do next. I know what I *hoped* he'd want . . . but being Lena's daughter *has* taught me *some* sense. You don't run off with an elvin Lord when you're sixteen and human. Rescuing him from the Lady was bad enough. I only hoped there wouldn't be an Incident. I knew Lena and Randal wouldn't exactly be pleased to find him on their doorstep, but I figured when I explained how much he needed help they'd understand.

If this doesn't sound like I'd thought it all out too clearly, it's true: I was really too worried about the Dance to put much thought into what would happen after. I wasn't even sure there'd *be* an after.

There certainly wouldn't be if Silvan and the lady didn't

even show up at the Ferret. I looked around, hard. They were a hard couple to miss. And they were nowhere in sight.

I was early, I thought. They weren't there yet. They weren't even coming. I'd gotten the day wrong. They'd been already and left.

They came in the door.

This time no one went down on their knees, but everyone was looking, human and elf. Farell Din himself went over and said something to the Lady that made her laugh.

The New Blood Review got going with "Free Me." They were ten times better than the band at the ball had been, did things with the music I would never have dreamed of. They had no singer, but I remembered the words:

Rope me to the wind and set me free,
Ten thousand volts is not enough
To free me . . .

The Lady and her Lord came onto the dance floor. In my stomach, someone was beating a cat to death. I kept thinking, Why did I wear these earrings, they look so dumb. . . .

Then I went up to Silvan and took his hands.

The Lady looked over her shoulder, amused. Then she must have realized what was happening. She shook her head at him, reached for his hand that wore her ring. But I held his hand safe in mine. I looked into his pale, still face. The music was too loud to hear anything, but I made my lips say, "I am not afraid."

Silvan's hands were impossibly cool, the bones almost weightless. Mine felt sweaty and grubby by contrast. Then I felt the tingle of wild magic in them, and the beat of the music got into my blood. . . .

I'll never dance like that again. But it was worth it, for the one night. Like my whole *body* was music, like the band couldn't play unless I was moving the beat. . . . I had my eyes closed a lot of the time, so as not to see the people watching me, and to better feel the bass in my bones, the shrill licks come off the top of my head. I didn't really care what I looked like, for the first time in my life. I got hot, the sweat ran down my chest. For once at the Ferret it felt like there was no one trying to dance in my space, and when I opened my eyes, I saw there wasn't. The whole floor around us was clear. Silvan was dancing elvin and liquid, putting little twists into the beat with his hands, his feet. It was great to watch, but I couldn't stop, and I didn't dare try to mirror him, for fear of losing what I had.

The band just kept going, riffing like crazy on that one tune, over and over, *free me, free me, free me . . .*

I smiled at him, and he smiled back. He didn't look that old. For a moment, we were just what we were supposed to be: two kids having fun, out free in the hottest spot in the World or out of it: the Dancing Ferret, Soho, Bordertown, Borderland, the Universe.

Then, with a flourish of silver, the Lady was there. She didn't touch him or me, just started dancing in the open space where we were. Her hair was braided all over her head, with silver bells woven in. You couldn't hear them, of course, but they trembled when she moved.

She looked better than both of us put together. I tried not to care. It wasn't *fun* she was having, just some old power probably my mother's age (*more,* if the stories about elves are true), trying to stay young by picking up some kid like Silvan, who'd probably never been to a decent club before in his life. . . .

As if she were pulling them in, the space around us started to close up with dancers. Everybody was on the floor, more people than I thought the Dancing Ferret could hold. They were crowding us out, so close it was hard to do anything but shuffle to the beat. And the beat was hard, now, all bass and drums, no lightness even of cymbals. Like there was no tune at all, just a steady thump like footsteps, a giant heart.

Now I wanted to stop. I couldn't even see Silvan. I couldn't see anything but some tall person's shoulder. For all I knew, he was gone, dropped out already, and I could stop. I was thirsty, and the bottoms of my feet ached. The beat was jerking me like a puppet, not *free me,* just *me—me—me—me—*

Then the treble, faint and faraway over the bass, sweet and clear . . . the jingle of silver bells, the Lady's laughter.

I stayed on my feet. I didn't lean on the other dancers. And when the music came back and the floor cleared down to normal, I was there and the Lady was there, and her Lord was gone. He was gone. He "gave it over" to me, and the Challenge was mine.

Still I didn't stop. I wanted to outlast her. The rules to the Challenge were strange to me, and he'd warned me something like this might happen. Since the Lady had entered the Dance, it might be that I had to go on to keep Silvan free from her. I wouldn't dance *with* her, but I'd dance against her. Nobody fresh from Elfland was going to outdance me. I was Bordertown, Dragon's Tooth Hill, and we bowed to no one.

It's pure charity to say I was really dancing. Moving to the music, maybe. My tunic was so wet it was sticking to me. But the Lady wasn't doing much better. More graceful, maybe, but not too exciting to watch anymore. The Glamour had gone out of it. It was going to end with two wet little heaps on the floor at this rate, I thought.

I'd reckoned without that good old elvin style.

She stopped.

Right at the end of a song, she simply threw back her head, brushed a few wisps of hair out of her eyes, and shrugged. Elegantly, of course.

I didn't know what to do. Had she thrown the contest? Or *was* there no contest? Maybe she just didn't think I was worth fighting with: no glory in beating some gawky little human girl.

Or maybe she'd been afraid to lose. Afraid to look sweaty and tired and as though she actually cared about anything. She didn't *care* about Silvan.

I saw him making his way to me through the press of people. His face was paler than even an elf's should be. Wordlessly, he took my hand. And he looked at me like there was something I should do. Something more.

I was scared to look at the lady, but I made myself do it. She was smiling, looking like she'd won. But she hadn't won. I'd won.

"I claim Silvan," I said to her.

She couldn't hear over the noise, but she knew what I'd said. The smile vanished from her face like the glue that had been holding it on had suddenly come unstuck.

"Take him," her lips moved. That was all. Then she turned away, back into the crowd that was already dancing to a new song.

We threaded our way out of the Dancing Ferret, out into the cool darkness of Carnival Street, still holding hands. I could feel the ring on his finger, his Lady's ring, elvin-cold against my skin. I didn't look to see if Scullion was following me. I'd won Silvan, and that was all that mattered. Nothing could hurt me tonight. An entire gang of Bloods could jump me; I'd break their heads and play dice with their teeth.

I led my Lord through the streets of Soho, past graffiti-glittering walls. He finally pulled me to a halt to lean against one of them, still catching his breath. He looked so fragile. There was none of that elvin arrogance. Had I really out-danced him? And didn't he know yet what I was?

I guess not. He pulled me to him like he was terribly cold and needed me to warm him. And I lifted my head and got that kiss I'd wanted so much at the ball.

Even now, it feels better to remember the way it was then. Magic, it felt like magic all through me. I'd never been so happy. I'd almost stopped being me. I felt grateful and triumphant, both at once.

That was all there was. His mouth was still on mine when I felt a tremendous crash on the back of my head, and the world fell away from me.

I came to in a blurry room full of sunlight. I was home. My parents were sitting next to my bed talking over my head, in the middle of a quiet argument.

". . . better that way," Randal was saying.

"Not this time, love," Lena said firmly. "She should know as soon as she—"

She stopped as soon as she saw my eyes were open.

"What?" I said hoarsely. "What's going on? Where's Silvan?"

"You're all right, honey, Scullion brought you home." Randal sounded real gentle, the way he did when I was truly young. It made me want to cry. "Here's something for you to drink. Let me help you sit up."

"My head hurts," I said, like a little girl. "What happened? Is Silvan all right?"

"He's fine," Lena said. "Drink your medicine."

I drank it, and then I went to sleep. Then the good-wife came and looked at my head, and made me tell her whether I could see things or not, and said I had a mild concussion and I'd be fine if I just rested. I was going to wait until they were all out of the room and then get up and find out what was going on, but instead I fell asleep again.

I woke up in the middle of the night. Lena was there,

dressed up like she'd just come in from a party. She was wearing my favorite scent, the one that smells like the red flowers that come up from the south sometimes, the real expensive ones that won't grow in Borderland.

"Mumma," I said, "what's going on?"

She answered me in her most grown-up voice, the one I usually hear only when she's addressing the Council or I've really loused up my schoolwork. "I'm afraid there's been some political trouble, and you got caught in the middle of it. Nobody blames you. It's not your fault."

That got me mad. "If you think rescuing somebody from a place he doesn't want to go back to is—is just *political trouble,* then you've got the stone heart! Did it ever occur to you to wonder how people *feel*? Or is all you think about your precious politics?"

"That's enough," she said in a voice so controlled it scared me. "Or we're both going to start crying, and I'd rather not do that. Is that what he told you? That you were *rescuing* him?"

I didn't like the way she said that. As if she felt sorry for me. "Well, of course!" I almost shouted. "What did you *think* I was doing?"

"Scullion knocked you on the head and brought you home. *He* thought you were kissing the elf Lord."

"Scullion! Scullion did that to me? I thought he was supposed to protect me!"

"He is," said my mother dryly. "I hate to bring politics into this, but had you thought about what would happen to the peace of Bordertown if a human girl ran off with a Lord defecting from beyond the Border? It was bad enough you Challenging the Lady in a crowded club with half Soho watching . . . but we're all right there, because nobody at the Dancing Ferret is likely to know you by sight. For all they know, with that hair, you could have been some elf punk. You certainly weren't *dressed* like the hill!"

I felt like I was choking. "So you had Scullion bop me on the head to prevent scandal! Was that to protect my good name, or yours and Randal's?"

"It was Scullion's idea. He says he recognized the Challenge song you were singing. He's half-elvin, he knows these things."

"And have you considered"—I tried to sound as calm and cold as Lena—"what's going to happen to Silvan without my protection?"

"Nothing's going to happen to Silvan," she said bitterly. I was amazed at the anger in her voice. "God, maybe Randal was right about this. I'm not sure I can do it. Charis . . . It wasn't true, any of it."

"What do you mean, it wasn't true? Are you trying to make me believe it didn't happen, now?"

"Shush. Just listen to me. The Lady came down from Elfland to make trouble. She doesn't like the independence of the Bordertown elves. She and the elves in our Council have been feuding for years. She thinks they're too close to us humans—even Windreed, to *her,* is 'too friendly.' I hate to sound like some Ho Street bigot, but it was a masterly piece of elvin trickery: she looked around for some way to make trouble, to cut a rift between the two communities. They found it in you. I don't know . . . the elves have an unerring instinct for the vulnerable, for what and who will hurt the most. Sometimes I think life is just a giant story for them, an exciting game to win.

"The plan all along was for you to run off with Silvan. Then the lady would raise the hue and cry, claiming quite rightly that a Bordertown human had desecrated elvin rituals, that you had tricked Silvan into thinking you were elvin . . . they knew, you see, about your hair. They must have heard about you before the M-Bassy Ball, somehow, and decided to try it there. And they nearly brought it off, too. If Scullion hadn't brought you home before you were recognized with Silvan, it would all be out in the open now. Of course we would have stood up for you, but it would be your word against theirs. And that was what they wanted, a fight between the two communities."

I didn't say anything.

"It would have hurt you very much," my mother went on, "much more than finding out this way, my darling, believe me."

My jaw was clenched so tight it ached. "No," I said. "I don't believe you. You're lying. Somebody's lying. Silvan needed me. She was going to m-marry him and make him live under the ground for the rest of his life or something. Maybe *she* was going to do all that stuff you say—maybe she made him go along with it—but he wasn't going to hurt me, he needed my help! You don't understand *anything.* I danced the Challenge and I won, and everything was going to be all right until *you* came along and spoiled it! You think I didn't know what I was doing—you *never* think I know what I'm doing!"

I was shouting by now; I guess I was hysterical or something. Anyway, Lena's voice cut through it like ice. "Do you think *he* didn't know what he was doing? He has magic, and he has beauty, and you didn't stand a chance. She wasn't going to marry him, no matter what he told you. Silvan is the Lady's brother."

I felt like the bed was melting away under me, and I was falling without moving. "Her—brother?"

"Do you think *I* don't know what I'm doing?" Lena said. "Do you think I haven't checked all my sources thoroughly, just because I can't tell you where I got all the information? Scullion has a lot of friends, and there are some elves on the Council—"

"All right," I said tightly, just to shut her up, to stop her from being so right, right, right all the time. "I believe you."

"Thank you," my mother said softly. "Charis . . . if it helps at all . . . we heard about the Challenge, about what you did. You were very brave, and very strong. We want you to know we're very, very proud of you."

"No," I said, holding on to my pillow for dear life, because if she didn't get out of there soon I was going to throw it at her. "No, it doesn't help. Not one stinking little bit."

So then she left, and I cried until I was too sick to cry anymore.

So none of it was true. Maybe if I tell myself this over and over again I'll get used to it and it'll stop hurting. Nobody needed me. I didn't help anybody. They made up a story they thought I'd fall for, and let me live in storyland for a while. That was real nice of them. And

HE WAS LAUGHING AT ME ALL THE TIME

HE WAS LAUGHING AT ME ALL THE TIME

Shit. I hate crying. I really do. Maybe I'll do some research on elvin customs and find out whether there really is a Lord and Lady, how he gets chosen and whether you can win somebody free of Elfland in a Dance Challenge, or is it all a crock of shit that sounds like what we think the elves are like and they're really up there smoking cigarettes and doing weird stuff with our cheese and lightbulbs and laughing at us all the time . . .

Only now I hate elves so much I never want to see any again; I don't even want to think about them. I'd better get over this or I'm going to wind up like those assholes from the World who think elves are going to steal their babies. Maybe I'd better go live in the World after all, where I don't have to worry about elves, or the Council, or anything.

I also hate my parents—not who they are, but what they

are. If I hadn't been their daughter, this wouldn't have happened to me. It wasn't just anybody's kid the elves wanted to make a fool of. I can't hate Scullion, because I haven't been out of the house, so I haven't seen him.

I certainly am going to be a busy girl, working so hard learning not to hate everybody. I won't have time for going dancing or stuff like that.

IV

The Lord and Lady are gone, and no one's created a scandal. It looks as though the peace of Bordertown is secure. Yay for our side.

Today a scruffy elvin punk came to the door with a parcel for me. It's a wooden box, carved in elf style with a pattern of leaves and waves. When you open it, there's a mirror set inside the lid. And in the box is a familiar silver ring on a green ribbon, and a lock of elvin silver hair.

Susan Palwick is the author of a number of distinguished short stories and the award-winning dark fantasy novel Flying in Place.

Jo's Hair

SUSAN PALWICK

You remember the story. Jo March, tomboy and hoyden, whose only beauty is her long chestnut hair, sells it for twenty-five dollars because her father lies ill in a hospital in Washington. He has not asked for twenty-five dollars, has not asked for anything, but Jo, good nineteenth-century daughter, knows that sacrifices are called for in such situations. Her father has sacrificed his comfortable home life to serve as a Civil War chaplain. Her mother has sacrificed her anger, and the other daughters their ambitions; little Beth will ultimately sacrifice her life. Jo, who does not yet wish to sacrifice her desires, sacrifices her hair instead: walks into a small shop where a small oily man cuts off her mane and gives her a small roll of bills, which she sends proudly to her father.

Her father does not want it. He never spends the money. When he comes home he tells the assembled family that in all Washington he couldn't find anything beautiful enough to buy with Jo's money, and Jo, sitting in the firelight, blushes, her eyes grown dim. Her parents and sisters, watching her, think her proud of her father's praise; and because she wants to please them, she tries to think so too. Deep down, though, some part of her knows that her sacrifice has been rejected as worthless: too crass, too material, too redolent of the flesh and the body, of the very things good daughters should never exchange for money. Jo's father does not want her hair or anything her hair has purchased.

She understands all this, bright girl that she is, although she never speaks of it. She grows more hair, and thinks only occasionally of the mane she sold. Dutiful daughter, she learns instead to make approved sacrifices. She stops writing, marries an older man with whom she founds a school, devotes herself to home and family. She never goes to Europe, never has an illicit romance, tastes the forbidden only through the adventures of the rambunctious boys she has raised, who are free to venture into the world. Jo has learned the limits of decorum.

But what of Jo's hair?

Here is Jo's hair in the window of the shop where she left it. It has been combed, braided, powdered, oiled, woven fantastically with flowers, a thing for fairyfolk or vain young girls. Along comes just such a young girl, with her even more worldly mother, both of them eager to buy the beauty Jo has so nobly, and with so little effect, sold for a few paltry pieces of paper.

"Look, Mama!" cries our new heroine, pointing at the beautiful plait in the window. "Just the thing for the ball!"

"It will do," her mother says with a nod, surveying Jo's hair with eyes used to assessing silks, satins, fine bonbons, the incomes and social standing of potential husbands. For fifty dollars she buys the hair Jo sold for twenty-five, and that night the young girl attaches Jo's hair to her own thick chestnut locks, just a shade darker than Jo's, and waltzes ecstatically in a brilliant green silk gown beneath even more brilliant crystal chandeliers. By the end of that year, Jo's lovely hair has shone in the light from many chandeliers, from the moon in summer rose gardens, from the blinding sun of midday boating expeditions. It has been admired by the cream of society, by fawning servants, and by a most satisfyingly long list of suitors, including the extremely rich, handsome, and dissipated young man upon whom the new owner of Jo's hair, and her mama, have rested their hopes for lo! these many waltzes.

The same Christmas day that Jo's father tells her he could find nothing to buy with her hair, the dissipated young man steals his first kiss from the worldly young lady, and strokes the smooth plait of Jo's hair, little dreaming that it once belonged to a poor clergyman's daughter. On the day Jo's sister Meg, to Jo's great grief, becomes engaged to a poor but honest tutor, Jo's hair is the central ornament in a costume which, before that evening is out, has been complemented by a dazzling diamond ring besides which even Jo's hair fades into insignificance.

And now, after a decorous three-year wait, Meg and the tutor decorously marry, as Jo mourns the first break in the circle of sisters. On that same day, the worldly young lady dies in childbirth—we would, of course, never dream of questioning whether the stillborn child was actually her husband's—and Jo's hair becomes the stolen property of a servant who carries it off with her into another household. As Jo dismisses the wealthy, dashing neighbor who so desperately wants to marry her, the housemaid who wears Jo's hair attempts—with far less success—to repulse the dishonorable advances of her gentleman employer. Jo flees her neighbor's heartbreak by going to New York to write sensation stories; the disgraced housemaid flees to a lying-in home and, after abandoning her baby on the steps of a church, finds herself reduced to acting bit parts in bad melodramas.

Now Jo's hair smells of greasepaint and cheap gin and the old, tired dust that collects in theaters. Scolded by Professor Bhaer—her destiny, her doom, the only desire she is allowed—for writing immoral trash, Jo resolves to be virtuous and puts away her pen. Little does she suspect that her hair, forever beyond virtue now, lies in a moldy trunk of stage properties a mere mile from the boarding house where, obeying her fate, she met the Professor.

She has more important things to worry about. Returning home to her family, she finds the saintly Beth dying a saintly death of tuberculosis. Grieving, Jo dutifully nurses her little sister, who counsels, as Victorian household saints always do, self-abnegation. "Be everything to Father and Mother when I'm gone," Beth says sweetly, "and if it's hard to work alone, remember that I don't forget you, and that you'll be happier in doing that than writing splendid books or seeing all the world."

Jo agrees, of course. How could she not? This is her first deathbed scene, and it moves her profoundly. Young as she is, she little guesses how many others there will be, how few things she will ever be able to do for herself if she devotes her life to keeping promises to the dead. Pierced by sorrow, valiantly struggling not to rebel against the drudgery of the life she has promised to lead, she stays at home and learns to dust.

Meanwhile, Jo's hair has, in a moment of sartorial desperation, been snatched out of its moldy backstage trunk by the woman who will eventually become the most famous diva of the age. As Beth dies, Jo's hair crosses the Atlantic on a luxury steamer. Jo wears mourning as her hair, adorned with blue gems, disembarks in London. Jo languishes at home, washing dishes and convinced that she is fated to be an old maid, as the actress wearing her hair sets out, in the company of a Lord addicted to opium and the perfume of women's bodies, for the mysterious East. Professor Bhaer miraculously reappears, and proposes to Jo under an umbrella on a gray, pouring afternoon, while Jo's hair hides demurely beneath a veil in Istanbul.

She marries Friedrich, of course—what choice does she have?—and embarks upon the Plumfield years, raising her sons and other people's sons, any sons she can find, raising them and teaching them and watching them leave her to marry, to go into business, to go West. Meanwhile, more people die: her mother, Meg's husband, various prim spinster neighbors. Jo, good Victorian wife, becomes an old hand at deathbed scenes.

Most of them are quite dull. Only one, of the many she must endure through the years, holds any interest for this tale. As Jo's father lies dying, he gives her back the twenty-five dollars she sent him, so very long ago, when she sold her hair. All these years, he has kept the roll of yellowed bills in a little leather bag. "Spend it on your boys," he tells her, and weeping, she promises him that she will, just as she promised Beth so long ago to live for her parents instead of herself.

But Jo doesn't spend the money on her boys. Instead, for a reason she cannot fully explain even to herself, she chooses not to spend the money at all. She wears the little bag around her neck, where it weighs on her like a millstone. If she were asked, she would say that, like her father, she cannot find anything beautiful enough to buy with the money. She isn't asked, however. No one notices or cares. Her countless boys have other interests, and Friedrich seems curiously distracted.

As it turns out, he has become infatuated with a local dairymaid, a recent immigrant from Germany who looks like a Valkyrie and makes superb sauerkraut, a skill Jo has never mastered. In due course, Friedrich and his new love run off to Berlin, where they open a restaurant. Jo struggles onward, heroically trying to run Plumfield alone. She acknowledges, although only to herself, a guilty relief when at last the school burns down, sacrificed to the wickedness of a blaspheming boy who insists on smoking cigars in bed.

Jo herself has, at last, sacrificed everything her father and Beth could have wished: her hopes, her health, her ambition, her idealism, any purely personal desires. She has been ground down to a suffering kernel of patience, that Victorian household staple—as crucial as bread, salt, and oil for the lamps—the woman who gives all and asks for nothing. In the process, she has outlived the era that molded her, has outlived the century itself. Jo has remained at home through the invention of Studebakers and submarines, of lightbulbs and airplanes, of motion pictures and federal income tax. Her lifetime has seen the sinking of the *Titanic,* the extinction of the passenger pigeon, and the hideous convulsions of the First World War.

When she was young and strong, all of this would have thrilled her; now it only inspires terror. Jo is obsolete, and she knows it. Selfless Victorian wives are going the way of the passenger pigeon. Friedrich has left her, her boys are scattered to the corners of the earth, and the women of her family who might have cared for her are dead, worn down by work and childbearing. Old and ailing now, Jo throws herself upon the mercy of a world she no longer understands, and repairs to the county poorhouse.

Jo's hair, meanwhile, has found its way into harems and whorehouses, palaces and parades: it has traveled by elephant through dim steaming jungles, by camel across the Sahara, by whaleboat across the Atlantic. It has been presented to the Queen in Buckingham Palace and crossed the Rockies on a mule; it has been admired in Paris salons and Colorado saloons. It has been mute witness to adulteries, betrayals, murders, political plots, the death of men in duels and women in childbirth. It has seen the world's greatest cities and smallest villages. Children have pulled on it, lovers have caressed it, heathen healers have cast spells with it, taking it for some holy shaman's charm.

As we rejoin Jo's hair, a dog in Windswept, Kansas, carries it away from its owner, a wandering scissor salesman who won it from a California undertaker in a poker game. The dog buries it under a tree. A few days later, a very young Kansas pirate, seeking gold, notices the signs of recent digging and unearths Jo's hair. Disappointed not to have found more glittering treasure, but as confident as any savage that this relic must have arcane magical powers, he gives it to his mother for her birthday.

"What a strange thing," she says, holding Jo's hair gingerly between thumb and forefinger.

"Don't you like it, Mama?"

"It's pretty," she says, eyeing the thick, dirty plait and feeling ashamed of her own sparse locks. "I'd say it's been knocking about a bit, though. The lady who grew it must've been a stunner. I wonder why she cut it off?"

"Maybe she was an imprisoned princess," says the small pirate hopefully.

His mother grunts. "Don't get many of those around here, dearie. Those books you read will be rotting your brain. A nun, maybe. Who knows?" She puts Jo's hair into a drawer, not wishing to hurt her son's feelings. If only she had some nice hair of her own to cut off. She's heard that people pay good money for hair.

In the county home, Mother Bhaer lies marooned in a thin white bed, her wrinkled hands plucking at the coverlet in front of her, her wrinkled white head—all its hair lost, long ago, to illness, age, grief—covered by a wrinkled white cap. A thin line of drool descends from one side of her mouth. She has just soiled the sheets.

In her more lucid intervals, she realizes that she has indeed achieved her ambition of becoming like Beth, for here she is, dying, tended by others. She knows now that everyone becomes like Beth, whatever they do in their lives or don't do. Had she written all the splendid books she ever wanted to write, had she traveled to her heart's content, still she would have arrived here at last. She has cheated herself for nothing; her self-denial has left her only the small pouch around her neck, holding the twenty-five dollars she has never spent.

For the moment, she has forgotten about the money, forgotten the meaning of the slight, familiar weight on her chest. For long stretches now, she forgets where she is and where she has been, forgets that she is dying, forgets, blessedly, all the things she has lost and the many more she has never had. She lies on her narrow bed, her eyes glazed; sometimes she calls out names—Friedrich, Beth, Marmee—and then, head cocked, falls silent, as if listening for an answer from a beloved voice. The voices that answer are never ones she knows.

And now here comes another voice Jo doesn't know, someone new to change the bedclothes, to feed Jo gruel and carry the bowl away afterwards, to open the window when the room needs airing and close it again when Jo gets too cold. "Good morning, Mother Bhaer," the new voice says, too loudly, and fragments of Jo's past come rushing upon her like pieces of an unwelcome dream.

"Please don't call me that. Call me Jo."

The new voice hasn't heard her. "There now, mum, we'll have you all comfy in a jiffy," it says, and lifts Jo to yank the linens off the bed. Jo sees now a beaming, ruddy face, very young, as guileless as a yearling colt's. When the young woman turns to reach for the clean sheets, Jo sees swinging below her white cap a thick chestnut braid.

"What beautiful hair you have," Jo says wonderingly. It reminds her of something, but she can't quite remember what.

The young woman laughs, deftly changing the bed beneath Jo's prone body. "This thing? This old rat's tail? Oh, it's a hairpiece, mum. My aunt in Kansas sent it to me for a lark; her son found it buried under a tree. Just fancy that. I don't even know why I wear it—the pins stick into my head and it itches something furious. Probably has bugs. It smells queer enough."

She proceeds to pull out the pins until the offending appendage comes free. She tosses it carelessly onto the clean bed next to Jo, and Jo considers asking her to put the thing somewhere else—if it does have bugs, Jo certainly doesn't want it there—but instead she reaches out and begins to stroke the braid as she would an animal. Then she lifts it to her cheek, caressing it.

"Don't it smell queer?" the nurse says. "My aunt said she couldn't figure out what it smelled like. Nothing you'd call bad, exactly—just strange. Hair *do* pick up smells like nobody's business, don't it? What do you think it smells like, mum?"

It smells like sunlight and cinnamon, like ambergris and attar of rose, like battlefields and bedrooms. It smells like musk and milk, fresh ink and old ivory; like pine needles, incense, horsedung, curry, and beer, like old books and new timber. It smells like mustard and meadow grass and moonshine, like savannahs and sourdough and the restless sea.

Jo feels her eyes filling with tears. "I'll give you twenty-five dollars for this," she says.

The nurse stares at her. "For *that?* That old thing? Oh now, mum, I'd be robbing you, I couldn't—"

"Yes, you could," Jo snaps, already fumbling with the bag

around her neck. "Here. Take it. Buy something you want. Buy something beautiful."

She thrusts the money into the young woman's hand and sends her away. After all these years, Jo at last knows that there was a reason why her father never spent the twenty-five dollars on himself, and why Jo never spent it on anyone else. A hank of dirty hair has renewed her faith in Providence.

The nurse, guiltily clutching the leather bag, lingers outside the door, her conscience battling with the part of her that has long coveted a grand feathered hat in one of the fancy stores downtown. Surely the old woman must be cracked, to give twenty-five dollars for a filthy, nasty plait of hair like that. And what if she suddenly comes to her senses, accuses the nurse of cheating or robbing her?

The nurse hefts the little bag in her hand: suspiciously light, this little bag. Maybe there's nothing inside. Maybe the old lady made that up about the twenty-five dollars. I'll just take a look, the nurse thinks, curious now. She opens the bag and shakes out what's inside: a few folded, faded, fragile pieces of paper, cracking and crumbling as she touches them. They may have been money once, but they won't buy anything now.

Poor old thing, the nurse thinks, overcome by pity, poor crazy old woman, her money's not even any good anymore. I won't tell her. I'll let her keep the hair, and I'll let her think she paid for it. These old people need their pride.

Every good tale needs three of something. Here, then, is our third deathbed scene: Jo, stretched out on her thin white bed with a look of peace after all these weary months. It is the dark hour before dawn, the same hour at which Beth died so many years ago. Someone has combed Jo's hair out onto the pillow, and the local minister—complacently aware of his virtue in having dragged himself here from a warm bed—is amazed to discover that the wrinkled white cap has hidden, all this time, a rich crop of chestnut hair, thick and shining, hair any girl would be proud to show off in a ballroom.

From somewhere comes a faint smell of horses, of French perfume, of the sea; the minister wrinkles his nose and waves a hand in front of his face. The new nurse must have left this stink in the room, little strumpet under her starched white uniform, so many of the young ones are like that, pretending to be pious when really—

His mind begins to wander into speculations about the lascivious curves beneath the new nurse's white frock. Fortunately for the state of his soul, the old woman on the bed stirs and suddenly opens her eyes, looking fixedly at something across the room.

"What is it?" demands the minister softly, recalled to his duty. Sometimes these old people, especially the women, have visions of Heaven when they die. That kind of thing has gone out of fashion now, and the minister misses it. He can still remember the days when entire families would crowd around the deathbed, waiting eagerly for a glimpse of the Beyond. He has heard the dying describe the loving face of God, the Shining Ones gathered to welcome them home, blessed Sweet Jesus waiting on the broad banks of that final river. He always respected those visions; with one son dead in a mangled motorcar and another never returned from the battlefields of Europe, he wants more desperately than ever to believe them. "Dear Mother Bhaer, can you tell me what you see?"

She doesn't answer, but begins to weep: tears of joy, the minister knows, a triumph of faith in the hereafter. He feels joy hovering in the room like so many ministering angels. "Tell me," he pleads solemnly, his voice taking on the exhortatory fullness it acquires only in the pulpit and at deathbeds. He leans forward and gazes prayerfully upwards, certain that he is about to receive some new assurance of Paradise. "Before you go, dear, dear Mother Bhaer, tell me what you see!"

"All the world," says Jo March, and smiles at him, and dies.

A winner of science fiction's Hugo Award, Harry Turtledove is widely acclaimed as the dominant writer of "alternate history" science fiction, such as his bestselling The Guns of the South *and his more recent* Ruled Britannia. *He also writes fantasy stories and novels, including* Between the Rivers, *the Videssos series, and comic fantasies like* The Case of the Toxic Spell Dump.

Not All Wolves

HARRY TURTLEDOVE

Archbishopric of Cologne: 1176

A full moon hung in the clear dark sky. Dieter raced through the streets of Cologne. Mud splashed under the pads of his feet. It flew up to stick in lumps in the matted fur of his tail. He turned sharply and dashed down a narrow, stinking alley.

Much too close behind him, someone cried, "There he goes! That way!" A score of men or more were hunting him. Their high, excited shouts reminded him of the baying of wolves.

Had he been in his own familiar body, he might have laughed, or cried, or both at once. In the wolf's shape he wore, he could only whimper. He tried to run faster.

Torches appeared at the mouth of the alley. They cast a flickering light down its length. Dieter's eyes saw that only as brighter grayness. A wisp of breeze brought him the smell of torchsmoke, and of his pursuers. He could smell their fear, and their resolve.

The men knew nothing of the wondrous things his nose

told him, any more than a deaf man could follow a minnesinger's song. But their eyes, now, were keener than his; they were many; and they could plan. More shouts rang out:

"There he is!" "Which way did he turn?" "To the left!" "No, to the right, you idiot!" "Yes, to the right! I saw him too!" "Klaus, Joachim, and Hans, up to the street of the tailors, and quickly! Don't let the cursed beast get through that way!"

And one more cry, over and over again: "Kill the werewolf!"

It's not my fault, Dieter wanted to explain. *I do no harm.* But when he opened his wolf's jaws, only a wolf's growls came out. And those wolf's jaws, he could not deny, held a full set of wolf's teeth. He could feel them, jagged against his tongue, which hung from the side of his mouth as he panted in the air he needed to run and run and run.

Inside the fleshy envelope of a wolf, though, he kept the wits he had as a boy. If the street of the tailors was still unblocked, he might yet break away from the pack (yes, that was the proper word, he thought) at his heels.

Too late, too late—he heard Klaus, Joachim, and Hans beat him to the corner. They all carried torches; two had clubs, and the other a woodcutter's ax. They looked this way and that. *Good,* Dieter thought. They did not know he was close by. He sprang at them. They were only three, after all, not twenty.

Two screamed like lost souls and fled. The third had more courage in him. His club thudded against Dieter's ribs. Pain flared, then died. Dieter's flesh mended with unnatural speed. Had the fellow thought to swing the torch, though, he might have done true harm.

Dieter gave him no chance to think of that. He snarled horribly and ran by. He was ahead of his pursuers again. But he was not free of them, as he had hoped. The brave man pounded after him, yelling. His cries, and the shrieks the other two were letting out, were sure to draw the rest of the mob.

All Dieter wanted was a place to be left alone to wait out the night. Come morning, he knew, he would be himself again: thirteen, an orphan, making his living as best he could, doing odd jobs for weavers and tanners, enamelers and smiths.

Was it four months ago the change had first come on him? Other changes started not long before then. His voice began to crack, and to deepen. Fine, fuzzy down appeared on his cheeks. The second- and third-hand tunics and breeches he wore seemed suddenly to bind, and to leave him bare at the wrists and ankles.

Every lad he knew went through those changes. But not every lad he knew turned into a wolf when the moon was full.

The first time it happened, by luck Dieter had been alone. Even after he struggled out of the clothes that no longer fit his new shape, he did not fully realize what he was. Not until he changed back at sunrise and saw the wolf's prints in the dirt of the empty stable where he'd spent the night did he begin to understand. And with understanding came fear.

The next night of the full moon, and the one after that, he had sought out deserted places to wait through the change. While he was a wolf, he had no urge to tear the throat out of every man and beast he saw: past stealing a flitch of bacon once, he had gone hungry on nights the change struck him. He also had no illusions about the townsfolk believing that.

He had been on his way to hide this time, too. But that fat fool of a swordsmith kept him working late, and the moon rose while he was still on the street.

A woman screamed. He could not really blame her. Had he seen someone turn from boy to wolf before his eyes, he thought he would have screamed himself. The hunt had been on ever since.

"Kill the werewolf!"

He was growing heartily tired of that cry. But the one that

came after made the hair along his spine stand up: "Aye, burn it in the old market square in front of St. Martin's church, as we did the wizard last year!"

The crowd, people said, had jammed the square. Dieter had not gone himself. He had no stomach for such spectacles. He had not escaped it altogether, though; the stench of burnt flesh lingered for days in front of the church. Even then, he had taken more notice of smells than most folk. *No wonder,* he thought.

He imagined himself—in wolf's shape or boy's, it would not matter—tied to a stake, with little yellow flames licking through the fagots toward his tender flesh. He threw back his head and howled, a long cry of fear and desolation.

The shouts behind him redoubled. Dogs yelped frantically. Lights appeared in windows as people fetched lamps or candles from beside their beds to try to see what was going on.

Some of them, Dieter knew, would join the chase. He should have kept quiet. But the mere idea of burning had ripped the wail from him. By God, they would *not* burn him!

By God! Hope ran through him. It was dizzying, so much so that he almost stumbled into a pile of garbage at the edge of the street. Surely a priest could lift this curse from him!

He seldom went to church. He had to worry about keeping his belly—if not full, then at least with something in it—on Sunday no less than any other day. But he knew where every church in the town was. They were likely places for work—and handouts.

Had he been next door to St. Martin's, he would not have gone there, not after the shouts of burning him in front of it. But St. Martin's lay close by the Rhine, far away from the ancient maze of streets he was running. This central part of Cologne, he had heard, went back to the legendary days of Rome.

Of Rome he knew nothing save the name. He did know he was near the church of St. Cacilien. If none of the men who hunted him was waiting down this street . . .

None was. He turned right, then left. There stood St. Cacilien's church, its doors open to the needy. No one, Dieter thought, had ever been more needy than he. He climbed awkwardly up the stairs—stairs were made for creatures with two legs, not four—and into the church.

It looked strange, and not just because he was seeing it only in shades of gray. Now his eyes were also lower to the ground. The pews seemed a forest around him.

In boy's shape, too, he hardly noticed the incense in the air. It was just part of how churches smelled. As a wolf, though, the bitterness of myrrh and frankincense's sharp spicy scent made his nose twitch and tingle. He gasped, then sneezed, once, twice, three times.

A priest was walking up the aisle to the altar. He carried a long staff with a crucifix on the end. At the sneezes, he whirled round in surprise. "Good health to—" he began, then stopped in horror when he saw who—or rather, what—had sneezed.

Dieter trotted toward him. He opened his mouth to ask the priest's blessing. That showed him the one flaw in his plan. As a wolf, he could not tell the man what he needed.

The priest saw only a great hairy beast rushing at him with gaping jaws. *"Lieber Gott!"* he gasped. With no other weapon he could reach, he swung his staff at the wolf.

The crucifix was silver. The blow hurt Dieter as much as if he had been human, and kept on hurting. Howling in pain and dismay, he whirled about and fled from the church, tail between his legs. "A wolf! A wolf!" the priest shouted behind him.

Some of the hunters were just drawing near St. Cacilien's. They yelled and pointed when they saw Dieter streak out.

They ran after him. His savage growl, though, made them think twice about coming close. Hurt as he was, he acted and sounded fiercer than before.

But the men did cut him off from the new market square. He growled, deep in his throat. So many streets led off the square, he would have had his choice of escape routes. Instead, his pursuers forced him away—and the priest's hue and cry would only bring more people out after him. Already he could hear new voices, smell new scents among those who chased him.

He was halfway down a street before it jogged to show him it had only the exit down which he had come. A tall, barred gate of stout oak timbers blocked the other end. He yelped and whimpered. He was trapped here. Too late to double back now; his pursuers had plugged the way out.

They knew it too. "We have him now!" one shouted. "He can't get into the Jews' quarter at night. Come on!"

Dieter snarled, this time at himself. He should have remembered that the Jews were closed off from the rest of the city between sunset and sunrise. The men were coming closer fast. He could not go back through them. He stood there, panting. Part of him, the exhausted part, wanted to lie down and give up.

Then he thought of the flames again. No, he could not let the hunters take him. He ran for the gate and flung himself upwards.

He had imagined himself easily clearing the timbers, landing lightly on the far side. His head and forelegs cleared, sure enough, but his belly slammed against the gate, hard enough to drive half the wind from him. He hung there a moment, stunned. His hind feet scrabbled for purchase. The wood was rough; his claws bit. Leaving skin and hair behind, he dragged himself over and fell like a stone to the ground.

His undignified scramble had let him be seen. "There he

went!" a man yelled from the other side of the gate. The fellow pounded on it with his fist. "Here, you damned Jews, open up!"

Dieter raced away. Now he had time to find a hiding place without any of his pursuers liable to spot him diving for cover. He would not keep that chance for long. Several men were battering at the gate, one, it sounded like, with an ax. "Open up!" they shouted at the top of their lungs. "You damned stupid Jews, there's a werewolf loose among you!"

That would make the gates open if anything did, Dieter thought. He knew he never hurried to do anything for people who cursed him and called him names. He suspected the Jews were no different from him in that, no matter that they had their own strange faith. But he would run if someone screamed, "Fire, you fool!" The Jews might swallow insults for the sake of hunting him down.

He rounded a corner, and almost ran into an old man who wore a bushy beard and a long black robe that flapped at his ankles. They both stopped, staring at each other. The old Jew did not run shrieking, as so many had.

Behind Dieter, clamor grew. Either someone would come open the gate or the men who hunted him soon would break it down.

The frozen tableau that gripped Dieter and the man could not last, not with shouts of "Werewolf!" flying thick and fast. Dieter was about to run when the old Jew spoke: "Come with me, and quickly!" He opened a door, gestured urgently.

Dieter hesitated. All the wild, wolfly instincts in him rebelled at trusting any man. The boy he still was had trouble believing anyone would want to help him in his present state. But the old man had not known he was coming. No trap could be waiting for him inside that house. And even if one somehow was, what could a frail graybeard do against any wolf, let alone a werebeast?

The sound of the gate creaking open decided him. His hunters were in the Jewish quarter, and the Jews likely would be after him too. Everyone was against him, save this one old man. He grabbed at that like a drowning man grabbing for a log. He darted inside.

The old man shut the door behind them. "Get under the table there," he said. When Dieter had, he draped a cloth over it that hung down to the floor on all sides. Then he lit a couple of candles at a little brazier and set them on the table. Dieter's world, the little square of it he could see, went from black to gray. The old man rustled about for another couple of minutes, then sat down. His knees pushed at the tablecloth.

"Now we wait," he said. Dieter whined softly to show he had heard.

They did not wait long. A knock came at the door. "Avram, are you there?" a man asked.

"Where else would I be, with the candles lit?" the old Jew said. "It's late, David. Why do you come around asking foolish questions?"

"Avram, will you please open up?" the other man, David asked. "Some of the good folk from outside the gate are with me. They are searching, they say, for a—a wolf."

The stool creaked as Avram rose. Dieter heard him open the door. "A wolf? In Cologne?"

"So they say," David told him. "They seemed most urgent—we thought it wiser to let them come in, no matter the hour."

"Is that the commotion I heard?" Avram sounded grumpy and disapproving. "It was loud enough to disturb my studies."

"Too bad, old Jew." Dieter shivered at the sound of the new voice—it belonged to the man who had dared swing a club at him. "When a werewolf is loose in the city, we don't care what we disturb to find it." Others shouted agreement.

"Well, I have seen no wolves, were or otherwise, gentlemen.

I've been at my books since sundown. May I go back to them?"

"Since sundown, you say? Why are your candles so long?" Dieter had to clamp his jaws shut to keep from whimpering in terror. Not only was this hunter a brave man, but also no one's fool.

Avram just shrugged; Dieter heard his robe rustle. "Because the last pair guttered out not long ago, and I lit these from them. Why else?"

"Hrmmp. You've seen or heard nothing out of the ordinary, you say?"

"Not till you came," Avram replied sharply.

"You watch your mouth, Jew, or you'll watch the few teeth you have left go flying into the mud." But after that, the man turned back to his comrades. "If this old bastard's been here all night, the cursed beast can't have snuck in. On to the next house." Dieter heard them tramping away.

Avram shut the door, walked back over to the table. He did not lift the cloth. Very softly, he said, "I'll stay down here reading until these candles fail. Don't come out till then. I'll leave a dish of water for you. You'd be wiser to stay the night here, I think. In the morning, in your proper shape, you'll have an easier time getting back to your own affairs."

Dieter wished he could answer in words. He thumped his tail against the floor. Avram grunted. The old Jew sat down, began turning pages and, every so often, muttering to himself.

When one candle went out, he got up. As he had promised, he poured water from a jug and set it by the table. He blew out the other candle. "Sleep well, wolf," he said. He went up the stairs in the dark.

Even though no one could see him now, Dieter did not come out for a long time. When at last he did, he bent his head over the bowl and lapped it dry, then slurped drops of water from his chin and whiskers with his tongue. Fleeing was thirsty work.

He went back under the table to sleep. If it grew light before he changed back to himself, he wanted the concealment the cloth would bring.

He woke to find one of his feet poking a table leg. One of his feet . . . It was hairless, clawless, with five toes all in a row. It was dirty, but pink under the dirt. He could see it was pink. "I'm Dieter," he whispered. His mouth formed words. He was a boy again.

He crawled out from under the table, stood up. He realized he was naked, and saw he had a small scar on his belly that had not been there before: a souvenir, he supposed, of his scramble over the gate.

He made a cloak of the tablecloth. He had just wrapped it around himself when old Avram came downstairs. "So that's what you look like, eh?" the old Jew said. He handed Dieter a bundle of clothes. "Here. Put these on. You're apt to look out of place, wearing table linen in the street."

The clothes were not new, but better than what Dieter was used to wearing. They fit well enough. As he dressed, Avram cut him cheese and bread for breakfast. He had not known how hungry he was until he saw he had finished before Avram was even half done with his smaller portion.

"Want more?" Avram asked.

"No, thank you." Dieter paused. "Thank you," he said again, in a different tone of voice.

The old Jew gave a gruff nod. "It should be safe now to go back to your part of the city, boy."

"Yes." Dieter started for the door, then stopped. He turned back to Avram. "May I ask you something?"

"Ask," Avram said round a mouthful of bread and cheese.

"Why did you save me?" Dieter blurted. "I mean—everyone

else who saw me wanted to kill me on sight. What made you so different from the rest of them?"

Avram sat silent so long on his stool that Dieter wondered if he had somehow offended him. At last the old Jew said slowly, "One thing you should remember always—you are not the only one ever hunted down Cologne's streets."

Dieter thought about that. He never really had before. Jews falling victim to mobs were just part of life in the city to him, like chamber pots being hurled into the street from second-floor windows or famine one year in four. The Jews, though, he realized, might not see it like that.

Indeed, Avram was going on, as much to himself as to Dieter, "No, lad, and not all wolves run on four legs, either. You ask me, the ones with two are worse. Keep clear of them, and you'll do all right." He opened the door.

Yesterday, Dieter thought as he stepped into the cool damp air of early morning, he would have had no idea what the old Jew was talking about. Now he knew. With a last nod to Avram, he started down the street. He would have to find some work to do if he expected to eat lunch.

Debra Doyle and James D. Macdonald are the authors of many works of SF fantasy, including the Mageworlds series of SF adventure novels and the Mythopoeic Fantasy Award–winning Knight's Wyrd. *"Stealing God" is one of a series of stories and novels starring Peter Crossman, Knight Templar in the modern world.*

Stealing God

DEBRA DOYLE AND JAMES D. MACDONALD

I was working the security leak at Rennes-le-Château when the word came down. The Rennes flub was over a hundred years old, but the situation needed constant tending to keep people off the scent. That's the thing about botches. They never go away.

Now I had new orders. Drop whatever I was doing and get my young ass over to New York mosh-gosh. Roger that, color me gone. I was on the Concorde out of Paris before the hole in the air finished closing behind me in Languedoc.

With the Temple paying my way, cost wasn't a worry. I had enough other things to think about. The masters weren't bringing me across the Atlantic just to chew the fat. We had plenty of secure links. Whatever this was, it required my presence.

Sherlock Holmes said that it was a capital mistake to theorize before one had information. My old sergeant, back when I was learning the trade, told me to catch some sleep whenever I could. I dozed my way over the Atlantic and didn't wake up until we hit JFK.

Customs inspection was smooth and uneventful—I had only one piece of carry-on luggage, with nothing in it that the customs people might recognize as a weapon. I took the third cab in the rank outside the terminal and was on my way. First stop was at The Cloisters in Fort Tryon Park, to pay my respects to the Magdalene Chalice. My arrival would be noted there, and the contact would come soon.

Outside the museum I got another cab to Central Park West. I made my way to the Rambles, that part of the park where the city can't be seen and you can almost imagine yourself in the wilderness.

Sure enough, a man was waiting. He wore the signs, the air, and the majesty. I made a quiet obeisance, just to go by the book, and he responded. But I didn't need any of the signals in order to recognize one of the two masters.

There are only three and thirty of us in the inner Temple, plus the masters. We're the part of the Temple that's hidden from all the other Knights Templar: the secret from the holders of the secrets, the ace up the sleeve. All of us warriors, all of us priests. We serve, we obey. When needed, we kick ass.

"Hello," he said. "It's been years."

"Sure has, John," I replied. "What's up?"

We spoke in Latin, for the same reason the Church does. No matter where you are or where you're from, you can communicate.

"There's a problem," he said. "Over on the East Side."

The Grail. It had to be. "Instructions?"

"Go in, check it out, report back."

"Anything special I'm looking for?"

"No," he said. "Just be aware that the last three people who got those same orders haven't reported in yet."

We nodded to each other and parted. I walked south. There are a bunch of hotels along Central Park South, and I wanted to hit the bar in one of them and do some thinking. For Prester John to be away from Chatillon meant that things were more serious than I'd suspected.

I sat in the bar at the Saint Moritz, drinking Laphroaig neat the way God and Scotland made it, while I wondered what in the name of King Anfortas could be going on over at the UN, and how I was going to check. Halfway down the bar another man sat playing with the little puddle of water that had collected around the base of his frosty mug of beer. He was drinking one of those watery American brews with no flavor, no body, and no strength to recommend it, though it had apparently gotten him half plowed regardless. After a minute or two I realized what had drawn my attention: He was tracing designs in the water on the bar.

Designs I recognized. Runes.

Did they think I was blind, I wondered, or so ignorant that I wouldn't notice? But I didn't perceive any immediate danger, and a sudden departure would tip my hand to whoever was watching. Maybe this guy was just a random drunk who happened to know his mystic symbols.

Sure, and maybe random drunks had nailed three other knights.

No, more likely he was a Golden Dawner or a Luciferian. Probably a Luciferian. Lucies have a special relationship with the Grail, or they think they do. I tipped up the last drops of Laphroaig, harsh on my tongue like a slurry of ground glass and peat moss, called for another shot, and drank half of it. The money lying by the shot glass would pay for my drink. I left the bar, left the hotel, turned east, and started walking. Leaving good booze unfinished is a venial sin, but that way it'd look like I'd just stepped over to the men's room and was coming back soon—good for a head start.

Halfway down the block I spotted a convenient bunch of construction barriers. I ducked behind them, and as soon as I was out of sight from the street, my left hand darted into my bag. A couple of seconds to work the charm and I stepped out onto the sidewalk, Tarnkappe fully charged and ready in my hand. My bag remained behind, looking for anyone without True Sight like a rotting sack of garbage.

There are only three Tarnkappen in the world, and I had one of them. Something like that can come in handy in my line of work, and it was about to come in handy again. I walked slowly until I was sure that anyone following me from the Saint Moritz was on my tail. Then I cruised eastward, window-shopping. Windows make great mirrors to show what's behind you—and sure enough, here came my runic friend, Mr. Beer.

I turned a few random corners to make certain he was following, then got into a crowd and slipped on the Kappe. A few seconds later, after a bit of fancy footwork to make sure that my location and method weren't revealed by a trail of people tripping over nothing, I leaned against the side of a building and watched to see what would happen next.

Mr. Beer was confused, all right. He cast up and down the street a bit, but pretty soon he figured out that he'd botched the job. He stepped into a phone booth, then punched in a string and spoke a couple of words. His face was at the wrong angle for lipreading, but I could guess what he was saying: "I lost him."

Maybe I couldn't see what he was saying, but I'd managed to get the number he'd dialed. The whole time he was on the phone, I was on the other side of the street with a small pair of binoculars. He hadn't shielded the button pad with his hand. Half trained—a Lucie, for sure.

I trailed him until he went into a hotel and up to a room. Then I slipped the Kappe into my back pocket and followed that up by slipping a few quick questions to people who didn't even know afterward that they'd been questioned. Before long I knew that Beer's name was Max Lang, that he spoke with a foreign accent, that he'd been there for one week and planned to stay for another, and that he tipped well.

I left him in the hotel. The trail had taken me to the Waldorf-Astoria in midtown. Might as well head over to the United Nations building. It was still early, with lots of light in the sky and lots of people on the sidewalk. I kept my eyes open, but I didn't pick up a tail.

I turned the problem over in my mind. Max Lang couldn't have found his way out of a paper bag if you gave him a map and printed instructions. So how did he find me in the bar? And how did he come to know the Therion rune sequence?

The UN building stands towering over FDR Drive, along the East River. Security there is tight by American standards, which means laughable for anyplace else in the world. Inside the building I knew which way to go, and I had passes that were as good as genuine to get me anywhere I needed.

I stood for a moment just inside the metal detectors at the front doors, feeling with my senses. Was there something wrong in the building? Nothing big enough to show up without a divination, and I doubted that the guards would let me get away with performing one here, even if they weren't bent to the left—and with three knights missing already, only a fool wouldn't assume that the guards were bent. Prester John doesn't use fools. I headed for the Meditation Room.

The Meditation Room was right where I'd left it last time I'd been in town. No obvious problems. I went in. Everything was still in place. There was the mural in the front of the room, with its abstract picture of the sun, half dark, and half light. Cathar symbolism, and Manichean before that. We kept the picture up there to remind the Cathars how wrong they'd been. And there was the Grail—a natural lodestone, cut and polished into a gleaming rectangular block.

Wolfram von Eschenbach let the cat out of the bag when he wrote *Parzival,* back in the twelve hundreds. Somehow he'd gotten the straight word on what the Grail looked like. According to the Luciferians, who claim to know the inside story, the Grail had been the central stone in Lucifer's crown, back before he had a couple of really bad days and got his dumb ass tossed out of Heaven. When Lucifer landed in Hell, they say, the Grail landed on Earth.

What *was* true was that the Grail had banged around the Middle East for quite a while—capstone of the Great Pyramid, cornerstone of the Temple of Solomon, that sort of thing. Back during the Crusades we'd been given the keeping of it. We never could hide the fact that there was a Grail, or that it was holy, but for a long time we tried to get people to go looking for dinnerware. Then someone talked. Somewhere, somehow, there was a leak. And blunders, like I said, never go away.

So far, though, everything looked all peachy-keen and peaceful at the United Nations. The room, the mural, the big chunk of polished rock. I pulled out a little pocket compass. Yep, that was still a lodestone over there.

One more test. I opened the little gold case in my pants pocket and slipped out a consecrated Host. I palmed it, then walked past the Grail on my way out of the room. My hand brushed the polished stone as I went by. Then I was out of the room, heading for the main doors and the street.

I raised my hand to straighten my hair, and as my hand passed my lips, I took the Host. Then I knew there was something really, desperately wrong. No taste of blood.

Hosts bleed when they touch the Holy Grail. Don't ask me how; I'm not enough of a mystic to answer. But I do know why—Godhood in the presence of Itself makes for interesting physical manifestations.

There was a stone back there in the Meditation Room. But either it wasn't the real Grail, or it wasn't holy anymore.

Whoever did this was far more powerful than I'd imagined.

They either had to smuggle a six-and-a-half-ton block of rock into the UN, and smuggle another six-and-a-half-ton block of rock out of there without anyone noticing, or they had to defile something that had never been defiled—not even on Friday the 13th, when some men with real power and knowledge had given it their best shot and come away with nothing but their own sins to show for the effort.

I had to report back. Prester John needed to know about this as soon as possible.

That was when they hit me, just as I stepped out onto the street. I felt a light impact on the side of my neck, like a mosquito. I slapped at it by reflex, but before my hand got there, my knees were already buckling. Two men moved in on either side of me, supporting me. My eyes were open, and I could see and remember, but my arms and legs weren't responding anymore.

"Come on," the man on my right said. "You're going for a little ride."

They walked me across the plaza, three men holding hands. No one looked twice. You see some funny things in New York.

They put me in the back of a limo. Another man was behind the wheel, waiting for them. The door shut and we pulled away from the curb. The guy on my right pushed my head down so I wasn't visible from outside, which meant I couldn't see where they were taking me, either.

We crossed a bridge—I could hear it humming in the tires—then slowed to join other traffic. I pulled inside myself and looked for where the poison was in my body. It was potent, but there couldn't be much of it. I could handle not-much.

With enough concentration some people can slow their heartbeat down to where doctors can't detect it. Other people can slow their breathing to where they can make a coffinful of air last a week. I concentrated on finding all the molecules of poison in my bloodstream and making Maxwell's Demon shunt them off to somewhere harmless.

Little finger of my left hand, say. Let it concentrate there and not get out.

The car was slowing again. Stopping. Too soon. I hadn't gotten all the poison localized yet.

They pulled me out of the backseat. We were on a dock, probably on Long Island. No one else was in sight. I could see now what was going to happen: Into the water, the current carries me away, I'm too weak to swim, I drown. The poison is too dilute, or it breaks down, or it's masked by the byproducts of decomposition and the toxicological examination doesn't find it at the autopsy.

They weren't asking any questions. Instead, we went out to the end of the pier, them walking and me being walked. Two of them held me out over the water while the third—the one who'd been the driver—spoke.

"We do not slay thee. Thy blood is not on us. We desire no earthly thing: Go to God with all ye possess. Sink ye or swim ye, thou art nothing more to us."

A roaring sounded in my ears, and I was falling forward. Water, cold and salt, rushed into my nose and mouth.

Human bodies float in salt water. *Concentrate on moving the poison. Give me enough control that I can float on my back . . .* I was sinking. The light was growing dim. I concentrated on lowering my need for oxygen, lowering my heartbeat, lowering everything.

Move the poison. Don't use air. Float.

Then it was working. I could feel strength and control return to my arms and legs. I was deep underwater. I opened my eyes and looked around. I saw shadow and pilings not too far away: the bottom of the pier.

Swim that way—slowly—keep the poison in the left little finger. Don't use air. Then float up.

I didn't dare gasp for breath when I got to the surface. For all I knew, my assailants were still up there waiting. Slowly, quietly, I allowed my lungs to empty, then fill again. I hooked my left arm around the nearest piling, then reached down with my right hand and undid a shoelace. I hoped I wouldn't lose the shoe.

Using the lace, I tied a tourniquet around my left little finger—now the drug couldn't get out—and reached down again to my belt. The buckle hid a small push-dagger, made of carbonite so metal detectors wouldn't pick it up. Don't let the material fool you; it's hard and sharp. I cut the end of my little finger, held the knife between my teeth, and squeezed out the poisoned blood. The blood came out thick and dark, trailing away in the water like a streamer of red. Then I unloosed the tourniquet and it was time to go.

The foot of the pier was set in a cement wall about seven feet high, but the wall was old and crumbling. I got a fingerhold, then a foothold. At last I was out of the water. I crawled up until I was lying on top of the wall, under the decking of the pier. Anyone looking for me would have to be in the water to see me. I stayed there, waiting and listening, for a hundred heartbeats, then two hundred, and heard nothing but waves lapping up against the wall.

A sound. A board creaked on the dock. They'd left someone behind, all right—someone waiting like I was, only not so quietly.

But those cowboys had been a little slack. Either they'd trusted their drug too much, or else it was really important to their ritual that I keep all my possessions. The end result was the same: I hadn't been searched. When I reached a hand down to my pocket, the Tarnkappe was still where I'd stuffed it when I'd gotten done with Max Lang.

A visit to Lang looked like it was in the cards. Later. There were other things to do first.

I put on the Kappe, then crawled out of my hiding place and up onto the shore. There he was, out on the pier: a man in a business suit, carrying a Ruger mini-14 at high port. I sat on the shore, hoping I'd dry out enough so that water drops splashing on the pavement wouldn't give me away. Or chattering teeth—the sun was heading down and it was going to get cold pretty soon for a man in wet clothes.

Whatever those lads had hit me with, it'd left me with the beginning of a king-of-hell headache. I ignored the discomfort and concentrated on the man on the pier. Who was he? I'd never seen him before.

I heard the second man coming before I saw him, tramping heavy-footed down the road to the pier. He walked out and greeted the first. This time I could read their lips: "Time to go . . . there's a meeting . . . yes, we both have to be there . . . forget him, he's gone."

They walked back off the pier and I swung in behind them, letting the sound of their footfalls cover mine.

They had a car parked up the way—not the one that had brought me here. This one had two bucket seats up in front and nothing behind. They got inside; I got up on the back bumper and leaned forward across the trunk, holding on with arms spread wide. The car pulled away. All I had to do now was stay on board until they got to wherever they were going. That, and hope the Tarnkappe didn't come off at highway speeds.

The first sign we came to told me that I was NOW LEAVING BABYLON, NEW YORK. Babylon. Figures. Nothing happens by chance, not when you have the Grail involved. It all means something. The trick is finding out what.

This pair wasn't real gabby. I'd hoped to do some more lipreading in the rearview mirror, but as far as I could tell they drove back to the Big Apple in stony silence. They took the Midtown Tunnel back in, then local streets to somewhere on the East Side around 70th street. That was where I had my next bit of bad luck.

Out on the highway, the Tarnkappe had stuck on my head like glue. But here in the concrete canyons, a side gust took it away and there I was in plain view on the back deck. All I could do was roll off and scuttle for safety between the rushing cars, while taxis screamed at me and bicycle messengers tried to leave tire stripes up my back.

I made it to the other side of the street. The Tarnkappe was gone, blown who-knows-where by the wind, and I couldn't make myself conspicuous by doubling back to look for it. A quick stroll around the corner, down one subway entrance and up another, and I was as safe as I could hope to be with my shoes squishing seawater.

I started out at a New Yorker's street pace for the spot where I'd ditched my bag. By now the sun was down for real and the neon darkness was coming up: a bad time of day for strangers to go wandering around Central Park. Me, I kind of hoped someone would try for a mugging. I had a foul mood to work off, and smashing someone's face in the name of righteousness would just about do the trick.

Nobody tried anything, and my bag was waiting where I'd left it. I changed clothes right there in the alley, and debated reporting in. But someone had gone to a lot of trouble to make me vanish, and I wanted the secret of my survival to be shared by the minimum number.

Sure, I had my orders. But blind obedience isn't what the Temple needs from the thirty and three. Distasteful as I found the possibility, I had to consider whether I'd been sold out from inside. If so, then reporting in would be a very bad idea.

Maybe those other three knights had figured things out the same way. They could be lying low and saying nothing until the situation clarified. But I didn't think it was likely. Odds were that they were sweating it out in Purgatory right now—like I'd be, if I didn't start taking precautions.

I began by using the kit in my bag to make a few changes to my appearance. No sense having everyone who'd already seen me recognize me the next time I showed up. Meanwhile, it was dinnertime, which meant there was a good chance that my Mr. Lang would be away from his room. A search might show me something useful. And when he got back from dinner, I wanted to ask him some questions.

The rooms at his hotel had those new-style keycards with the magnetic strip. Some people think the keycards are secure, and they'll probably stop the teenagers who bought a Teach Yourself Locksmithing course out of the back of a comic book. The one on Lang's room didn't even slow me down.

Lang wasn't out, after all. He was in the room, but I wasn't going to get any answers out of him without a Ouija board. He was naked, lying on his back in the bathtub. Someone had been there before me—someone with a sharp knife and a sick imagination.

I dipped my finger in the little bottle of chrism I carry in my tote and made a quick cross on his forehead.

"For thy sins I grant thee absolution," I muttered—wherever he'd gone, he needed all the help he could get. Lucies aren't famed for their high salvation rate.

Then I searched the room, even though whoever had taken care of Lang would have done that job once already. Aside from the mess in the bathtub, the contents of the hotel room didn't have much to say about anything, except maybe the banality of evil: no address books; no letters or memos; no telltale impressions on the memo pad. Nothing of any interest at all.

Then I found something, taped to the back of a drawer. My

unknown searcher had missed it. Or maybe he'd left it behind, having no use for it—he hadn't used bullets on Lang, only the knife. But there it was, a Colt Commander, a big mean .45 automatic.

I checked it over. Five rounds in the magazine, one up the spout. Weapon cocked, safety off. I lowered the hammer to half-cock and took the Colt with me, stuffing it in my waistband in the back, under the sport coat I was wearing. That lump of cold metal made me feel a lot better about the rest of the evening.

One more thing to do: I picked up the room phone, got an outside line, and punched in the number Lang had called that afternoon. After two rings, someone picked it up.

"International Research," said a female voice.

"This is Max," I said, my voice as muffled as I could make it. "I'm in trouble."

Then I hung up.

Before I left the room, I opened the curtains all the way. Then I eased myself out of the hotel and over to a vantage point across the street, where a water tower on a lower building gave me a view of the room I'd just left. The bad guys who'd tried to drown me hadn't taken my pocket binoculars, either. Those were good optics—when I used the binocs to look across the street, it was like I was standing in the hotel room.

I waited. The wind was cold, and a little after one in the morning it started to rain. It was just past 4 A.M., at that hour before dawn when sick men die, when I spotted something happening.

Across the street the door eased open, then drifted shut. A woman walked into the room. She was tall, slender, and stacked. Black lace-up boots, tight black jeans, tight black sweater. Single strand of pearls. Red hair, long enough to sit on, loose down her back. A black raincoat hung over her right arm. She was wearing black leather gloves. In her left hand she had a H&K nine-millimeter. Color coordinated: The artillery was black, too.

She did a walk-through of the room. Nothing hurried. I watched her long enough that I could recognize her again, and then I was sliding down from my perch. The lady had carried a raincoat. If she planned to go out into the weather, I was going to find out where she was headed. My guess was that she was from International Research, whoever they really were.

I was betting that she'd come out the main door. So I did a slow walk up and down the street, one sidewalk and then the other, before I spotted her through the glass in the lobby, putting on that coat. Then she was out the revolving door and away.

One nice thing about New York is that it's possible to follow someone on foot. The car situation is so crazy that no one brings a private vehicle onto the island if they can help it. She might still call a cab, but if she did, so could I. I've never yet in my career told a cabbie to "Follow that car," but there's a first time for everything.

I wasn't going to get the chance tonight. A limo was cruising up the street at walking speed, coming up behind the lady in black. I recognized it. The boys who'd grabbed me yesterday had used that car or one just like it to carry me out to Babylon for sacrifice.

The car stopped and the two clowns in the back got out. They looked like the same pair of devout souls who'd invited me to a total-immersion baptism. It was time for me to join the fun. I angled across the rain-soaked street, pulling that big-ass Colt into my hand as I went.

The two goons had caught up with the lady, but she wasn't going as quietly as I had the day before. Maybe they'd missed with their drugged dart—she was muffled to the nose in her raincoat, with the collar turned up. Or maybe they wanted her talkative when they got wherever they were going. No matter. They were distracted, and the driver was watching the show.

I came up beside the window out of his blind spot. Using the .45 as a pair of knucks, I punched right through the glass into the back of his head. Then I pulled the door open and him out with it, spilling him onto his back in the street. I kicked him once on the point of the chin while he lay there.

"For these and all thy sins I absolve thee," I muttered, making a cross over him with the Colt.

The whole thing hadn't taken more than a couple of seconds, and now it was time to go help the lady. Generally speaking I'm not the kind of knight who goes around rescuing damsels in distress—but I wanted to talk with this one, and keeping her alive was the only way to go.

I used the roof of the car as a vaulting horse and landed feet first on top of one of the goons, bringing him down with me in a tangle of arms and legs. It took me a second to extricate myself, with elbows, knees, and the heavy automatic smashing into my man along the way. He got in a couple of good licks, then gave up all interest and started holding what was left of his nuts.

Meanwhile the lady in black was doing the best she could. But her little nine-millimeter was caught under the raincoat, and the man who had her was too strong. He'd thrown an arm around her neck in the classic choke come-along and was dragging her into the backseat. Maybe he hadn't noticed that the driver wasn't there anymore.

I took him in the back of the skull with the butt of the Colt Commander. He slipped to the ground to join his moaning pal.

"Come on!" I yelled at the lady. "Let's get out of here!"

"Where to?" she gasped.

"Into the car."

I slid behind the wheel—the keys were still in the ignition and the engine was turning over—and slammed the driver's-side door. The lady didn't argue. She got in beside me and closed the other door, and I took off from the curb.

I made a left turn across traffic into a side street, and said, "Where to, sister?"

"Who are you?"

Rather than give her an answer, I said, "The cops are gonna be all over this block in a couple of minutes—I saw the doorman go running inside like a man with 911 on his mind. You got a safe place to go?"

She gave an address down in SoHo. I drove to the address, ditched the car, and went with her up to an apartment: third floor of a brownstone, three rooms and a kitchen. I hoped she was in a rent-controlled building, or this place would be costing her a pretty.

The apartment was almost empty: nothing but a coffeemaker in the kitchen, a couple of sofas, and a bed, all visible from right inside the front door.

"Take a seat," she said. "I'll make coffee."

She stripped off her coat and turned to hang it on a peg by the door. When she turned back, the little nine-millimeter was pointing right between my eyes. I'd stuffed the .45 into my waistband in back again, to keep her from getting nervous. Her get nervous? That was a laugh.

"You've missed three recognition signals," she said. "You aren't from Section. So how's about you tell me who you are?"

"People call me Crossman," I said. "Peter Crossman."

"Is that your real name?"

"No, but it'll do. I'm the connection for midtown. You want coke, you call me."

"Your kind isn't known for making citizen arrests," she said. The muzzle of the nine-millimeter never wavered, even though from the way her chest was going up and down she had to be nervous about something. "What did you think you were up to tonight?"

"Someone who doesn't work for me using muscle in my territory, that interests me. Let one bunch get away with it, pretty soon it's all over town that Crossman's gone soft, and they're all trying to move in. Can't let that happen."

"So—" she started, but never finished. A knock sounded on the door.

"Maggie," came a voice from outside. "Maggie, I know you're in there. Open up."

She made the little pistol vanish. "Come on in—it isn't locked."

The door swung open, and I got a sinking feeling in my guts. The Mutt and Jeff act waiting on the landing were the same pair who'd given me the ride back to town the day before. The watchers from the dock in Babylon. I didn't think they recognized me—the Tarnkappe had kept me invisible at first, and then I'd changed my face. I was glad now that I'd taken the precaution.

They came in. They were wrapped in dripping raincoats—no way of telling what kind of firepower they were carrying underneath, but it would take 'em a while to pull anything clear. The first guy, the short one, nodded over at me. "Who's the meat?"

"A guy named Crossman," Maggie said. "He's some kind of drug lord. Showed up tonight and pulled my buns out of a bad situation while you two were sucking down cold ones in some bar."

"Get rid of him," the second guy said.

"No, I think I want him to stay." She looked at me. "You do want to stay, don't you? I'll let you buy me a drink after all this is over."

"Yeah," I said. "I want to stay."

That was the truth. This whole affair was getting more interesting by the minute. And as for buying that drink—I couldn't help wondering what sort of temptation she had in mind for me to resist.

She started to say something else, and that was when the door to the apartment flew open again. This time it was the two guys from the street—the ones who had tried to stuff Maggie into their car, the same ones who'd grabbed me outside the UN. One of them was carrying a Remington Model 870. The other was lugging a Stoner. They both looked pissed off.

They didn't bother with the formalities.

"One of you bastards," the guy with the Stoner said, "knows something we want to know. So we aren't going to kill you now. But we have other ways of finding out, so don't think we'll hesitate to shoot you if we have to. So. Who's going to tell me: Where's the Holy Grail?"

"It's in Logres, asshole," said Maggie's shorter guy.

The new arrival with the riot gun butt-stroked him across the room. He went down hard.

"I sure hope he wasn't the only guy who knew," Remington said, "or the rest of you are going to have a really rough time. Who wants to give us a serious answer?"

Maggie was standing beside and a little behind me. I felt something soft and warm pressing into my hand while everyone else was looking at the guy on the floor. It felt like a leather bag with marbles inside. I took it and made it vanish into my front pants pocket.

Stoner looked at me—maybe he'd seen me move. "Don't I know you from somewhere?"

I shook my head a fraction of an inch one way and then the other. "I don't think so."

I wasn't as scared as I hoped I looked, but things weren't shaping up too good. The new guys hadn't disarmed anyone yet, and neither weapon was pointing right at me, but with my piece tucked into my waistband in back, I wouldn't have put a lot of money on getting it clear before they could turn me into Swiss cheese with ketchup. Besides, I wanted these gents alive. Someone knew where the Grail was, and all of these jokers looked like they knew more than I did.

"Lay off," Maggie said. "This one's your basic crook I picked up. You don't want him, you want me."

Whatever they were after, odds were it was in that little sack—at least Maggie thought it was. But I knew better. You don't carry a six-point-five-ton block of lodestone around in a leather drawstring bag.

"Yeah, sister, we want you," Remington said. "What were you doing at the Waldorf tonight?"

"Visiting a friend. Got a problem with that?" She'd drifted a little away from me. Maybe no one remembered she'd ever gotten close.

"Do you have it?"

"No. It isn't here."

Even the guys with the long guns were treating Maggie with respect—she must rate in someone's organization, I thought. Meanwhile, she was getting close to the light switch. I kept watch out of the corner of my eye, ready to make my move when she made hers.

"Where is it?" Remington said again.

She drifted another step sideways. "Do you know the stone-yard for St. John the Divine?"

Then her elbow smashed backward against the switch and the lights went out. I leaped over the sofa in a flat dive, rolled, and came up crouching in the corner near the window, with my back to the wall and the .45 in a two-hand grip in front of me.

I heard a nine-millimeter go popping off where Maggie had been standing, and an answering roar from the Remington—

both of them laid over the stitching sound of the Stoner firing full auto.

That about did it for my ears. Too much gunfire and you're hearing bells ring an hour later. Of course, now the bad guys couldn't hear me, either. But my eyes were adjusting to the dark, and anyone standing up in front of the windows would be silhouetted against the skyglow.

I started duckwalking in the direction of the door, keeping my head low. My foot hit something hard. I reached down with my right hand, my left holding the .45 steady in front of me. It was the Stoner. The barrel was warm, which was more than you could say about the hand that held it. No pulse in the radial artery. I mouthed an absolution and continued moving along the wall.

Over by the window, another shadow was moving—a male, standing, with the distinctive shape of a pump-action in his hands. The weapon was swinging in slow arcs across the room. It stopped—he'd seen something. He started raising the shotgun to his shoulder.

I drew a careful bead on him. "Go in peace to love and serve the Lord," I muttered, and pulled the trigger.

Then I was rolling away, because a scattergun like the Remington doesn't need much aiming. But I needn't have worried—I saw his shadow drop in that boneless way people get when they're shot. A .45 yields a 98 percent one-shot kill rate. If I hit him . . . well, I don't miss often.

I fetched up against someone very soft and very warm—Maggie, waiting in the shadows by the other corner. She reached up and flipped the lights back on.

I stood flattened against the wall and looked around. Stoner and Remington had both bought their parts of the farm. Maggie's two pretty boys were hugging the carpet and playing possum—at least they'd been smart enough not to be targets.

The tall one got to his feet.

"You found it?" he said to Maggie. "Come on, let's get over there."

"It isn't so far," Maggie said. "In fact it's—"

"Shut up," I said. "These two jokers aren't on your team."

"What do you mean?"

She was bringing the nine-mike-mike to bear on me. I pointed my own weapon at the floor, so she wouldn't get the wrong idea and make a hasty move, and nodded at the pair of corpses.

"How do you think the Bobbsey Twins over there found this place?" I asked. "They sure didn't follow us. I bet these two guys brought 'em along, and were going to play good cop/bad cop with us."

"But—" Maggie began.

"He's right, you know," the shorter one said. He produced an Uzi and brought it up to cover us. "Put down your weapons."

There comes a time when you know you've lost. I dropped my piece. Maggie did the same. The guy with the Uzi nodded at his buddy.

"Fred, pick them up."

The tall one—Fred, I guess his name was—stepped forward and bent over to pick up the handguns.

Shorty was still talking to Maggie. "The Grail isn't at St. John the Divine. We already checked. So I'm afraid I'll have to search you—several times, in a variety of positions. Unless you tell me where the Grail is right now. The truth and no tricks."

Maggie shook her head. "I don't think so."

"A pity," said Shorty. "You'll still be a Bride of Christ—you just won't be a virgin Bride of Christ—and you'll wind up telling me anyway."

"I don't know where it is," Maggie said.

"Then all my work will be for nothing," Shorty said, but he was grinning as he said it.

"Please," I said, trying to make my voice sound like I was scared witless. "I don't know what any of this is about. Please let me go—"

"Shut him up," Shorty said.

At least I'd gotten his eyes on me instead of Maggie. And Fred was coming up, his pistol in one hand, mine in the other. That's when I kicked him, a reaping circular kick, taking him in the throat. It raised him to his feet and set him stumbling backward.

Shorty fired—but someone should have taught him how to shoot. His round missed me, though I could feel the wind of it past my cheek and the answering spatter of plaster from the wall. I dove forward, spearing Fred in the belly with my head. Shorty's second shot took his partner between the shoulder blades as Fred was driven backward into him.

Then all three of us went down, and a moment later it was over. I rolled onto my back. Maggie was standing over me.

"You've been hit."

"I don't think so." But when I looked down at myself, sure enough there was blood pouring out, soaking the pocket where I'd put her bag—and where I kept my supply of Hosts. The Hosts were bleeding.

At that moment I knew. And looking into her eyes, I could tell she knew, too.

"It really was the Grail," she said.

"Looks like. Let's get out of here before the cops show up."

"Where to?"

"I'll introduce you to a man," I said. "You'll like him."

We left. The first police car arrived, lights flashing, when we were halfway down the block.

As dawn was breaking over a soggy New York morning, I was in the Rambles again. Prester John was waiting.

"Here it is," I said, tossing the sack to him. He opened the bag and rolled out the gemstones inside it.

"Yes," he said. "The substance is here, though the accidents have changed." The accidents. I should have thought of that back at the UN, when the Host that touched the meditation stone didn't bleed. A wafer, when it's transubstantiated, still has the outward appearance—the accidents—of a flat bit of unleavened bread, while its substance is the body of Christ. In the same way, the Grail's substance—whatever it is that makes it truly the Grail—now had the accidents of a handful of precious stones.

John looked back up at me, his hand clenching around the Grail. "Who's your friend?"

"Sister Mary Magdalene," she said. "From the Special Action Executive of the Poor Clares. I presume you're with the Temple?"

Prester John inclined his head.

"Pleased to meet you," she said. "We'd heard that there was some hanky-panky going on, especially when the Cathar Liberation Army started moving people into town."

"I can fill in the rest," I said. "Maggie's group was infiltrated by the Cathars, just before they got sold out themselves by the Luciferians. That's where Max Lang fits in. The Lucies had been contracted to grab the Grail because they were the only ones besides us who could handle it. Lang carried a bag of jewels in—swapped the substance of the jewels into the lodestone and the substance of the Grail into the jewels—and walked out. That gave them the Grail, but once the Lucies had it, they didn't want to turn it over, at least not to the Cathars. You remember what kind of mess there was last time *they* owned it."

"As if you can speak of anyone owning the Grail," Prester John said. "You're right: Lang must have transubstantiated the Grail into this little sack of jewels, and left the stone in the Meditation Room transubstantiated into a hunk of rock."

It all made sense. It also explained how the Lucies had smuggled six and a half tons of lodestone into and out of the UN—they hadn't. Nobody had carried anything through security that was bigger and heavier than a bag of marbles.

Prester John was shaking his head thoughtfully. "I wonder what made them think they could get away with it?"

"Maybe there's some truth to those stories about Lucifer's crown," I said. "The Lucies sure think so. And the Cathars knew they'd never get close working on their own, so they hired the Luciferians to do the dirty work for them. Then Lang got cold feet. Maybe he saw a vision or something. It's been known to happen. He was working up his nerve to return the Grail when he got hit."

"Lang had swallowed the stones," Maggie said. "I got 'em back. We'd been running electronic intelligence ops on the Lucies for a while. We intercepted one call yesterday afternoon that alerted us, and another call last evening from the hotel. That's when I got sent in. He was messed up enough when I got there that nobody's going to notice a few cuts more."

"Who was it who nailed him?" Prester John said.

"The Cathars," I said. "They'd figured out by then that he was trying to double-cross them."

"Any thoughts on how to get the Grail back to its rightful shape and rightful place?" John said. "We'll have to set new wards, too, so this won't happen again."

"That's your problem," I said. "Maybe you could hire the Lucies yourself. Me, I've got a social engagement. I promised Maggie a drink and I'm going to find her one."

"Hang on," Prester John said. "You're a priest. She's a nun. You can't go on a date."

"Don't worry," I said. "I won't get into the habit."

One of America's best-known writers for younger readers, Jane Yolen is the author of over two hundred books, ranging from picture books like Owl Moon *to novels like* Sister Light, Sister Dark *and* Briar Rose. *Her work has won most of the awards in the fantasy field, including the Nebula Award and the World Fantasy Award.*

Mama Gone

JANE YOLEN

Mama died four nights ago, giving birth to my baby sister Ann. Bubba cried and cried, "Mama gone," in his little-boy voice, but I never let out a single tear.

There was blood red as any sunset all over the bed from that birthing, and when Papa saw it he rubbed his head against the cabin wall over and over and over and made little animal sounds. Sukey washed Mama down and placed the baby on her breast for a moment. "Remember," she whispered.

"Mama gone," Bubba wailed again.

But I never cried.

By all rights we should have buried her with garlic in her mouth and her hands and feet cut off, what with her being vampire kin and all. But Papa absolutely refused.

"Your Mama couldn't stand garlic," he said when the sounds stopped rushing out of his mouth and his eyes had cleared. "It made her come all over with rashes. She had the sweetest mouth and hands."

And that was that. Not a one of us could make him change

his mind, not even Granddad Stokes or Pop Wilber or any other of the men who come to pay their last respects. And as Papa is a preacher, and a brimstone man, they let it be. The onliest thing he would allow was for us to tie red ribbons round her ankles and wrists, a kind of sign like a line of blood. Everybody hoped that would do.

But on the next day, she rose from out her grave and commenced to prey upon the good folk of Taunton.

Of course she came to our house first, that being the dearest place she knew. I saw her outside my window, gray as a gravestone, her dark eyes like the holes in a shroud. When she stared in, she didn't know me, though I had always been her favorite.

"Mama, be gone," I said and waved my little cross at her, the one she had given me the very day I'd been born. "Avaunt." The old Bible word sat heavy in my mouth.

She put her hand up on the window frame, and as I watched, the gray fingers turned splotchy pink from all the garlic I had rubbed into the wood.

Black tears dropped from her black eyes, then. But I never cried.

She tried each window in turn and not a person awake in the house but me. But I had done my work well and the garlic held her out. She even tried the door, but it was no use. By the time she left, I was so sleepy, I dropped down right by the door. Papa found me there at cockcrow. He never did ask what I was doing, and if he guessed, he never said.

Little Joshua Greenough was found dead in his crib. The doctor took two days to come over the mountains to pronounce it. By then the garlic around his little bed to keep him from walking, too, had mixed with the death smells. Everybody knew. Even the doctor, and him a city man. It hurt his mama and papa sore to do the cutting. But it had to be done.

The men came to our house that very noon to talk about

what had to be. Papa kept shaking his head all through their talking. But even his being preacher didn't stop them. Once a vampire walks these mountain hollars, there's nary a house or barn that's safe. Nighttime is lost time. And no one can afford to lose much stock.

So they made their sharp sticks out of green wood, the curling shavings littering our cabin floor. Bubba played in them, not understanding. Sukey was busy with the baby, nursing it with a bottle and a sugar teat. It was my job to sweep up the wood curls. They felt slick on one side, bumpy on the other. Like my heart.

Papa said, "I was the one let her turn into a night walker. It's my business to stake her out."

No one argued. Specially not the Greenoughs, their eyes still red from weeping.

"Just take my children," Papa said. "And if anything goes wrong, cut off my hands and feet and bury me at Mill's Cross, under the stone. There's garlic hanging in the pantry. Mandy Jane will string me some."

So Sukey took the baby and Bubba off to the Greenoughs' house, that seeming the right thing to do, and I stayed the rest of the afternoon with Papa, stringing garlic and pressing more into the windows. But the strand over the door he took down.

"I have to let her in somewhere," he said. "And this is where I'll make my stand." He touched me on the cheek, the first time ever. Papa never has been much for show.

"Now you run along to the Greenoughs', Mandy Jane," he said. "And remember how much your mama loved you. This isn't her, child. Mama's gone. Something else has come to take her place. I should have remembered that the Good Book says, 'The living know that they shall die; but the dead know not anything.' "

I wanted to ask him how the vampire knew to come first

to our house, then, but I was silent, for Papa had been asleep and hadn't seen her.

I left without giving him a daughter's kiss, for his mind was well set on the night's doing. But I didn't go down the lane to the Greenoughs' at all. Wearing my triple strand of garlic, with my cross about my neck, I went to the burying ground, to Mama's grave.

It looked so raw against the greening hillside. The dirt was red clay, but all it looked like to me was blood. There was no cross on it yet, no stone. That would come in a year. Just a humping, a heaping of red dirt over her coffin, the plain pinewood box hastily made.

I lay facedown in that dirt, my arms opened wide. "Oh, Mama," I said, "the Good Book says you are not dead but sleepeth. Sleep quietly, Mama, sleep well." And I sang to her the lullaby she had always sung to me and then to Bubba and would have sung to Baby Ann had she lived to hold her.

"Blacks and bays,
Dapples and grays,
All the pretty little horses."

And as I sang I remembered Papa thundering at prayer meeting once, "Behold, a pale horse: and his name that sat on him was Death." The rest of the song just stuck in my throat then, so I turned over on the grave and stared up at the setting sun.

It had been a long and wearying day, and I fell asleep right there in the burying ground. Any other time fear might have overcome sleep. But I just closed my eyes and slept.

When I woke, it was dead night. The moon was full and sitting between the horns of two hills. There was a sprinkling of stars overhead. And Mama began to move the ground beneath me, trying to rise.

The garlic strands must have worried her, for she did not come out of the earth all at once. It was the scrabbling of her long nails at my back that woke me. I leaped off that grave and was wide awake.

Standing aside the grave, I watched as first her long gray arms reached out of the earth. Then her head, with its hair that was once so gold now gray and streaked with black and its shroud eyes, emerged. And then her body in its winding sheet, stained with dirt and torn from walking to and fro upon the land. Then her bare feet with blackened nails, though alive Mama used to paint those nails, her one vanity and Papa allowed it seeing she was so pretty and otherwise not vain.

She turned toward me as a hummingbird toward a flower, and she raised her face up and it was gray and bony. Her mouth peeled back from her teeth and I saw that they were pointed and her tongue was barbed.

"Mama gone," I whispered in Bubba's voice, but so low I could hardly hear it myself.

She stepped toward me off that grave, lurching down the hump of dirt. But when she got close, the garlic strands and the cross stayed her.

"Mama."

She turned her head back and forth. It was clear she could not see with those black shroud eyes. She only sensed me there, something warm, something alive, something with the blood running like satisfying streams through the blue veins.

"Mama," I said again. "Try and remember."

That searching awful face turned toward me again, and the pointy teeth were bared once more. Her hands reached out to grab me, then pulled back.

"Remember how Bubba always sucks his thumb with that funny little noise you always said was like a little chuck in its hole. And how Sukey hums through her nose when she's baking bread. And how I listened to your belly to hear the baby. And how Papa always starts each meal with the blessing on things that grow fresh in the field."

The gray face turned for a moment toward the hills, and I wasn't even sure she could hear me. But I had to keep trying.

"And remember when we picked the blueberries and Bubba fell down the hill, tumbling head-end over. And we laughed until we heard him, and he was saying the same six things over and over till long past bed."

The gray face turned back toward me and I thought I saw a bit of light in the eyes. But it was just reflected moonlight.

"And the day Papa came home with the new ewe lamb and we fed her on a sugar teat. You stayed up all the night and I slept in the straw by your side."

It was as if stars were twinkling in those dead eyes. I couldn't stop staring, but I didn't dare stop talking either.

"And remember the day the bluebird stunned itself on the kitchen window and you held it in your hands. You warmed it to life, you said. To life, Mama."

Those stars began to run down the gray cheeks.

"There's living, Mama, and there's dead. You've given so much life. Don't be bringing death to these hills now." I could see that the stars were gone from the sky over her head; the moon was setting.

"Papa loved you too much to cut your hands and feet. You gotta return that love, Mama. You gotta."

Veins of red ran along the hills, outlining the rocks. As the sun began to rise, I took off one strand of garlic. Then the second. Then the last. I opened my arms. "Have you come back, Mama, or are you gone?"

The gray woman leaned over and clasped me tight in her arms. Her head bent down toward mine, her mouth on my forehead, my neck, the outline of my little gold cross burning across her lips.

She whispered, "Here and gone, child, here and gone," in a voice like wind in the coppice, like the shaking of willow leaves. I felt her kiss on my cheek, a brand.

Then the sun came between the hills and hit her full in the face, burning her as red as earth. She smiled at me and then there was only dust motes in the air, dancing. When I looked down at my feet, the grave dirt was hardly disturbed but Mama's gold wedding band gleamed atop it.

I knelt down and picked it up, and unhooked the chain holding my cross. I slid the ring into the chain, and the two nestled together right in the hollow of my throat. I sang:

"Blacks and bays,
Dapples and grays . . ."

and from the earth itself, the final words sang out,

"All the pretty little horses."

That was when I cried, long and loud, a sound I hope never to make again as long as I live.

Then I went back down the hill and home, where Papa still waited by the open door.

Author and musician Charles de Lint's beat is the fantastic in the everyday: magic loose on the city streets. Much of his work, including the story below, is set in and around the imaginary North American city of Newford, and follows a large and shifting cast of characters. Newford novels include Moonheart, Memory and Dream, Trader, The Onion Girl, *and* Spirits in the Wires. *He won the World Fantasy Award for* Moonlight and Vines, *one of several collections of shorter Newford stories.*

The Bone Woman

CHARLES DE LINT

No one really stops to think of Ellie Spink, and why should they?

She's no one.

She has nothing.

Homely as a child, all that the passing of years did was add to her unattractiveness. Face like a horse, jaw long and square, forehead broad; limpid eyes set bird-wide on either side of a gargantuan nose; hair a nondescript brown, greasy and matted, stuffed up under a woolen toque lined with a patchwork of metal foil scavenged from discarded cigarette packages. The angularity of her slight frame doesn't get its volume from her meager diet, but from the multiple layers of clothing she wears.

Raised in foster homes, she's been used, but she's never experienced a kiss. Institutionalized for most of her adult life, she's been medicated, but never treated. Pass her on the street and your gaze slides right on by, never pausing to register the difference between the old woman huddled in the doorway and a bag of garbage.

Old woman? Though she doesn't know it, Monday, two weeks past, was her thirty-seventh birthday. She looks twice her age.

There's no point in trying to talk to her. Usually no one's home. When there is, the words spill out in a disjointed mumble, a rambling monologue itemizing a litany of misperceived conspiracies and other ills that soon leave you feeling as confused as she herself must be.

Normal conversation is impossible and not many bother to try it. The exceptions are few: The odd pitying passerby. A concerned social worker, fresh out of college and new to the streets. Maybe one of the other street people who happens to stumble into her particular haunts.

They talk and she listens, or she doesn't—she never makes any sort of a relevant response, so who can tell? Few push the matter. Fewer still, however well intentioned, have the stamina to make the attempt to do so more than once or twice. It's easier just to walk away; to bury your guilt, or laugh off her confused ranting as the excessive rhetoric it can only be.

I've done it myself.

I used to try to talk to her when I first started seeing her around, but I didn't get far. Angel told me a little about her, but even knowing her name and some of her history didn't help.

"Hey, Ellie. How're you doing?"

Pale eyes, almost translucent, turn toward me, set so far apart it's as though she can only see me with one eye at a time.

"They should test for aliens," she tells me. "You know, like in the Olympics."

"Aliens?"

"I mean, who cares who killed Kennedy? Dead's dead, right?"

"What's Kennedy got to do with aliens?"

"I don't even know why they took down the Berlin Wall. What about the one in China? Shouldn't they have worked on that one first?"

It's like trying to have a conversation with a game of Trivial Pursuit that specializes in information garnered from supermarket tabloids. After a while, I'd just pack an extra sandwich whenever I was busking in her neighborhood. I'd sit beside her, share my lunch, and let her talk if she wanted to, but I wouldn't say all that much myself.

That all changed the day I saw her with the Bone Woman.

I didn't call her the Bone Woman at first; the adjective that came more immediately to mind was fat. She couldn't have been much more than five-one, but she had to weigh in at two-fifty, leaving me with the impression that she was wider than she was tall. But she was light on her feet—peculiarly graceful for all her squat bulk.

She had a round face like a full moon, framed by thick black hair that hung in two long braids to her waist. Her eyes were small, almost lost in that expanse of face, and so dark they seemed all pupil. She went barefoot in a shapeless black dress, her only accessory an equally shapeless shoulder bag made of some kind of animal skin and festooned with dangling thongs from which hung various feathers, beads, bottlecaps and other found objects.

I paused at the far end of the street when I saw the two of them together. I had a sandwich for Ellie in my knapsack, but I hesitated in approaching them. They seemed deep in conversation, real conversation, give and take, and Ellie was—

knitting? Talking *and* knitting? The pair of them looked like a couple of old gossips, sitting on the back porch of their building. The sight of Ellie acting so normal was something I didn't want to interrupt.

I sat down on a nearby stoop and watched until Ellie put away her knitting and stood up. She looked down at her companion with an expression in her features that I'd never seen before. It was awareness, I realized. She was completely *here* for a change.

As she came up the street, I stood up and called a greeting to her, but by the time she reached me she wore her usually vacuous expression.

"It's the newspapers," she told me. "They use radiation to print them and that's what makes the news seem so bad."

Before I could take the sandwich I'd brought her out of my knapsack, she'd shuffled off, around the corner, and was gone. I glanced back down the street to where the fat woman was still sitting, and decided to find Ellie later. Right now I wanted to know what the woman had done to get such a positive reaction out of Ellie.

When I approached, the fat woman was sifting through the refuse where the two of them had been sitting. As I watched, she picked up a good-sized bone. What kind, I don't know, but it was as long as my forearm and as big around as the neck of my fiddle. Brushing dirt and a sticky candy wrapper from it, she gave it a quick polish on the sleeve of her dress and stuffed it away in her shoulderbag. Then she looked up at me.

My question died stillborn in my throat under the sudden scrutiny of those small dark eyes. She looked right through me—not the drifting, unfocused gaze of so many of the street people, but a cold, far-off seeing that weighed my presence, dismissed it, and gazed further off at something far more important.

I stood back as she rose easily to her feet. That was when I realized how graceful she was. She moved down the sidewalk as daintily as a doe, as though her bulk was filled with helium, rather than flesh, and weighed nothing. I watched her until she reached the far end of the street, turned her own corner and then, just like Ellie, was gone as well.

I ended up giving Ellie's sandwich to Johnny Rew, an old wino who's taught me a fiddle tune or two, the odd time I've run into him sober.

I started to see the Bone Woman everywhere after that day. I wasn't sure if she was just new to town, or if it was one of those cases where you suddenly see something or someone you've never noticed before and after that you see them all the time. Everybody I talked to about her seemed to know her, but no one was quite sure how long she'd been in the city, or where she lived, or even her name.

I still wasn't calling her the Bone Woman, though I knew by then that bones were all she collected. Old bones, found bones, rattling around together in her shoulderbag until she went off at the end of the day and showed up the next morning, ready to start filling her bag again.

When she wasn't hunting bones, she spent her time with the street's worst cases—people like Ellie that no one else could talk to. She'd get them making things—little pictures or carvings or beadwork, keeping their hands busy. And talking. Someone like Ellie still made no sense to anybody else, but you could tell when she was with the Bone Woman that they were sharing a real dialogue. Which was a good thing, I suppose, but I couldn't shake the feeling that there was something more going on, something if not exactly sinister, then still strange.

It was the bones, I suppose. There were so many. How

could she keep finding them the way she did? And what did she do with them?

My brother Christy collects urban legends, the way the Bone Woman collects her bones, rooting them out where you'd never think they could be. But when I told him about her, he just shrugged.

"Who knows why any of them do anything?" he said.

Christy doesn't live on the streets, for all that he haunts them. He's just an observer—always has been, ever since we were kids. To him, the street people can be pretty well evenly divided between the sad cases and the crazies. Their stories are too human for him.

"Some of these are big," I told him. "The size of a human thighbone."

"So point her out to the cops."

"And tell them what?"

A smile touched his lips with just enough superiority in it to get under my skin. He's always been able to do that. Usually, it makes me do something I regret later, which I sometimes think is half his intention. It's not that he wants to see me hurt. It's just part and parcel of that air of authority that all older siblings seem to wear. You know, a raised eyebrow, a way of smiling that says, "You have so much to learn, little brother."

"If you really want to know what she does with those bones," he said, "why don't you follow her home and find out?"

"Maybe I will."

It turned out that the Bone Woman had a squat on the roof of an abandoned factory building in the Tombs. She'd built herself some kind of a shed up there—just a leaning, ramshackle affair of castoff lumber and sheet metal, but it kept out the weather and could easily be heated with a woodstove in the spring and fall. Come winter, she'd need warmer quarters, but the snows were still a month or so away.

I followed her home one afternoon, then came back the next day when she was out to finally put to rest my fear about these bones she was collecting. The thought that had stuck in my mind was that she was taking something away from the street people like Ellie, people who were already at the bottom rung and deserved to be helped, or at least just left alone. I'd gotten this weird idea that the bones were tied up with the last remnants of vitality that someone like Ellie might have, and the Bone Woman was stealing it from them.

What I found was more innocuous, and at the same time creepier, than I'd expected.

The inside of her squat was littered with bones and wire and dog-shaped skeletons that appeared to be made from the two. Bones held in place by wire, half-connected ribs and skulls and limbs. A pack of bone dogs. Some of the figures were almost complete, others were merely suggestions, but everywhere I looked, the half-finished wire-and-bone skeletons sat or stood or hung suspended from the ceiling. There had to be more than a dozen in various states of creation.

I stood in the doorway, not willing to venture any further, and just stared at them all. I don't know how long I was there, but finally I turned away and made my way back down through the abandoned building and out onto the street.

So now I knew what she did with the bones. But it didn't tell me how she could find so many of them. Surely that many stray dogs didn't die, their bones scattered the length and breadth of the city like so much autumn residue?

Amy and I had a gig opening for the Kelledys that night. It didn't take me long to set up. I just adjusted my microphone, laid out my fiddle and whistles on a small table to one side, and then kicked my heels while Amy fussed with her pipes and the complicated tangle of electronics that she used to amplify them.

I've heard it said that all Uillean pipers are a little crazy—that they have to be to play an instrument that looks more like what you'd find in the back of a plumber's truck than an instrument—but I think of them as perfectionists. Every one I've ever met spends more time fiddling with their reeds and adjusting the tuning of their various chanters, drones and regulators than would seem humanly possible.

Amy's no exception. After a while I left her there on the stage, with her red hair falling in her face as she poked and prodded at a new reed she'd made for one of her drones, and wandered into the back where the Kelledys were making their own preparations for the show, which consisted of drinking tea and looking beatific. At least that's the way I always think of the two of them. I don't think I've ever met calmer people.

Jilly likes to think of them as mysterious, attributing all kinds of fairy-tale traits to them. Meran, she's convinced, with the green highlights in her nut-brown hair and her wise brown eyes, is definitely dryad material—the spirit of an oak tree come to life—while Cerin is some sort of wizard figure, a combination of adept and bard. I think the idea amuses them, and they play it up to Jilly. Nothing you can put your finger on, but they seem to get a kick out of spinning a mysterious air about themselves whenever she's around.

I'm far more practical than Jilly—actually, just about anybody's more practical than Jilly, God bless her, but that's another story. I think if you find yourself using the word magic to describe the Kelledys, what you're really talking about is their musical talent. They may seem preternaturally calm offstage, but as soon as they begin to play, that calmness is transformed into a bonfire of energy. There's enchantment then, burning onstage, but it comes from their instrumental skill.

"Geordie," Meran said after I'd paced back and forth for a few minutes. "You look a little edgy. Have some tea."

I had to smile. If the Kelledys had originated from some mysterious elsewhere, then I'd lean more toward them having come from a fiddle tune than Jilly's fairy tales.

"When sick is it tea you want?" I said, quoting the title of an old Irish jig that we all knew in common.

Meran returned my smile. "It can't hurt. Here," she added, rummaging around in a bag that was lying by her chair. "Let me see if I have something that'll ease your nervousness."

"I'm not nervous."

"No, of course not," Cerin put in. "Geordie just likes to pace, don't you?"

He was smiling as he spoke, but without a hint of Christy's sometimes annoying demeanor.

"No, really. It's just . . ."

"Just what?" Meran asked as my voice trailed off.

Well, here was the perfect opportunity to put Jilly's theories to the test, I decided. If the Kelledys were in fact as fey as she made them out to be, then they'd be able to explain this business with the bones, wouldn't they?

So I told them about the fat woman and her bones and what I'd found in her squat. They listened with far more reasonableness than I would have if someone had been telling the story to me—especially when I went on to explain the weird feeling I'd been getting from the whole business.

"It's giving me the creeps," I said, finishing up, "and I can't even say why."

"La Huesera," Cerin said when I was done.

Meran nodded. "The Bone Woman," she said, translating it for me. "It does sound like her."

"So you know her."

"No," Meran said. "It just reminds us of a story we heard when we were playing in Phoenix a few years ago. There was a young Apache man opening for us, and he and I started comparing flutes. We got on to one of the Native courting flutes which used to be made from human bone and somehow from there he started telling me about a legend they have in the Southwest about this old fat woman who wanders through the mountains and arroyos, collecting bones from the desert that she brings back to her cave."

"What does she collect them for?"

"To preserve the things that are in danger of being lost to the world," Cerin said.

"I don't get it."

"I'm not sure of the exact details," Cerin went on, "but it had something to do with the spirits of endangered species."

"Giving them a new life," Meran said.

"Or a second chance."

"But there's no desert around here," I said. "What would this Bone Woman be doing up here?"

Meran smiled. "I remember John saying that she's as often been seen riding shotgun in an eighteen-wheeler as walking down a dry wash."

"And besides," Cerin added, "any place is a desert when there's more going on underground than on the surface."

That described Newford perfectly. And who lived a more hidden life than the street people? They were right in front of us every day, but most people didn't even see them anymore. And who was more deserving of a second chance than someone like Ellie, who'd never even gotten a fair first chance?

"Too many of us live desert lives," Cerin said, and I knew just what he meant.

• • • • • • • •

The gig went well. I was a little bemused, but I didn't make any major mistakes. Amy complained that her regulators had sounded too buzzy in the monitors, but that was just Amy. They'd sounded great to me, their counterpointing chords giving the tunes a real punch whenever they came in.

The Kelledys' set was pure magic. Amy and I watched them from the stage wings and felt higher as they took their final bow than we had when the applause had been directed at us.

I begged off getting together with them after the show, regretfully pleading tiredness. I *was* tired, but leaving the theater, headed for an abandoned factory in the Tombs instead of home. When I got up on the roof of the building, the moon was full. It looked like a saucer of buttery gold, bathing everything in a warm yellow light. I heard a soft voice on the far side of the roof near the Bone Woman's squat. It wasn't exactly singing, but not chanting either. A murmuring, sliding sound that raised the hairs at the nape of my neck.

I walked a little nearer, staying in the shadows of the cornices, until I could see the Bone Woman. I paused then, laying my fiddlecase quietly on the roof and sliding down so that I was sitting with my back against the cornice.

The Bone Woman had one of her skeleton sculptures set out in front of her and she was singing over it. The dog shape was complete now, all the bones wired in place and gleaming in the moonlight. I couldn't make out the words of her song. Either there were none, or she was using a language I'd never heard before. As I watched, she stood, raising her arms up above the wired skeleton, and her voice grew louder.

The scene was peaceful—soothing, in the same way that the Kelledys' company could be—but eerie as well. The Bone Woman's voice had the cadence of one of the medicine chants I'd heard at a powwow up on the Kickaha Reservation—the same nasal tones and ringing quality. But that powwow hadn't prepared me for what came next.

At first I wasn't sure that I was really seeing it. The empty spaces between the skeleton's bones seemed to gather volume and fill out, as though flesh were forming on the bones. Then there was fur, highlighted by the moonlight, and I couldn't deny it any more. I saw a bewhiskered muzzle lift skyward, ears twitch, a tail curl up, thick-haired and strong. The powerful chest began to move rhythmically, at first in time to the Bone Woman's song, then breathing of its own accord.

The Bone Woman hadn't been making dogs in her squat, I realized as I watched the miraculous change occur. She'd been making wolves.

The newly animated creature's eyes snapped open and it leapt up, running to the edge of the roof. There it stood with its forelegs on the cornice. Arching its neck, the wolf pointed its nose at the moon and howled.

I sat there, already stunned, but the transformation still wasn't complete. As the wolf howled, it began to change again. Fur to human skin. Lupine shape, to that of a young woman. Howl to merry laughter. And as she turned, I recognized her features.

"Ellie," I breathed.

She still had the same horsy features, the same skinny body, all bones and angles, but she was beautiful. She blazed with the fire of a spirit that had never been hurt, never been abused, never been degraded. She gave me a radiant smile and then leapt from the edge of the roof.

I held my breath, but she didn't fall. She walked out across the city's skyline, out across the urban desert of rooftops and chimneys, off and away, running now, laughter trailing behind her until she was swallowed by the horizon.

I stared out at the night sky long after she had disappeared, then slowly stood up and walked across the roof to where the Bone Woman was sitting outside the door of her squat. She tracked my approach, but there was neither welcome nor dismissal in those small dark eyes. It was like the first time I'd come up to her; as far as she was concerned, I wasn't there at all.

"How did you do that?" I asked.

She looked through, past me.

"Can you teach me that song? I want to help, too."

Still no response.

"Why won't you *talk* to me?"

Finally her gaze focused on me.

"You don't have their need," she said.

Her voice was thick with an accent I couldn't place. I waited for her to go on, to explain what she meant, but once again, she ignored me. The pinpoints of black that passed for eyes in that round moon face looked away into a place where I didn't belong.

Finally, I did the only thing left for me to do. I collected my fiddlecase and went on home.

Some things haven't changed. Ellie's still living on the streets, and I still share my lunch with her when I'm down in her part of town. There's nothing the Bone Woman can do to change what this life has done to the Ellie Spinks of the world.

But what I saw that night gives me hope for the next turn of the wheel. I know now that no matter how downtrodden someone like Ellie might be, at least somewhere a piece of her is running free. Somewhere that wild and innocent part of her spirit is being preserved with those of the wolf and the rattlesnake and all the other creatures whose spirit-bones *La Huesera* collects from the desert—deserts natural and of our own making.

Spirit-bones. Collected and preserved, nurtured in the belly of the Bone Woman's song, until we learn to welcome them upon their terms, rather than our own.

One of the newer writers on the fantasy scene, Andy Duncan has already won two World Fantasy Awards and published a collection with the intimidating title Beluthahatchie and Other Stories.

Liza and the Crazy Water Man

ANDY DUNCAN

She was long done singing, but the schoolhouse was still full of her voice. It flowed into the corners. It washed along the ceiling and the floorboards. It surged against the backs of the farmers and mill workers as they shuffled out the door. It claimed all the space they had occupied. It crowded them, ready to pour out, into the cool night, and roll freely across the face of the mountain.

The woman who owned the voice sat on the edge of the little stage and shook out her hair of silver and gold, raked her fingers through it once, twice, as she sweated in the lamp's kerosene glow. I stood there in the dimness, sweltering and damp, my tie undone. The people leaving whooped and laughed, but I feared to say a mumbling word. No room was left in that place for my voice.

So, wordlessly, I stepped into the circle of light, and held out my business card. It was all the offering I had.

Alvin Pleasants, Charlotte office
CRAZY WATER CRYSTALS COMPANY
of Minerals Wells, Texas
"Making weak men strong since 1880"
Sponsor of "CRAZY BARN DANCE"
Saturday nights on WBT

She read the card gravely and thoroughly, as if it were bad news from far away. Then she handed it back and smiled. "Thank you," she said, "but Aunt Kate and I have no need of laxatives. Thank you again, and good night."

"It's not a laxative," I said. "It's an all-purpose tonic."

"Is it, now? That sounds much more interesting. If you'll excuse me?" She picked up her guitar case, hoisted it onto one hip to get a better hold, then swung it between us and headed for the door. I followed and matched her stride, for she was as tall as I was. I had not driven halfway up the mountain called Yandro just to go back to Charlotte empty-handed, however pleasant the drive in springtime.

All my other leads had come to nothing: a mandolin player in Blowing Rock, a gospel quartet in North Wilkesboro, two fiddling brothers in Boone. None wanted to be broadcast all over the Carolinas on a fifty-thousand-watt station in between advertisements for Crazy Water Crystals. None wanted to pick up and move to Charlotte and become famous, like the Monroe Brothers and the Delmore Brothers and Fiddlin' Arthur Smith. None even wanted a steady radio salary. The year was 1936, and I apparently no longer could get 1931 mileage out of the phrase "ten dollars a week."

I kept right alongside as she swept through a knot of people on the porch. "Good night, fellas," she said. "I'll see y'all in church."

"Evening, Liza."

"Good night, Liza."

"Take care, Liza."

They stared at me as I kept pace, nearly a trot, down the steps and into the parking area. She walked right through the middle of a terrible snarl of wagons and shying mules and Model T's that churned around in circles slinging gravel. She looked neither to left nor right, as if charmed. I had seen this in mountain women before, this grim set of the jaw, this purposeful, loping gait, as if all slopes were steep. But I soon stopped comparing other mountain women to Liza Candler.

I tried my usually surefire sales pitch: I told the truth. "You have a voice like the voice of the mountain." I said, panting. "I want to put that voice on the radio. I don't want to sell you anything. I just want people to hear your voice."

"They hear me now," she said.

"Not many, though. How often do you play a dance like this? Once a week? I doubt it. Once a month, more like? And always for the home folks. The same people, month after month, year after year."

"Don't you like the same people, month after month, year after year? Do you change the people you like every month, like shifts at the furniture plant? And do you aim to run alongside me all the way home like a haint?"

I stopped and watched her stalk on down the road. "No, I thought you'd stop and talk to me, so I could offer you a ride."

"I ain't stopping," she said, her checked dress indistinct in the dark, "but if you drive up alongside me and open the door I might get in."

I ran back for the Packard.

"And then," she called after me, "we can see what Aunt Kate has to say."

• • • • • • • •

All the way up the road, I worked on her.

"You could come to Charlotte, stay for a week, visit the studio, get to know people, do a Crazy Water show on Saturday night, see how you like it. See how much mail comes in. Heck, I know people at RCA Victor. I could set up a recording session for you while you're in town. Do you know that Mainer's Mountaineers made eighteen thousand dollars last year for a half-hour's work in Charlotte? Just for 'Maple on the Hill'? They earned a half-cent in royalties off every record sold. How about that?"

Liza had her eyes shut and her head out the window, so that her hair streamed out behind. She had a profile like a cameo brooch. "A lot of people must have no music of their own," she said, "if they'll pay good money to try to hang on to somebody else's."

In the front parlor of the Candler place sat an ancient woman in a rocking chair, her feet propped on the gate of a cold iron stove. We walked in as she pushed a pinch of snuff into her mouth with one hand and snapped shut a small pouch with her other. She wore a tattered sweater, a gingham bonnet, and square eyeglasses as thick and grimy as windshields. Behind her, a gleaming shotgun leaned against the wall.

"Hello, Aunt Kate!" Liza cried, so loudly that I jumped. "This is Mr. Alvin Pleasants, from down in Charlotte."

Aunt Kate tucked the pouch into an apron pocket, pulled her eyeglasses down to the tip of her nose, and tilted her head back to look at me. Then she grunted and leaned sideways, slowly reached out behind, groped the air in the vicinity of the shotgun.

"No, Aunt Kate!" Liza yelled. "He ain't a fella! He wants to put me on the radio! He works for WBT!"

"Actually, I work for the Crazy Water Crystals Company, but

I do have an office at WBT. And I know the Monroe Brothers personally." I sat on the edge of a horsehair davenport, which pricked me something awful, and handed Aunt Kate a brochure. "Here's a copy of WBT's Official Radiologue, the seasonal programming schedule, compliments of Crazy Water Crystals." Aunt Kate bent over the brochure and scanned it with the tip of her nose. Liza looked at me meaningfully. Her eyes were gray. "Oh, I'm sorry," I said, and I began to yell, too. "It's a copy of the station's schedule! A gift for you!"

Aunt Kate slowly looked up at me and asked, very quietly, "Who in the world raised you to holler inside the house any such a way?"

I glared toward where Liza had been. I heard her bustle around the next room, humming. "I'm sorry, ma'am. Your niece gave me the impression that you were deaf."

Aunt Kate swatted the air. "Shoot. Ain't no telling what that gal will come up with. But if you know so much about radios, how 'bout turn on that one over there?" She pointed at a cathedral set across the room. "It's time for my story."

I turned the knob, heard a familiar click, then felt the vibration as the tubes started to warm up. As Liza walked in, tying back her hair, the radio started that slide-whistle sound that said the station would arrive in just a few seconds.

"Aunt Kate," Liza asked, at a normal volume, "haven't you wanted to visit Aunt Oese in the TB sanitarium in Charlotte?"

"You know I have, honey," Aunt Kate said. "Just been waiting on you to take a notion to come with me."

"Then I reckon I might as well come do your program," Liza told me. "Just for one show, of course."

The station faded in on a commercial: "If you care for your loved ones' laundry, banish tattletale gray with Fels Naphtha! Yes, banish tattletale gray with Fels Naphtha!"

"Good night, Aunt Kate," Liza said, and kissed the old

woman on the cheek. "Mr. Pleasants said he'd be happy to keep you company while you listen to your story."

"I did?"

"Good night, Mr. Pleasants," Liza said, standing in the doorway. "I hope that laxative company pays you well to drive around the countryside and bother people."

I enunciated carefully. "It's an all-purpose tonic."

"Is that so? Good night to you once again. I do hope you enjoy the program." She watched me through the narrowing crack, and I watched her, until the door thunked shut between us.

"And now—*The Romance of Helen Trent!* The real-life drama of Helen Trent, who, when life mocks her, breaks her hopes, dashes her against the rocks of despair, fights back bravely, successfully, to prove what so many women long to prove in their own lives: that because a woman is thirty-five—or more—romance in life need not be over. That romance can begin at thirty-five!"

As the organ music trilled, Aunt Kate leaned forward and puckered, sucked in her cheeks, squeezed a big dark drop from between her lips, and let it plop into a half-full Kiwi shoe-polish tin at her feet. She daubed her lips with a corner of her apron and sat back. The rocker and a floorboard creaked in harmony. The horsehair in the davenport worked its way a little further into me, as if to seize and haul me down into the brocade, fix me in that parlor forever.

Two months later, on the afternoon I met Liza and her aunt at the train station, my boss was pan-fried drunk. Had I know that, I might not have been so eager to drop Aunt Kate at the boardinghouse and whisk Liza immediately up to the station, hell-bent to show her the glories of radio. As I threw open the door to Mr. Ledford's office, I realized my error.

"Oh, dear," I said.

Empty bottles of Crazy Water's chief competitor, Peruna, formed three rows of pickets that guarded three sides of his desktop from all corners. Despite the mutter and jerk of the electric fan atop the file cabinet, the office was sweltering, and Ledford's ever-present homburg sagged over his ears like a deflated pudding. He gazed sightlessly forward, his expression placid, mournful, and expectant of all bad things. I timidly introduced Liza, and in reply his bullfrog voice rasped even more than usual.

"Good afternoon, Miss Candler," Ledford said. "Please forgive me, but I am drunker than Cooter John."

"There is no need to apologize," Liza said, "but who, pray tell, is Cooter John?"

"Cooter John does not exist," Ledford said. "He is a mythic figure, a wraith with a legendary capacity for drink."

"Thank you," Liza said.

I cleared my throat. "Probably we should come back later," I said. "Mr. Ledford sometimes likes to sample the competitors' products, just to, uh, investigate the market."

"I no longer wonder that Peruna sells so well," Ledford said. "It virtually sells itself, in all its smoothness and guile." He lurched sideways, rummaged in his trash can, and came up with a clutch of empty Peruna boxes. "If you will excuse me," he said, "I have box tops to redeem."

"You can talk to Miss Candler later," I said, hastily. "Maybe I could show her around downtown? Come back here just before *Briarhopper Time,* so she can watch the broadcast?"

Ledford flapped a hand at us, and we fled.

Out on the sidewalk, we walked into a hot breeze of exhaust fumes. We had to raise our voices to be heard over the rattles and growls of the Model T's and Model A's and the clangs of the street-cars that slid along the tracks in the middle of the traffic. Many of the Ford drivers seemed to keep one hand on the wheel and one on the horn, judging from all those honks and bleats. Drivers clawed at their collars, mopped their faces with handkerchiefs, wriggled out of suit jackets as their mindless automobiles rolled forward. Businessmen with briefcases, farmers in overalls, packs of dirty-faced children jaywalked at will, trotted from sidewalk to sidewalk, dodged the three streams of vehicles. Kids skipped merrily in front of the streetcars as the cowcatchers jabbed their shins.

"I am so sorry," I said for about the fifteenth time.

"I quite understand," Liza said.

"I handle all the talent—the singers, musicians, specialty acts. I don't have anything to do with the business side. But Mr. Ledford spends all his time dealing with the head office in Texas, and all he hears from them is sell, sell, sell. He gets discouraged. Me, I just listen to a lot of music. Good afternoon, Mr. Jennings!" I waved at the portly, gray-haired man at the rolltop desk in the lobby of the Union National Bank. He just glared back.

"Not very friendly," Liza said.

"He can't afford to be. He's the president of the bank. After the Crash, when so many other banks closed their doors, he moved his desk into the lobby and started handling all withdrawals personally. That's what kept him in business, probably—bullying people into not withdrawing their money."

On the next corner, a skinny young man with an open valise at his feet held swatches of cloth draped across his forearms. Around his neck dangled a ribbon of measuring tape. "Made-to-measure suits!" he cried. "A complete suit for a five-dollar deposit! Sir, that's a fine suit you have—couldn't you use another just like it? Have a good day, sir. Made-to-measure suits! Hi, Alvin, how's the boy?"

"Can't complain, Cecil, can't complain. Wife and kids all right?"

"Just fine, Alvin. That job lead I had last week went south, but hey, something will turn up. No, no need to linger, Alvin—

you bought three suits off me last month, and I know you haven't worn through the pants yet. Beg your pardon, ma'am."

"Come by the station sometime, Cecil. We'll go downstairs and get a bite to eat. The family, too, if you like."

"I appreciate it, Alvin. I'll see you. Made-to-measure suits! Just like mine, only twenty-three fifty! Nice cool seersucker, only eight ninety-five!"

We crossed the street in silence. I felt that if I looked around at Liza, she simultaneously would turn to look at me, and the thought made me flush as if it had happened. Instead, I waved at Mr. Tate, who draped a towel across a customer's face as we passed his shop—five white men in tilted chairs, five Negro men in a row behind. Mr. Tate grinned and ran his hand through his nonexistent hair, a visual reminder that I should come in for a trim.

Finally Liza asked, "If you own so many suits, Mr. Pleasants, why have I seen you in only one?"

I jammed my hands into my pockets. "Maybe some people need new suits more than I do," I said. I watched the cracks in the pavement go past.

To my surprise, Liza cut in front of me and walked backward for a few paces, so that we faced each other. She studied my face the way a fiddler studies the bow, the way a mill worker studies the thump of the shuttle and loom. Then she whirled and dropped back alongside me.

"Mr. Pleasants," Liza said, "I'd be honored if you were to buy me a cup of coffee."

The Star Lunch had only a couple of other patrons—wrong time of day—and so Ari Kokenes gave Liza the royal treatment. He poured her coffee and fussed over her. Up front, I leaned over the display case and peered at the pastries, but my reflection got in the way. I rubbed my chin. I thought I had shaved myself raw that morning, but now my face felt and looked like an empty burlap sack.

"How about some of the baklava, Illona?" I asked. "And two forks, maybe?" I looked up. Ari's daughter shrank from the counter, dark eyes wide as she looked past me. I turned just as Earl Gillespie seized my shoulder and breathed Sen-Sen into my face.

"Cheer up, Alvin, you'll curdle the cream." He slapped my back and barked a laugh. "Just a joke, pal, just a joke. Hi, Illona, how's my ready steady?"

Illona silently busied herself with the baklava and a small square of wax paper. She wrapped and unwrapped and wrapped it again, her eyes downcast. She moved her body as little as possible. If Earl watched her long enough, she'd dwindle down to nothing.

"Wait up for me, willya, Alvin?" Earl asked. "I need your help, okay? Great." Earl blew a kiss at Illona, winked at me, and barreled onward past Ari, who stood at attention at the end of the counter. "Use your phone, Ari? Great," Earl said, without a glance at the man.

"Sure, Mr. Gillespie, whatever you say," Ari said without enthusiasm. He slapped the countertop with the end of his towel and looked at me fast and blank, as if I had been replaced by a stranger.

I paid Illona and smiled at her until she flashed one in return. As I turned away, she had a hurried conversation with her father in Greek, maybe one sentence apiece, and then dashed into the back. The beaded curtain danced behind her.

As Earl watched my progress across the room, he rocked on his toes, jingled change in his pockets, and shouted into the telephone's mouthpiece as if the nearly empty Star Lunch were Grand Central at noon. "Get me WBT, please." I shoved my chair around between him and Liza, with my back to the phone. As he blew a long wolf whistle, I tipped my hat up and tried to square my shoulders to make them wider.

"Who's that," Liza stated.

"The announcer who says, once a week, 'For fifty-six years, Crazy Water has come to the aid of the weak and ailing, and it has made them men and women ready to face life's hardships.' "

"He does have that look about him," Liza said.

"Damn these people!" Earl cried. "Can't anyone answer a phone anymore? Can't anybody do an honest day's work? Has the whole world gone union?"

"Who's he calling that's so important?"

"Himself," I said.

Adelaide must have picked up, finally, because Earl dropped his normal deep radio voice and went into an exaggerated nasal twang. "Yes, please, is Mr. Gillespie in? Mr. Earl Gillespie? No? Could you please ask him to call Monica at Metro-Goldwyn-Mayer as soon as possible?" I pictured Adelaide at the other end as she rolled her eyes and drew shaded triangles on her blotter. "I'll be on the lot until three, West Coast time. Tell him I'm at the bungalow. Yes, he has the number. Thank you so much." He hung the earpiece back on its cradle and walked over, showing Liza all his teeth and slicking back his hair with one hand.

"You aren't fooling anybody, Earl," I said. "One day while you're busy chasing shopgirls at the five and dime, you're gonna get a real phone call, and Adelaide will just think it's you and laugh and hang up."

He didn't look at me. "You forget your manners, Alvin. Aren't you going to introduce me to your friend?"

I sighed. "Earl Gillespie, Liza Candler." Liza nodded just enough to acknowledge her name. "Liza Candler, Earl Gillespie." Earl bowed with an Errol Flynn flourish. "What do you need, Earl? We got to go."

"Now where in the world did Alvin Pleasants, of all people, find a pretty gal like you?" Earl turned a chair around and straddled it, his arms crossed over the back, and fished in the little jar on the table for a toothpick. "I've seen him drink coffee with street peddlers and hillbilly bands and nigger barbers, but never with anyone as high-class as you."

"I reckon you don't know him too well, then."

Her gaze would have frozen a smarter man, but Earl, like any mule, sometimes needed an ax handle. He just looked her over and shoved a toothpick into his mouth and chewed it with slow relish. "Yes, indeed. Alvin's outdone himself this time. Let's see now. You surely aren't a nigger barber. I don't see you carrying anything on your person to sell. So I'd say you must be a singer. And if you sing as pretty as you eat that pastry, why then I bet they've already put you on a record or two, am I right? I sure would like to hear one. Oh, yeah, that's it, I was right. See her blushing, Alvin, you see that?"

I saw it, and I was surprised. "Miss Candler? Are you all right?"

"I *tried* recording before," Liza blurted. "It didn't work out, that's all."

"What do you mean it didn't work out?" I asked. "They didn't *like* you?"

She stabbed me a look. "I'll have you know Mr. Peer said I could sing the clouds across the sky." Right then, her voice was almost as flat as Aunt Kate's. Almost.

Earl grinned as he watched us go back and forth.

"Peer?" I repeated. "Ralph Peer? You recorded for the top field producer in the country?"

"Oh, I was just a youngun," Liza said, laughing a little. "It must have been five years gone." She stabbed a stray pistachio with her fork, glanced at me, sighed and went on. "I was visiting some cousins down here in the flats, and we saw the ad in the paper, and we just went over there and sang and that was it. Just some giggly mountain gals out having fun, clomping around in our brogans, tracking in mud. Mr. Peer was just being nice to us 'cause it was the end of the day. They were glad to get rid of us, I bet." She smiled real quick at me and then at Earl and then at me, and then she let it go and turned to look at something on a shelf that had all of a sudden become plumb fascinating.

Earl cleared his throat. "You ever met a real-life radio star before, Liza honey? Why don't you come up to the studio while we do the Briarhopper show this afternoon? Just tell 'em you're there to see me, they'll let you right in."

"C'mon, Earl," I said, "save it for the bungalow. And if you've got a favor to ask me, ask it."

"Oh, it's not big, Alvin," Earl said, swiveling his head around at me like a turtle. "Not worth interrupting a nice conversation. You need to slow down and enjoy yourself more. But since you asked, I'm working on next month's banquet for the Alf Landon campaign at the Hotel Charlotte. I thought it'd be nice to have some local musicians perform before all the speeches. Might help people's dinners set better. You suppose some of your hillbilly friends would be interested in that? I figured I'd ask you before I asked anyone else, just as a favor."

"I seriously doubt it, Earl. How much you gonna pay?"

"Now, Alvin. Remember, this is a benefit. Everyone's donating their time and energy. I am, and Colonel Macon, and Mrs. Steere, and everyone else. It'd be a little unfair if the musicians wouldn't donate their time, too."

"They make little enough money working for Colonel Macon and Mrs. Steere in the mills all day long," I said. "Now you want 'em to work for those same people at night, and do it for free? Forget it, Earl. Besides, I don't know any hillbillies, myself included, who would donate to the Landon campaign so much as a—a cold cup of coffee."

That said, I drank the rest of mine, flustered again. Both Earl and Liza looked at me. So did Ari, in a sense, even with his back turned. He stayed scrupulously within earshot and rearranged bottles of olive oil with great industry.

"Why, Alvin," Earl said. "I'm surprised at you. Saying such anti-American things in front of this impressionable young woman. You don't want her to think you've bet on a losing horse, do you?"

It was like batter turning golden in a pan. Liza suddenly beamed at Earl as if his mask had dropped off and revealed Clark Gable. "A losing horse, Mr. Gillespie?" She reached across the table and touched Earl's forearm, just long enough to rivet his attention.

"There's no doubt about it, young missy," he said. "All the papers say it's over, it's Landon over Roosevelt two to one." He proceeded to tell us how much better off the mill workers would be without government meddlers and Communist labor agitators, and how the Democrats in Washington kept finding new ways to pick an honest man's pockets. "Do you know they plan to assign a number to every worker in America, and fingerprint everybody, and issue dog tags? It'll be just like prison. Just like Russia."

"That sure is scary, Mr. Gillespie," Liza said. "In fact, I'd say you're the scariest man I've met in Charlotte. I believe we've got to be going, isn't that right, Mr. Pleasants? But I wish you and Governor Landon luck, Mr. Gillespie."

"Thank you, thank you, Miss Candler," Earl said, and rose with us. "Hey, Alvin. Alvin! About that banquet—"

"I already told you to forget it, Earl."

"Did I forget to mention," Earl said, as he examined the frayed end of his toothpick, "that the performers would be welcome to help themselves to the buffet? Prime rib? Shrimp cocktail? Peach melba? All the trimmings?"

I stood there, my hat halfway to my head. Ari waited, holding open the door.

"Can they take home leftovers?" I asked. I looked not at Earl but at the tiles beneath my feet.

"I don't see why not," Earl said. "No sense in it going to waste."

"I'll ask around," I said. "I'll see what I can do."

Outside, the three smallest Kokenes kids jumped rope on the sidewalk. Patent-leather shoes smacked the pavement to the rhythm of a singsong chant:

"Roosevelt's in the White House, waiting to be elected, Landon's in the garbage, waiting to be collected, Alf Alf Alf Alf Arf Arf Arf Arf, Roosevelt's in the White House . . ."

Earl glared at Ari, who shrugged broadly and smiled. One gold tooth sparkled in the sun. "Who knows where kids hear such things?" he said, and lifted his hands in resignation.

Earl grunted, tipped his hat to Liza, and strode away. He gave the jump rope a wide berth.

"We'll see you later, Ari," I said. I walked off in the opposite direction from Earl, even though he was bound for the station like us.

Halfway down the block, I said, "I'm sorry about that, too," assuming Liza was beside me. She was. I added: "I guess I'm sorry about everything today. Earl sure pushes my buttons, though. He knows my weaknesses."

"I'd call them strengths," Liza said. As she walked, she traced the brick wall alongside with her finger.

Briarhopper Time aired live each weekday afternoon right before *The Lone Ranger.* Although their sponsor was Crazy Water's chief competitor, I had to admit that the Briarhoppers were one of the most popular bands at WBT, among the staff as well as among the public. When Liza and I got back to the station that evening, just as the show began, we joined about a dozen people gathered in the corridor outside the studio to watch the show through the soundproof plate glass.

From the loudspeaker above our heads came the familiar opening—"Do y'all know what 'hit is? 'Hit's Briarhopper Time!"—and then the first licks of "Hop Along Peter." Eventually, Earl Gillespie, on the other side of the glass, stepped up to the microphone, and Liza watched him attentively.

"Have a nice walk?" asked Ledford, who gnawed the tip of a new cigar beside me. He looked considerably more focused.

"Mr. Ledford," Liza asked, "could I please borrow your lighter?"

"But of course," Ledford said, and handed it over.

"I didn't know you smoked, Miss Candler," I said.

"I don't," she said, and walked away with the lighter.

"Hey," Ledford said. She disappeared around the corner. He looked at me like he expected me to sprint after her.

In the studio, Earl had launched into a commercial. His lips moved on the other side of the plate glass; his dulcet voice crackled through the loudspeaker. "And now a word from the Consolidated Drug Trade Products Company of Chicago, Illinois, home of the wondrous laboratories that gave the world Radio Girl perfume, Kolorbak hair dye, and Zymole Trokeys cough drops."

The studio door in the far wall opened, and Liza sashayed through, ushered by a smiling security guard who held the door and waved to get Earl's attention. Liza high-stepped over microphone cords as she approached Earl, the hem of her dress swinging.

Ledford's cigar drooped in his mouth.

Earl beamed at Liza and glanced up from his script at every other word to mug and preen. She smiled and waved, wiggling her fingers like a little girl.

"Friends, does your medicine chest include a bottle of Peruna? Yes, I said Peruna—that's P-E-R-U-N-A, the all-purpose wonder tonic that so many of your friends and neighbors rely upon when they feel under the weather."

Liza stood directly in front of him, still smiling. Earl winked at her, oblivious as she slowly raised the lighter.

"I'm sure all you Briarhopper fans out there don't need a reminder that for each Peruna box top you send in, you get a photograph of everyone's favorite hillbilly band—the Briarhoppers!—absolutely free and suitable for framing."

Liza flicked the lighter aflame, and apparently jammed an important cog in Earl's mind.

"But right now I want to address the, the medicinal benefits of—of Peruna, which is safe and effective for adults as well—I mean, for children as well as adults."

Liza set the top of Gillespie's script on fire and walked away, smiling and waving at me. What else? I waved back. The paper rushed into flame like it was soaked in Peruna, and Gillespie desperately tried to speed up his last few lines.

"Mothers and fathers, when your little ones wake up with a stomachache or a chill you'll want a bottle of Peruna on hand won't you?" He held a torch by his fingertips. "Of course you will! Sleep better tomorrow night because you have Peruna in your medicine chest that's P-E-R-U-N-A just-ask-for-it-by-name-and-now-we-return-to-the-Briarhopper-show! Shoot!" he hissed, and dashed his flaming script to the floor as the band solemnly stepped forward and began "More Pretty Gals Than One." A technician ran over and tried to kick apart the ashes quietly, like a soft-shoe dancer in a medicine show.

"What a pro," Ledford said. "Note how he said 'shoot' and not 'shit,' and turned away from the microphone just in case? Read all the copy before it burned up, too. He does have talent, the son of a bitch. Thank you, ma'am," he told Liza, and accepted his lighter with a little bow.

"I just set your announcer on fire," Liza said. "Aren't you mad?"

"No, ma'am," Ledford said. "He's our announcer only on Saturday nights. On weekdays he works for the competition, and I happily consign him to the flames."

I watched through the glass as Gillespie bolted. "On the other hand," I said, "this might be a good time to go out and get a sandwich." I hustled Liza toward the elevators as Gillespie charged into view around the corner, holding his hand and cursing.

"Hold the car!" I cried.

As the door on the cage slid shut, I heard Ledford say: "You hush that bad talk, Earl. No one buys tonic off a cussing man."

Half a floor down, I asked Liza, "That damn fool stunt was for me, wasn't it?"

"You can have it if you like," she said with a grin.

I laughed. "Okay, I'll take it, then."

"Done."

"Done." We shook hands violently, as if pumping water, and then hollered laughing like younguns. The operator gripped the handle and shook his head.

I showed her around town, what town there was. The old U.S. Mint had been moved out to Eastover and reopened as an art museum, of all things, the first in the state, so I took her there out of civic duty. I showed her that the eye of the eagle above the door was really the taillight off a Ford, and she agreed that was the best part of the museum. We watched airplanes land and take off at Douglas Field, and I told her how Mayor Douglas made a big speech at the dedication about the brilliant future of air travel and then, when invited to go up in one of the things, replied, "Thank you, no." We went to the kiddie matinee at the State Theater, the New York Grand before talkies, because Johnny Mack Brown was signing autographs in between episodes of *Rustlers of Red Dog*. Those younguns were screaming wild, and if their popguns had been loaded, why I wouldn't have given you a nickel for the life of Johnny Mack Brown. Then we ate fifteen-cent hamburgers and drank five-cent Cokes at the Canary Cottage, the cheapest good place in town, and from there went over to the Hotel Charlotte. We couldn't afford to do anything there but sit on the plush furniture in the massive, marbled lobby, watch people go by, and enjoy the curious breeze that constantly stirred the palms no matter the weather outside. We sat on facing sofas, sprawled our arms along the backs, and took up as much free space as we could.

"If anybody tries to run us off," I said, "tell them we answer only to J. Edgar Hoover."

After a while, I ran out of jokes and other things I felt comfortable saying, and so I just sat with my chin on my fist, listened to Liza talk, and watched her finish a cup of cider that she had bought at a sidewalk stand down the street.

She jiggled the straw up and down in the ice. "Just what are you smiling about, Mr. Pleasants?"

"About a song, actually."

She laughed and looked at her cup. "Oh, I bet I know what it is." Then she sang the first few lines:

"The prettiest girl
That ever I saw
Was sipping cider
Through a straw."

And just that snippet of a silly little ditty nearly filled that lobby, her voice was so clean and full and true. The whole place got a little quiet to make way for that voice, and heads turned and looked our way, through ferns and around fluted columns.

"Is there any song you can't make beautiful?" I asked. "We sang that song a thousand times, and yet I'd never heard it before now."

"Who's 'we'?" she asked.

I fidgeted and checked my nails. "Oh, a band I used to be in. Years ago. We toured around. That was our most requested song, believe it or not. Grove Keener—it was his band, Grove's band—he used to call it our 'signature tune,' can you believe it? Like we were Les Brown's big band at Duke. We'd do that song three times, some nights, before the audience would let us go."

"Tell me," Liza said. She curled her legs up beneath her on the sofa, her gray eyes for a second turning wide and somehow reproachful, as if what I said hurt. Then her crooked, dimpled smile crept out again. "Tell me what it was like."

"Being in a band?"

"Yes."

"Okay." I took a deep breath, and then I told her.

Back before Roosevelt, but after the Crash, I worked at the Gastonia mill five days a week and spent the other two days on the road with the Carolina Cavaliers. Seems like they were the same two days, over and over and over again. Each Friday evening we piled into Ira Cannon's Model A, all six of us and our instruments, and jolted along a hundred miles of dirt roads and mud tracks to get to some crossroads in the middle of nowhere with a thrown-away schoolhouse.

A couple of farm boys would carry the desks outside and stack them against the wall to clear a dance floor. The sun would sink behind the mountain long before showtime, so the boys also lighted kerosene lamps and situated them someplace in the school so that they wouldn't get knocked over and burn the place down like in Tobaccoville in '29.

If the show was announced on the radio the week before, maybe some neighbor called the station and invited us to supper, but if not, we stopped on the way at a general store. The man at the store, because we were musicians, stared at each bill, front and back, and tugged at its corners before folding it into his cash drawer.

Later, outside the schoolhouse, we sat on the running board of the car and ate Nabs, sardines, sweet rolls, Co-Colas, whatever we'd bought. Usually I bought a few inches of baloney, say, and Ira bought some crackers, and so on, and then we portioned it out. We didn't look at each other or actually ask for anything, just nodded and said, "Much obliged."

Later we sat on the car or in the grass, smoked and listened to the crickets. With about twenty minutes till showtime and no customers in sight, we started making light of ourselves.

"Well, fellas, I wonder what tunes these cows would like to hear?"

"I just remembered, Greta Garbo's doing a fan dance tonight at the barbershop down in Valmead. No wonder we got no crowd. Bad timing, boys."

But with about five minutes to go, we saw lanterns flash like lightning bugs on the slopes all around, and heard faint talk and laughter in the pasture on one side and the woods on the other, and then a long string of cars hauled up the grade, and ten minutes after that, people packed that schoolhouse so thick, you'd think the attraction was indeed Garbo instead of a bunch of worn-out mill hands singing songs everyone knew already.

When it all ended, a couple of hours later, we divvied up the till. Fifty cents apiece on a good night, with maybe a dime extra for Grove 'cause it was his band and a dime extra for

Ira 'cause it was his car. Then we all climbed into the Ford and rattled back to Charlotte, just in time to go on the air live on WBT's six A.M. farm show. That Saturday evening, if we were lucky and had the work, we were on the road again. Sometimes I put on my dress shoes Friday afternoon and didn't get the chance to take them off again until late Sunday night. Then back to the mill on Monday, of course.

In my dreams I'd try to play a tune on a spindle, feed into a loom a pearl-inlay guitar.

"Did you record?" Liza asked. She looked at her cider, now mostly water, and set the cup on the coffee table with strange deliberation, as if where she set it mattered.

"No," I said. "The band has, though, since I left 'em. In fact, they're scheduled to cut some sides tomorrow morning. In fact—" I gnawed my thumbnail.

"In fact, what?"

"In fact, I talked to the RCA Victor people just today. They had a cancellation in tomorrow's schedule, right after the Carolina Cavaliers. They said that based on my glowing recommendation, they would—"

"Oh," she said.

"—pencil you in, if I called them back by five. And then I wondered whether I should call Grove, to see if he and the boys could record a second session, as your backup band. And to lend you, you know, moral support."

We sat there and looked at each other.

"I appreciate your eventually getting around to telling me this," Liza said.

"You're welcome."

She took a deep breath. "Call them."

"I did," I said. "That's why I waited so long to tell you."

• • • • • • • •

The RCA Victor studio, at the Southern Radio Corporation offices on Tryon Street, was a big cleared-out storage room. Crates of Victrolas and radio sets were stacked along the walls of the nearest corridor. Liza and I sat on the floor in this narrowed passage, surrounded by dozens of men and women who talked, smoked, and tuned. They cradled guitars, fiddles, mandolins, banjos, washboards, jugs. A string-bass player stood with his arm around the waist of his ungainly instrument. They looked like an awkward couple waiting for a dance to start.

All the musicians wore their stage clothes: embroidered western shirts, white cowboy hats, neckerchiefs. The members of the Woodlawn String Band stood out in their stiff new overalls and bow ties. Everyone's outfits looked crisp and clean, except for a few mud-spattered pants cuffs. Not everyone could afford the streetcar.

"I don't know why we get so dressed up to record," a banjo player once told me. "No matter how good we sound, won't no one be able to see us. Maybe we dress up out of respect for the folks who sang the songs before we did."

Liza asked me, a little too loudly: "How come everyone looks like Gene Autry? I didn't know there were so many cowboys in North Carolina."

"There aren't any," I said, "but the new Gene Autry picture has a Charlotte band in it, and everybody here has seen it about a dozen times. To these folks, *Ride Ranger Ride* is not a Gene Autry picture but a Tennessee Ramblers picture that has Gene Autry in it. Now everybody tries to look like the Tennessee Ramblers."

Liza asked, "If they're a Charlotte band, how come they call themselves the Tennessee Ramblers? Are they from Tennessee?"

"No. Crazy Water Crystals brought them down from, uh, Rochester, New York, I believe."

"Well, where'd they get Tennessee from?"

I sighed. "I swear I don't know, Miss Candler. It's all show business, and I just don't have time to explain show business to you on this day and in this place."

Liza laughed. "Well, I'll be sure and quiz you later about all this Hollywood business, Mr. Laxative Man."

"I'll thank you not to call me Mr. Laxative Man. I'm a talent scout. I do not fool with laxatives. Besides, it's an all-purpose tonic. Ah, hell. I would like to know whether you pester the life out of your Aunt Kate like this. Is that why her face has closed up like a fist?"

"You can just hush about Aunt Kate, and what's wrong with you this morning anyway? You've been too sour to live." She squinted at me like the sun was in her eyes. "I swear I believe you're more nervous than I am."

"Yes, I'm nervous," I said. "You're about to step into that room and try to lay across a sheet of wax a voice that's the most beautiful sound in God's world. If these people like it, they'll roll it up like a sausage and run it through a press and stack copies of it in trucks like pulpwood and sell them for a few cents apiece, and you don't even know these people. To be honest with you, Miss Candler, I don't know whether they deserve to hang on to a voice like yours, or even to sully it with their fingers as it passes."

We looked at each other steadily.

"I believe I judge people pretty well, Mr. Pleasants," Liza whispered. "I don't think you need to worry at all."

I heard a pair of brogans scrape along, and Aunt Kate stood over us, blocking out the light, looking even more grim than usual. It is a thousand wonders she didn't empty that sanitarium.

"I just saw a streetcar run over a dog and keep on going," she said. "This place you live in is a bad place, Mr. Pleasants. This place you live in is the last place God made."

A bald man in a sweat-blotted shirt banged through a door a few yards down the hall. "Candler!" he read off his clipboard. "Liza Candler? We're ready for you, Miss Candler."

Liza didn't budge. She still looked at me. She didn't look scared, exactly; that would have been all right, that I would have understood. She looked at me as if I had forgotten the words in the middle of a duet.

"You'd best get up, ma'am," a fiddle player told her. "Get it over with."

I reached out a hand to help her up. She looked at it a moment, then grabbed it.

"Are you Miss Candler? I'm Frye Gooding, with RCA Victor. Pleased to meet you. Hello there, Alvin. Good to see you again."

"Yeah, nice to see, uh . . ." But Gooding already had swept her away, talking in her ear as if he were telling loud secrets: He had fallen behind schedule because some people kept blowing take after take, and he really wished more entertainers would learn at least the rudiments of the recording process, but now time was of the essence, he was sure she'd understand; and all the while he tap, tap, tapped her in the small of her back with his clipboard as he herded her toward the studio door. I followed them, waggling my fingers. Quite a grip that woman had. Thought for a second she wasn't going to let go.

I looked up just before I bumped into them. Aunt Kate had blocked all of us with a broomstick arm thrust across the doorway. Her eyes were shut and her face balled up like she smelled something awful.

"Dear Lord," she called, "smile upon Liza, your daughter, who pleases You so each Sunday with 'The Great Speckled Bird' and other hymns in Your name, and be with her as she sings for these strange New York men in their dark room full of machines. Amen."

"Amen," Liza muttered, and ducked beneath Aunt Kate's arm.

Bolts of black monk's cloth covered the walls and the ceiling. A lone microphone, the size and shape of a billy club, hung at eye level from the ceiling in the middle of the room. A technician cinched it up a bit on its cord, and when he let go, it swung slowly like a pendulum, not enough to stir the stifling air. The musicians stood around it, instruments at the ready: two fiddles, banjo, mandolin, guitar, upright bass. I stepped forward and shook the guitarist's slick, damp hand.

"Good to see you, Alvin," Grove Keener said.

I shook hands all around. "Morning, boys. How's everyone?"

"You shoulda brought your guitar, Alvin," Ira Cannon said. "A band can't never have too many guitars."

"I brought something better than that worn-out old guitar," I said. "Fellas, if you can't say anything else good about me when I'm gone, at least tell people that I'm the man who introduced you to Liza Candler."

After the introductions, Liza and Grove and the others huddled for a few minutes to run down the songs she had selected. As I expected, the Cavaliers knew all of them. I made myself scarce, perched on a stool behind the sound engineers' equipment, which looked like a dismantled tractor motor spread across a series of tables. Then Gooding gave the performers their final instructions. This was old hat to the Cavaliers, and they fidgeted and joked around, but Liza solemnly listened to every word.

"First you'll hear one buzz. Sid, let them try on that buzz for size. . . . Got that? Okay, then we'll have a wait—of a few seconds or a few years, depending on that damned equipment, ha ha, right Sid?—and then you'll hear two buzzes right together. Like this . . . After those buzzes, count to two—one Mississippi, two Mississippi—then go ahead, 'cause I'll be pointing at you, and we'll be recording by then. Any questions?"

"Mississippi's been sorta bad luck for us," Grove said.

"Yeah," Ira said. "The last time we played in Mississippi, the audience left in the middle of the show 'cause someone's cow had got out."

Grove asked, "Would you mind if we counted 'One Jimmie Rodgers, two Jimmie Rodgers' instead?"

"Hell, you can count 'One Liza Candler, two Liza Candler' if you want to. Just count to two before you sing. Okay? All set? Here we go. . . ."

The wait between buzzes was about a year and a half. I held my breath. Then the fiddlers, poised with their elbows up, drew their bows across their strings and pulled the rest of the band along. I watched the music, the way you can see it happen if you pay attention to the fingers and the strings and the flash of the picks, until Liza started singing, when the whole dark, close, choking box of a studio was replaced by other sights.

"Let us pause in life's pleasures
And count her many tears
Oh we all share in sorrow with the poor."

I saw Mr. Jennings braced for the worst at his rolltop desk, and I saw padlocked front doors all over Charlotte, at bank after bank—the Merchants and Farmers, the Independence National, even the First National in its brand-new twenty-one-story skyscraper. Against its titanic brass doors, a small boy listlessly bounced a ball.

"It's a song that'll linger
Forever in our ears
Oh hard times come again no more."

I saw a tall but neat stack of furniture on a sidewalk. A man and a woman sat upright at opposite ends of the sofa, their children between them. All stared straight ahead at nothing. On the porch, a deputy nailed up a sign with a series of hammer blows.

"It's a song this side of the weary
Hard times, hard times,
Come again no more."

I saw hundreds of people in a slow single file around the Salvation Army building. Sawhorses funneled them into the side entrance, where women in uniforms handed them each a bowl and a spoon. Two blocks down the street, a newcomer with a valise hurried to get in on the end of the line. It was Cecil, measuring tape flapping around his neck.

"Many days you have lingered
Too long around my door
Oh hard times come again no more."

And it went on like that, for the rest of that song and for the next three songs, too. When the session ended I felt a hand clamp my shoulder. I jerked like a hare and suddenly rushed back into my body. My foot had fallen asleep, and my rear end hurt from the stool.

"Some people come in and do take after take, use up nearly all the wax," Gooding said. "But I never saw such a flawless session as this."

"It ain't natural," an engineer said, rapt in the roll of the wax cylinder.

"New York won't believe it," Gooding said. "This woman could be bigger than the Carter Family. Where in the world did you find her, Alvin?"

"A lot of people have asked me that," I said. Liza and the

band and the technicians talked excitedly and slapped each other on the back and hugged each other. I do believe Ira cried, there beneath that suspended microphone. I glanced around and saw Aunt Kate, posted with folded arms beside the door. She looked like she wanted to show pride but was too sad to do it, as if Liza had just sung a solo at a funeral.

Charlotte wasn't a big town, then or now, and word got around. I talked Liza up a bit myself. That Saturday night, a good half-hour before the *Crazy Barn Dance* went on the air, the corridor outside the studio filled not only with the usual Monroe Brothers fans but also with Grove Keener and his boys, a bunch of other musicians, numerous members of the Kokenes family, and several of the reporters from the *Charlotte News*. The reporters, as a group, hailed Mr. Tate when he arrived, fresh from the barbershop.

"Why so many damn newspapermen?" Ledford growled as he stared through the control-room window. "Burke Davis, and Shipp, and Cash—and there's Hargrove, too. What is this, a press conference? Since when did any of those eggheads get interested in hillbilly music?"

"What?" I said. "Oh. Well, I showed Liza around the *News* office yesterday, and they got more interested than usual. Especially in the threat of a party afterward. What time's it?"

"Quit asking," Ledford said. "And sit down, willya? I see enough marching in the newsreels."

I couldn't sit down. I roamed the control room, picked my way over electrical cables and boxes of equipment, got into people's way, bumbled and fumbled and tried not to stare at Liza. She sat smiling in a folding chair across the studio, where she chatted with the Monroes and with George Crutchfield, the guest announcer. I was too anxious even to enjoy the news that Earl Gillespie had called in sick at the last minute. "Probably burnt up with fever," Ledford said. "*Please,* Alvin, sit down."

"Have a spoonful of Peruna," Aunt Kate said, her back to us. She stood in front of the window like a fence post in gingham, and said nothing else before the show began.

The red light flashed once, twice, then burned hellish and steady. The Monroe Brothers sang "What Would You Give in Exchange for Your Soul?" George Crutchfield talked about the wondrous virtues of Crazy Water Crystals. Then I had to sit down.

"This is a song for my Aunt Kate," Liza said, with a smile into the iron bloom of the microphone. She turned aside a little and coughed, so that I died for a second or two. Then she returned the smiles of Charlie Monroe on her left, Bill Monroe on her right. They nodded at each other over her head, and commenced the simple, familiar tune, Charlie on guitar and Bill on mandolin. Liza smiled at me, and at Aunt Kate, and at me again, through the plate glass and began to sing the hymn as no one on the airwaves had sung it before.

"What a beautiful thought I am thinking
Concerning a great speckled bird.
Remember her name is recorded
On the pages of God's holy word."

When the song ended, I continued to listen to it. The Monroe Brothers swapped banter with Crutchfield. Liza stood to one side, tightened her guitar strings, and waited for her next song cue. I still listened to the song that had ended.

Ledford interrupted. "I mightily wish we had a clear-channel station," he said. "Fifty thousand watts blankets the Southeast, but some places still won't be able to tune in to Miss Candler tonight."

"Mr. Pleasants?" One of the technicians held out the earpiece of the wall phone. "Call for you, Mr. Pleasants."

"Huh? Me?"

"It's Mr. Gooding. From RCA Victor."

Aunt Kate turned to watch me as I made my way over. "Hello?" I cupped a hand over my other ear. "Hello, Frye?"

No preamble, no pleasantries. "Alvin, I just got off the phone with New York. I sent 'em the rolls immediately, special courier."

"Oh, really? That was fast. So tell me, tell me, what did they think?"

His voice quavered. "They don't know what to think, Alvin. And frankly, I don't know what to think either."

"What's wrong? Didn't they like the record?"

"They liked it fine. What they could hear of it."

"I don't follow. Did something go wrong?"

"I'll say it went wrong. Not a word of Liza's singing got recorded. Not a word, Alvin! It's the damndest thing—"

"Oh, for—Jesus, Frye, what the hell kind of operation are you running, anyway?" The others looked at me quizzically. "I mean, I expected better from Victor, for God's sake. This is awful. She will be so, so disappointed. Well, you'll just have to give her another chance on another date, with some equipment that actually works—"

"Alvin, you don't get me. Listen to what I'm saying. There was nothing wrong with the equipment. It picked up everything. Everything except the girl."

"You've lost me," I lied, much more quietly.

"It picked up every sound in that studio—the coughing and shifting around between numbers, the cues I gave the technicians, the buzzers, every note the Cavaliers played. Whenever they joined in at the choruses, that came through loud and clear, too. But there's no female voice on the record *anywhere.* I tell you, Alvin, it's as if she wasn't in the room."

"But of course she was in the room. I mean, we were there, we saw her. Frye, this is crazy."

"You think I don't know that, Alvin? You think I can't tell that for myself? I listened to her on the earphones the whole time the wax rolled. You should see me here, whiskey all down my tie because I can't hold my hand still long enough to take a shot. You should come over here and stumble around in the dark with the rest of us, among thousands of dollars of equipment dismantled and flung all over the floor of the studio, and no problems anywhere that we can see. You should see some of the top sound engineers in the country cross themselves and mumble about haints and witchcraft—witchcraft, Alvin! The evil eye! In the year of our Lord nineteen hundred and thirty-six!"

"Frye. Calm down."

He cut his voice to nearly a whisper. "I asked you before, and I'll ask you again—Where did you find that woman? But this time, Alvin, I don't want to know the answer."

Then he hung up.

In the studio, Crutchfield made another pitch for Crazy Water Crystals. I waved my hands wildly, like a controller at Douglas Field, until I got Liza's attention. Then I pointed toward the door to the corridor.

"Alvin. What's up?"

"Call Adelaide," I told Ledford as I headed out. "Call anybody with their radio on. Hell, call Earl. Ask 'em what they just heard broadcast. Ask 'em if it sounded all right."

"Alvin—"

"Boss, please, do it! Aunt Kate can explain." I vaulted the rail and landed beside the steps in the middle of the corridor, just as Liza shoved open the steel, red-lighted studio door.

"What in the world?" she said. "I have to be back in there in about two minutes—"

"RCA Victor called."

She froze.

"This happened five years ago, didn't it? This is why your session with Peer just 'didn't work out,' isn't it? Liza, what does this mean? *Why can't your voice be recorded?*"

"We don't know," Aunt Kate said. She stood in the control-room doorway and stared down at us.

"I can speak for myself!" Liza cried, then closed her eyes and took a deep breath and said, more calmly: "I have heard tell that in the old stories, the women and the men with powers wouldn't show up in mirrors, wouldn't be reflected if they looked into a pool. Maybe this is the same thing, only they didn't have all this fancy equipment back when those stories got told. . . . I don't know. . . ."

"An angel won't never show up in no photograph," Aunt Kate said.

"I'm not an angel!" Liza said. "And I'm not a witch either! I want to sing to people, Alvin. I want to perform, and record, and travel all around. *I want what you had, what you gave up.* For the past five years, I've been scared even to leave Yandro—knowing what I knew about myself—but when you came for me—I thought it might be—a sign—"

I nodded, eyes wide. "It was. That's exactly right. It was as much a sign as either of us ever will get in our lives. You did right to come."

Ledford poked his head out of the door, behind Aunt Kate's shoulder. "Alvin, Adelaide says it's coming through loud and clear, no problems at all. Now what in the world did you—Miss Candler, you best get back into that studio this very *instant*!"

She whirled and dashed for the studio door. When she reached it, she looked back around, her eyes like stars, her hair astream around her face, and she told me: "Yes. I was right to come." She slammed back through the door, and I stood in the corridor as those words whipsawed into me just the same as if she had sung them.

I don't remember how I got to the street, elevator or stairs or window or wings, but I remember the screech of tires and the horns and the shouts as I ran from one sidewalk to the other, back and forth, into diners and cigar stores and newsstands, and reached across people to wrench radio knobs until I heard what I needed so desperately, and so on all the way down the block, leaving a wake of shouts and jeers and laughter and a street filled with Liza's song.

I am proud to say that Liza sang in my presence just about every day for more than forty years of marriage, and in all those days I never heard her hit a note that wasn't true and good and fine. She did some radio, and she played a right many shows all around. I still get a few letters from people in the Carolinas and Virginia and Tennessee, folks who heard her in person years ago in Asheville or Greensboro or Union Grove or especially the Merle Watson Festival, that big mess of a crowd in North Wilkesboro she sang to in the last year of her life. Before she went on, she stood in the wings, in front of a big upright fan that made her hair float like a gray cloud, and I came back from the edge of the stage and reported at least one whole county out there on the hillside, and she smiled and said, "Well, Mr. Laxative Man, I reckon I'll just do like always, and pretend I'm singing to you."

It's a hard job to write these people back and say that Liza's gone, but I take the opportunity to reassure them that she ever existed at all, that their memories have not played tricks on her voice, and that's what everybody really wants anyway.

Liza traveled with me all over the mountains after I quit Crazy Water Crystals and got on with the Smithsonian. We must have lugged my equipment into every hollow in the Appalachians, every schoolhouse dance and fiddlers' convention, trying to record and transcribe everything we could before it all vanished, before it all headed to Nashville and turned into Crazy Water and Martha White Flour and Purina Dog Chow and whatever else needs selling today. People that want to hear about all that would be just as well served to go to the fourth floor of Wilson Library in Chapel Hill. All my tapes are in their Southern Folklife Collection, along with thirty-seven thousand other recordings. Gospel choirs, washboard and Jew's-harp pickers, fiddlers, bluesmen, string bands, medicine-show pitchmen. So much music otherwise gone from the world.

I'm up there in the library about once a week myself. Takes me about near forever just to walk across Franklin Street these days, and I feel like a spectacle with my walking stick and my gray suit and hat, while skateboarders and tattooed women parade around me. But the young folks on the fourth floor know me and bring me whatever tapes I want to hear, and then they leave me alone as best they can. But I can tell they're nervous. They're afraid I'll just up and die with my headphones on, there in my favorite booth, the one with the framed receipt on the wall. I've got the numbers memorized: For song royalties in the last quarter of 1928, Pop Stoneman received $161.31, including $1.63 for 340 copies of "Prisoner's Lament." I wonder whether Pop Stoneman ever knew, even for a second, how lucky he was to make even a nickel off a lament.

I sit in that booth and listen to Mainer's Mountaineers and Fisher Hendley's Carolina Tar Heels and the Crazy Bucklebusters and Dorsey and Howard, the Dixon Brothers. I listen to "Wreck on the Highway" and "Let Me Be Your Salty Dog" and "Cocaine Blues" and "Let the Church Roll On" and "What Would You Give in Exchange for Your Soul?" So many others.

I know them all by heart, but I need to hear them just the same.

And no matter what else I listen to beforehand, I always end up with one of the Liza tapes. I made dozens of them, with every new technology that came along, over the course of forty years. When I finally handed them over, all carefully dated and labeled just like the others, the librarians thought there was some mistake. They wondered why in the world I would record the zing of crickets, the bark of a distant hound, the scrape of a chair, and sometimes a cough.

That's all I heard on the tapes as well, to begin with. But as the years pass, my ears get better. Nowadays I hardly strain at all to hear "Hard Times" and "The Great Speckled Bird" and even

The prettiest girl
That ever I saw
Was sipping cider
Through a straw.

When I'm slumped in that booth, and the librarians creep past me thinking I've died or at least nodded off, I'm really just listening to a voice that never falters or fades, a voice that fills the library and the campus and the world and the mountain and the schoolhouse and yet finds room for me, calls me out of the dark and to the edge of the stage, to Liza in a kerosene glow.

Sherwood Smith is the author of Wren to the Rescue, Crown Duel, *and other fantasy novels for young readers. She has also co-written several science fiction novels with Andre Norton, and she co-authored the space-opera Exordium series with Dave Trowbridge.*

Mom and Dad at the Home Front

SHERWOOD SMITH

Before Rick spoke, I saw from his expression what was coming.

I said the words first. "The kids are gone again."

Rick dropped onto the other side of the couch, propping his brow on his hand. I couldn't see his eyes, nor could he see me.

It was just past midnight. All evening, after we'd seen our three kids safely tucked into bed, we'd stayed in separate parts of the house, busily working away at various projects, all of them excuses not to go to bed ourselves—even though it was a work night.

Rick looked up, quick and hopeful. "Mary. Did one of the kids say something to you?"

"No. I had a feeling, that was all. They were so sneaky after dinner. Didn't you see Lauren—" I was about to say *raiding the flashlight and the Swiss Army knife from the earthquake kit* but I changed, with almost no pause, to "—sneaking around like . . . like Inspector Gadget?"

He tried to smile. We'd made a deal, last time, to take it

easy, to try to keep our sense of humor, since we knew where the kids were.

Sort of knew where the kids were.

How many other parents were going through this nightmare? There had to be others. We couldn't be the only ones. I'd tried hunting for some kind of support group on the Internet—*Seeking other parents whose kids disappear to other worlds*—and not surprisingly the e-mail I got back ranged from offers from psychologists for a free mental exam to "opportunities" to MAKE $ IN FIVE DAYS.

So I'd gone digging again, this time at the library, rereading all those childhood favorites: C. S. Lewis, L. Frank Baum, Joy Chant, Ruth Nicholls, and then more recent favorites, like Diana Wynne Jones. All the stories about kids who somehow slipped from this world into another, adventuring widely and wildly, before coming safely home via that magic ring, or gate, or spell, or pair of shoes. Were there hints that adults missed? Clues that separated the real worlds from the made-up ones?

"Evidence," I said, trying to be logical and practical and adult. "They've vanished like this three times that we know about. Doors and windows locked. Morning back in their beds. Sunburned. After the last time, just outside R.J.'s room you saw two feathers and a pebble like nothing on Earth. You came to get me, the kids woke up, the things were gone when we got there. When asked, the response was, and I quote, 'What feathers?' "

But Rick knew he had seen those feathers, and so we'd made our private deal: Wait, and take it easy.

Rick rubbed his hands up his face, then looked at me. And broke the deal. "What if this time they don't come back?"

We sat in silence. Then, because there was no answer, we forced ourselves to get up, to do chores, to follow a normal routine in hopes that if we were really, really good, and really, really normal, morning would come the same as ever, with the children in their beds.

I finished the laundry. Rick vacuumed the living room and took the trash cans out. I made three lunches and put them in the fridge.

I put fresh bath towels in the kids' bathroom.

At one o'clock we went to bed and turned out the light but neither of us slept; I lay for hours listening to the clock tick, and to Rick's unhappy breathing.

Dawn. I made myself get up and take my shower and dress all the while listening, listening . . . and when I finally nerved myself to check, I found a kid-sized lump in each of the three beds, a dark curly head on each pillow. R.J.'s face was pink from the Sun—from *what* Sun?—and Lauren had a scrape on one arm. Alisha snored softly, her hands clutching something beneath the bedclothes.

I tiptoed over and lifted the covers. Her fingers curled loosely around a long wooden wand with golden carving on its side. If it wasn't a magic wand, I'd eat it for breakfast.

Alisha stirred. I laid her covers down and tiptoed out.

"A magic wand?" Rick whispered fiercely. "Did you take it?"

"Of course not!" I whispered back. "She'd have woken up, and—"

"And what?" he prompted.

I sighed, too tired to think. "And would have been mad at me."

"Mad?" Rick repeated, his whisper rising almost to a squeak. "Earth to Mary—*we* are the parents. *They* are the kids.

We're supposed to keep them safe. How can we do it if they are *going off the planet every night*?"

I slipped back into Alisha's room. She had rolled over, and the wand had fallen off the mattress onto her blue fuzzy rug.

I bent, my heart thumping so loud I was afraid she'd hear it, closed my fingers round the wand, and tiptoed out.

"Hmm." Rick waved it back and forth. It whistled—just like any stick you wave in the air—but no magic sparks came out, no lights, no mysterious hums.

"This has got to be how they get away," Rick murmured, holding the wand up to his nose and sniffing. "Huh. Smells like coriander, if anything."

"Except how did they get away the first time?"

"Good question."

I felt my shoulders hunch, a lifetime habit of bracing against worry.

Rick grimaced. "I know what you're thinking, and I'm thinking it too, but maybe it's okay. Maybe the other world isn't a twisted disaster like ours."

"But—why *our* kids?"

Rick shrugged, waving the wand in a circle. "Found by a kid from another world? Some kid who knows magic, maybe?" His voice suspended, and he gave me a sort of grinning wince. "Kid magician?" He laughed, the weak, unfunny laugh that expresses pain more than joy. "Listen to me! Say those words to any other adult and he'll dial 1-800-NUTHOUSE."

I gripped my hands together, thinking of my kids, and safety. I said, "Touch it on me."

"What?" Rick stared.

"Go ahead. If it sends me where they go—"

Rick rubbed his eyes. "I'm still having trouble with the concept. Right. Of course. But we'll go together." His clammy left hand closed round my equally damp fingers, and with his right he tapped us both on our heads.

Nothing happened.

Rick looked hopeful. "Maybe it's broken."

"I don't think we're that lucky," I muttered, and went down to fix breakfast.

The kids appeared half an hour later, more or less ready for school. The looks they exchanged with each other let me know at once that they were worried—desperately—about something.

Then three pairs of brown eyes turned my way.

"Um, Mom?" R.J. said finally, as he casually buttered some toast. "Did you, uh, do housecleaning this morning? You know, before we woke up?"

"No," I replied truthfully, watching his toast shred into crumbs. He didn't even notice.

"Did you, like, find any, um, art projects?" Lauren asked.

"Art projects?" I repeated.

R.J. frowned at his toast, then pushed it aside.

Alisha said, "Like a stick. For a play. A play at school— Uhn!" This last was a gasp of pain—someone had obviously kicked her under the table. Her eyes watered, and she muttered to Lauren, "What did you do that for?"

"The play was last month, remember?" Lauren said in a sugary voice, rolling her eyes toward me. "Mom helped paint scenery!"

I fussed with my briefcase, giving them sneakier looks than they were giving me, as I watched them trying to communicate by quick whispers and pointing fingers. Rick came in then, looked at us all, and went out again—and I could hear him turning a laugh into a cough.

••••••••

"You all reminded me of a bunch of spies in a really bad movie," Rick said later, when I was driving us to our respective workplaces. He grinned. "All squinting at each other like—"

"Rick." I tried not to be mad. "It is *our kids* we're spying on. Lying to. I feel terrible!"

He said, "I don't. At least they're home—"

"They're not at home. They're at school."

"They're safe. The wand's in the trunk of the car, by the way. And as soon as I can, I'm going to take the damn thing out and burn it, and make sure the kids *stay* safe."

I sighed as I drove past palm trees and billboards—the once-reassuring visual boundaries of mundane reality. Mundane made sense. It was safe, because there were no reminders in that everyday blandness that the rules we make to govern our lives are not absolute, and that safety is an illusion.

I dropped Rick off at his printshop. Sighed again when I parked the car.

And I sighed a third time when I sat down at my computer, punched up Autocad, and stared at the equations for the freeway bridge I was supposed to be designing.

When we got home, the first sign that Something Was Up was the house—spic and span. Usually housecleaning is something that gets done when Rick and I feel guilty, or when it's gotten so cluttered and dusty I turn into the Wicked Bitch of the West and dragoon everyone into jobs.

I knew, of course, that they'd given the place a thorough search—but at least they hadn't made a mess. I considered this a Responsible Act, and brought it up to Rick later, when we got ready for bed. And didn't a Responsible Act deserve one in return?

"Very responsible," he agreed. "Won't it be a pleasant, refreshing change to sleep the entire night, knowing they are safely in their beds?"

"Did you destroy the wand?" I asked.

He studied the ceiling as though something of import had been written there. "No. Not yet. But I will."

Home life was normal for about a week.

At least on the surface.

The kids tried another surreptitious search, more oblique questions, and then finally they just gave up. I know the exact hour—the minute—they gave up because they really gave up. Not just their secret world, but everything. Oh, they ate and went to school and did their homework, but the older ones worked with about as much interest and enthusiasm as a pair of robots, and Alisha drifted about, small and silent as a little ghost.

I hated seeing sad eyes at dinner. We cooked their favorite foods. Rick made barbequed ribs and spaghetti on his nights, and I fixed Mexican food and Thai chicken on my nights—loving gestures on our part that failed to kindle the old joy. R.J. and Lauren said "Please" and "Thank you" in dismal voices, and picked at the food as though it were prune-and-pea casserole.

Alisha didn't talk, just *looked*.

I avoided her gaze.

Eight days later I passed by Lauren's room with a stack of clean sheets and towels, and heard soft, muffled sobs. Her unhappiness smote my guilty heart and I was soon in our room snuffling into my pillow, the clean laundry laying on the carpet where I'd dropped it.

We're the parents. They are the kids.

That's what Rick had said.

I got up, wiped my face on one of those clean towels, and went back—not sure what I'd say or do—but I stopped when I heard all three kids in Lauren's room.

"I can't help it." Lauren's voice was high and teary. "Queen Liete was going to make me a maid of honor to Princess Elte—my very best friend! Now we've missed the ceremony!"

"You can't miss it, not if you're the person being ceremonied." That was Alisha's brisk, practical voice. Even though she's the youngest, she's always been the practical one.

"Celebrated," R.J. muttered. "How much time has passed there? What if they think we don't want to come back? That we don't care any more? Brother Owl was going to teach me shape-changing on my own, without his help!"

Lauren sniffed, gulped, and cried, "I wish you hadn't picked up that stupid wand, Alisha. I wish we'd never gone. It's so much worse, being stuck here, and *remembering*."

"I don't think so." That was R.J.'s sturdy voice. "Somebody got the wand, but nothing can take away what I remember. Riding on the air currents so high, just floating there. . . ."

"Learning a spell," Alisha put in, "and seeing it *work*. Knowing that it had to be us, that we made all the difference."

"You're right," Lauren said. The tears were gone. "Only for me the best memory was sneaking into the Grundles' dungeon. Oh, I hated it at the time—it was scarier than anything I'd ever done—but I knew I *had* to get Prince Dar out and, being a girl, and an outworlder, and a very fast runner, I was the *only one* who could get by those magic wards. I liked that. Being the only one who could do it."

"Because of our talents," Alisha murmured longingly.

"Because we saw the signs, and we believed what we saw," R.J. added, even more longingly.

Gloomy silence.

I tiptoed away to pick up the towels and sheets.

• • • • • • • •

Rick was in the garage, supposedly working on refinishing one of the patio chairs, but I found him tossing the sander absently from hand to hand while he stared at R.J.'s old bicycle.

"You haven't burned the wand," I guessed.

He gave his head a shake, avoiding my eyes. "I can't."

"I think we ought to give it back," I said.

He looked up. His brown eyes were unhappy, reminding me terribly of R.J.'s sad eyes over his untouched dinner.

"They're our kids," I said. "Not our possessions." I told him what I'd overheard.

"Talents," he repeated when I was done.

I said, "What if Alisha had been born with some incredible music talent? She'd be just as lost to us if she were at some studio practicing her instrument eight hours a day, or being taken by her music coach to concerts all over the country."

"She'd be safe," Rick said.

"Not if some drunk driver hits her bus—or a terrorist blows up her concert hall. We taught them to be fair, and to be sensible. But to be totally safe in this world we'd have to lock them in a room. The world *isn't* totally safe. I wish it were."

Rick tossed the sander once more from hand to hand, then threw it down onto the workbench. "They lied to us."

"They didn't lie. Not until the wand disappeared. And we lied right back."

"That's love," Rick said. "We did it out of love. Our duty as parents is to keep them safe, and we can't possibly protect them in some world we've never even seen!"

"Think of Lauren, making friends. For five years we've worried about her inability to make friends—she's never fit in with the kids at school."

"She needs to learn to fit in," Rick said. "In this world. Where we live."

I felt myself slipping over to his way of thinking, and groped for words, for one last argument. "What if," I said. "What if those people from the other world find their way here, but they only have the one chance—and they offer the kids only the one chance to go back? Forever? What if we make them choose between us and that world? They've always come back, Rick. It's love, not duty, that brings them back, but they don't even know it, because they've never been forced to make that choice."

Rick slammed out of the garage, leaving me staring at R.J.'s little-boy bike.

I was in bed alone for hours, not sleeping, when Rick finally came in.

"I waited until Alisha conked off," he said, and drew in a shaky breath. "Damn! That kid racks up more under-the-covers reading time than I did when I was a kid, and I thought I was the world's champ."

"You put the wand back?" I asked, sitting up.

"Right under the bed."

I hugged my knees to my chest, feeling the emotional vertigo I'd felt when Lauren was first born, and I stared down at this child who had been inside me for so long. Now a separate being, whose memories would not be my memories. Whose life would not be my life.

And Rick mused, "How much of my motivation was jealousy, and not just concern for their safety? I get a different answer at midnight than I do at noon."

"You mean, *why didn't it ever happen to me?*"

His smile was wry.

They were gone the next night, of course.

It was raining hard outside, and I walked from room to silent room, touching their empty beds, their neatly lined-up books and toys and personal treasures, the pictures on their walls. Lauren had made sketches of a girl's face—Princess Elte? In R.J.'s room, the sketches were all of great birds, raptors with beaks and feathers of color combinations never seen in this world. He'd stored in jewelry boxes the feathers and rocks he'd brought back across that unimaginable divide.

Alisha's tidy powder-blue room gave nothing away.

The next morning I was downstairs early, fixing pancakes, my heart light because I'd passed by the three rooms and heard kid-breathing in each.

I almost dropped the spatula on the floor when I looked up and there was Alisha in her nightgown.

She ran to me, gave me a hug round the waist. "Thanks, Mom," she said.

"Thanks?" My heart started thumping again. "For pancakes?"

"For putting it back," she said. "I smelled your shampoo in my room that day, when the wand disappeared. But I didn't tell the others. I didn't want them to be mad."

I suddenly found the floor under my bottom. "Your dad put it back," I said. "We were in it together. We didn't mean to make you unhappy."

"I know." Alisha sat down neatly on the floor next to me, cross-legged, and leaned against my arm, just as she had when she was a toddler. "We didn't tell you because we knew you'd say no. Not to be mean. But out of grownup worry."

"We just want to keep you safe," I said.

She turned her face to look up at me, her eyes the color of Rick's eyes, their shape so like my mother's. "And we wanted to keep you safe."

"Ignorance is not real safety," I pointed out. "It's the mere illusion of safety."

Alisha gave me an unrepentant grin. "How many times have you said about us, *they're safer not knowing?*" she retorted, and then she added, "That's why we always go at midnight, and we're only gone a couple of hours. We can do that because the time there doesn't work like here."

"But another *world*. How can we set safety rules? We don't know what happens." I held her tightly against me.

"You send us to school," Alisha said, pulling away just a little, so she could look at me again. "You don't know what happens there. Not really."

I thought back to my own school days, and then thought of recent media orgies, and felt my heart squeeze. "True. But we're used to it. And habit and custom are probably the strongest rules we know. Can we go with you to the other world? Just to see it?" I asked.

Alisha shook her head. "There's a big spell. Prevents grown-ups, because of this big war in the past. Only kids can cross over—not even teenagers. One day we'll be too old. I know you'll be real sorry!"

I tried to laugh. It wasn't very successful, but we both smiled anyway. "It's not every set of parents who have kids who cross worlds—you'll have to give us time to get used to it."

She hugged me again, and flitted away to get dressed.

"R.J. has taken to telling me stories," Rick said a few days later. "Not—quite—admitting anything, just offering me these stories instead of me reading to him."

Only Lauren went about as if nothing were different, everything were normal. Keeping the other world secret was important to her, so we had to respect that, and give her the space to keep it.

"Alisha told me more about magic," I said that next week.

The kids were gone again. A spectacular thunderstorm raged like battling dragons outside. We didn't even try to sleep. We sat in the kitchen across from each other, hands cradling mugs of hot chocolate. Rick had put marshmallows in it, and whipped cream, and just enough cinnamon to give off a delicious scent.

"Magic." He shook his head.

"The amazing thing is, it sounds a lot like the basic principles of engineering."

"I think R.J. has learned how to turn himself into a bird," Rick said, stirring the marshmallows round and round with his finger. "They fly in a flock, and watch for the Grundles, who I guess have a bad case of What's-yours-is-mine as far as other kingdoms are concerned." His smile faded, and he shook his head. "Nothing will be the same again, Mary—we can't even pretend to be a normal family."

"Is anybody?" I asked. "I mean, really?"

What *is* normal?

We live in our houses and follow schedules and pick jobs that are sensible and steady and keep the bills paid, but in my dreams I fly, as I did when I was small.

"The universe is still out there just beyond the palm trees and malls and freeways," I said. "And the truth is we still don't really know the rules."

What we do know is that we love our children, will always love them, until the stars have burned away to ash, and though parents are not issued experience along with our babies' birth certificates, we learn a little wisdom and a lot of compromise as the children grow.

Rick said slowly, "Well, I hope Lauren and her sword-swinging princess pal are kicking some serious Grundle butt."

We remember how to laugh.

Like the story below, Emma Bull's 1987 debut novel War for the Oaks *is about young musicians in the modern world who come up against unexpected magical doings—no surprise, since Bull is herself a musician and performer of considerable gifts. Among Bull's other works are the acclaimed science fiction novel* Bone Dance *and the Borderlands novel* Finder.

A Bird That Whistles

EMMA BULL

The dulcimer player sat on the back steps of Orpheus Coffeehouse, lit from behind by the bulb over the door. His head hung forward, and his silhouette was sharp against the diffused glow from State Street. The dulcimer was propped against his shoulder as if it were a child he was comforting. I'd always thought you balanced a dulcimer across your knees. But it worked; this sounded like the classical guitar of dulcimer playing. Then his chin lifted a little.

"'Twas on one bright March morning, I bid New Orleans adieu,
And I took the road to Jackson town, my fortunes to renew.
I cursed all foreign money, no credit could I gain,
Which filled my heart with longing for the lakes of Pontchartrain."

He got to the second verse before he stopped and looked up. Light fell on the side of his face.

"I like the bit about the alligators best," I said stupidly.

"So do I." I could hear his grin. " 'If it weren't for the alligators, I'd sleep out in the woods.' Sort of sums up life." He sounded so cheerful, it was hard to believe he'd sung those mournful words.

"You here for the open stage?" I asked. Then I remembered *I* was, and my terror came pounding back.

He lifted the shoulder that supported the dulcimer. "Maybe." He stood smoothly. I staggered up the steps with my banjo case, and he held the door for me.

In the full light of the back room, his looks startled me as much as his music had. He was tall, slender, and pale. His black hair was thick and long, pulled into a careless tail in back, except for some around his face that was too short and fell forward into his eyes. Those were the ordinary things.

His clothes were odd. This was 1970, and we all dressed the way we thought Woody Guthrie used to: blue denim and workshirts. This guy wore a white T-shirt, black corduroys, and a black leather motorcycle jacket that looked old enough to be his father's. (I would have said he was about eighteen.) The white streak in his hair was odd. His face was odd; with its high cheekbones and pointed chin, it was somewhere out beyond handsome.

But his eyes—they were like green glass, or a green pool in the shadow of trees, or a green gemstone with something moving behind it, dimly visible. Looking at them made me uncomfortable; but when he turned away, I felt the loss, as if something I wanted but couldn't name had been taken from me.

Steve O'Connell, the manager, came out of the kitchen, and the green-eyed man handed him the dulcimer. "It's good," he said. "I'd like to meet whoever made it."

Steve's harried face lit up. "My brother. I'll tell him you said so."

Steve disappeared down the hall to the front room, and the green eyes came back to my face. "I haven't forgotten your name, have I?"

"No." I put my hand out, and he shook it. "John Deacon."

"Banjo player," he added. "I'm Willy Silver. Guitar and fiddle."

"Not dulcimer?"

"Not usually. But I dabble in strings."

That's when Lisa came out of the kitchen.

Lisa waited tables at Orpheus. She looked like a dancer, all slender and small and long-boned. Her hair was a cirrus cloud of red-gold curls; her eyes were big, cat-tilted, and gray; and her skin was so fair you should have been able to see through it. I'd seen Waterhouse's painting *The Lady of Shalott* somewhere (though I didn't remember the name of the painter or the painting then; be kind, I was barely seventeen), and every time I saw Lisa I thought of it. She greeted me by name whenever I came to Orpheus, and smiled, and teased me. Once, when I came in with the tail-end of the flu, she fussed over me so much I wondered if it was possible to get a chronic illness on purpose.

Lisa came out of the kitchen, my heart gave a great loud thump, she looked up with those big, inquiring eyes, and she saw Willy Silver. I recognized the disease that struck her down. Hadn't she already given it to me?

Willy Silver saw her, too. "Hullo," he said, and looked as if he was prepared to admire any response she gave.

"Hi." The word was a little breathless gulp. "Oh, hi, John. Are you a friend of John's?" she asked Willy.

"I just met him," I told her. "Willy Silver, Lisa Amundsen. Willy's here for open stage."

He gave me a long look, but said, "If you say so."

I must have been feeling masochistic. Lisa always gets crushes on good musicians, and I already knew Willy was one.

Maybe I ought to forget the music and just commit seppuku onstage.

But you can't forget the music. Once you get the itch, it won't go away, no matter how much stage fright you have. And by the time my turn came—after a handful of guys-on-stools-with-guitars, two women who sang *a capella* for too long, a woman who did Leonard Cohen songs on the not-quite-tuned piano, and the Orpheus Tin-and-Wood Toejam Jug Band—I had plenty of stage fright.

Then Willy Silver leaned over from the chair next to me and whispered, "Take it slow. Play the chord progression a couple of times for an intro—it'll settle you down."

I looked up, startled. The white streak in his hair caught the light, and his eyes gleamed green. He was smiling.

"And the worst that can happen isn't very bad."

I could embarrass myself in front of Lisa . . . and everyone else, and be ashamed to ever show my face in Orpheus again. But Willy didn't look like someone who'd understand that.

My hands shook as if they had engine knock. I wanted to go to the bathroom. Steve clumped up onstage, read my name from the slip of paper in his hand, and peered out into the dark room for me. I hung the banjo over my shoulder and went up there to die for my art.

I scrapped the short opening I'd practiced and played the whole chord progression instead. The first couple measures were shaky. But banjos give out a lively noise that makes you *want* to have a good time, and I could feel mine sending those messages. By the time I got around to the words, I could remember them, and sing them in almost my usual voice.

"I got a bird that whistles, honey, got a bird,
Baby, got a bird that will sing.
Honey, got a bird, baby, got a bird that will sing.

But if I ain't got Corinna, it just don't mean
It don't mean a natural thing."

At the back of the room, I could just see the halo of Lisa's hair. I couldn't see her face, but at least she'd stopped to listen. And down front, Willy Silver sat, looking pleased.

I did "Lady Isabel and the Elf Knight" and "Newry Highwayman." I blew some chords and forgot some words, but I lived through it. And people applauded. I grinned and thanked them and stumbled off the stage.

"Do they clap because they like what you did," I asked Willy, "or because you stopped doing what they didn't?"

Willy made a muffled noise into his coffee cup.

"Pretty darn good," said Lisa, at my elbow. I felt immortal. Then I realized that she was stealing glances at Willy. "Want to order something, now that you're not too nervous to eat it?"

I blushed, but in the dark, who could tell? "PB and J," I told her.

"PB and J?" Willy repeated.

We both stared at him, but it was Lisa who said, "Peanut butter and jelly sandwich. Don't you call them that?"

The pause was so short I'm not sure I really heard it. Then he said, "I don't think I've ever been in a coffeehouse where you could order a peanut butter and jelly sandwich."

"This is it," Lisa told him. "Crunchy or smooth, whole wheat or white, grape jelly or peach preserves."

"Good grief. Crunchy, whole wheat, and peach."

"Non-conformist," she said admiringly.

He turned to me when she went toward the kitchen. "You *were* pretty good," he said. "I like the way you sing. For that last one, though, you might try mountain minor."

"What?"

He got an eager look on his face. "Come on," he said, sprang out of his chair, and led the way toward the back.

We sat on the back steps until the open stage was over, and he taught me about mountain minor tuning. His guitar was a deep-voiced old Gibson with the varnish worn off the strategic spots, and he flat-picked along with me, filling in the places that needed it. Eventually we went back inside, and he taught me about pull-offs. As Steve stacked chairs, we played "Newry Highwayman" as a duet. Then he taught me "Shady Grove," because it was mountain minor, too.

I'd worked hard at the banjo, and I enjoyed playing it. But I don't think I'd ever been aware of making something beautiful with it. That's what those two songs were. Beautiful.

And Lisa moved through the room as we played, clearing tables, watching us. Watching him. Every time I looked up, her eyes were following his face, or his long fingers on the guitar neck.

I got home at two in the morning. My parents almost grounded me; I convinced them I hadn't spent the night raising hell by showing them my new banjo licks. Or maybe it was the urgency with which I explained what I'd learned and how, and that I had to have more.

When I came back to Orpheus two nights later, Willy was there. And Lisa, fair and graceful, was often near him, often smiled at him, that night and all the nights after it. Sometimes he'd smile back. But sometimes his face would be full of an intensity that couldn't be contained in a smile. Whenever Lisa saw that, her eyes would widen, her lips would part, and she'd look frightened and fascinated all at once. Which made me feel worse than if he'd smiled at her.

And sometimes he would ignore her completely, as if she were a cup of coffee he hadn't ordered. Then her face would close up tight with puzzlement and hurt, and I'd want to break something.

I could have hated him, but it was just as well I didn't. I wanted to learn music from Willy and to be near Lisa. Lisa wanted to be near Willy. The perfect arrangement. Hah.

And who could know what Willy wanted?

Fourth of July, Independence Day 1970, promised to be the emotional climax of the summer. Someone had organized a day of Vietnam War protests, starting with a rally in Riverside Park and ending with a torchlight march down State Street. Flyers about it were everywhere—tacked to phone poles, stuck on walls, and all over the tables at Orpheus. The picture on the flyers was the photo taken that spring, when the Ohio National Guard shot four students on the Kent State campus during another protest: a dark-haired woman kneeling over a dead student's body, her head lifted, her mouth open with weeping, or screaming. You'd think a photo like that would warn you away from protesting. But it gives you the feeling that someone has to do something. It gets you out on the street.

Steve was having a special marathon concert at the coffeehouse: Sherman and Henley, the Rose Hip String Band, Betsy Kaske, and—surprise—Willy Silver and John Deacon. True, we were scheduled to go on at seven, when the audience would be smallest, but I didn't care. I had been hired to play. For money.

The only cloud on my horizon was that Willy was again treating Lisa as one of life's non-essentials. As we set up for the show, I could almost see a dotted line trailing behind Willy that was her gaze, fixed on him.

Evening light was slanting through the door when we hit the stage, which made me feel funny. Orpheus was a place for after dark, when its shabby, struggling nature was cloaked with night-and-music magic. But Willy set his fiddle under his chin, leaned into the microphone, and drew out with his bow one sweet, sad, sustained note. All the awareness in the room—his, mine, and our dozen or so of audience's—hurtled to the sharp point of that one note and balanced there. I began to pick the banjo softly, and his note changed, multiplied, until we were playing instrumental harmony. I sang, and if my voice broke a little, it was just what the song required:

"The sun rises bright in France, and fair sets he,
Ah, but he has lost the look he had in my ain country."

We made enough magic to cloak *three* shabby coffeehouses with glamour. When I got up the nerve to look beyond the edge of the stage, sometime in our fourth song, we had another dozen listeners. They'd come to line State Street for the march, and our music had called them in.

Lisa sat on the shag rug in front of the stage. Her eyes were bright, and for once, her attention didn't seem to be all for Willy.

Traditional music mostly tells stories. We told a lot of them that night. I felt them all as if they'd happened to friends of mine. Willy seemed more consumed by the music than the words, and songs he sang were sometimes almost too beautiful. But his strong voice never quavered or cracked like mine did. His guitar and fiddle were gorgeous, always, perfect and precise.

We finished at eight-thirty with a loose and lively rendition of "Blues in the Bottle," and the room was close to full. The march was due to pass by in half an hour.

We bounded offstage and into the back room. "Yo," said Willy, and stuck out his right hand. I shook it. He was touched with craziness, a little drunk with the music. He looked . . . not quite domesticated. Light seemed to catch more than usual in his green eyes. He radiated a contained energy that could have raised the roof.

"Let's go look at the street," I said.

We went out the back door and up the short flight of outside stairs to State Street. Or where State Street had been. The march, contrary to the laws of physics governing crowds, had arrived early.

Every leftist in Illinois might have been there. The pavement was gone beneath a winding, chanting snake of marchers blocks and blocks and *blocks* long. Several hundred people singing, "All we are saying / Is give peace a chance," makes your hair stand on end. Willy nudged me, beaming, and pointed to a banner that read, "Draft Beer, Not Boys." There really were torches, though the harsh yellow-tinted lights of State Street faded them. Some people on the edges of the crowd had lit sparklers; as the line of march passed over the bridge, first one, then dozens of sparklers, like shooting stars, arced over the railings and into the river, with one last bright burst of white reflection on the water before they hit.

I wanted to follow the march, but my banjo was in the coffeehouse, waiting for me to look after it. "I'm going to see what's up inside," I shouted at Willy. He nodded. Sparklers, fizzing, reflected in his eyes.

The crowd packed the sidewalk between me and Orpheus's front door, so I retraced our steps, down the stairs and along the river. I came into the parking lot, blind from the lights I'd just left, and heard behind me, "Hey, hippie."

There were two of them, about my age. They were probably both on their school's football and swimming teams; their hair was short, they weren't wearing blue jeans, they smelled of Southern Comfort, and they'd called me "hippie." A terrible combination. I started to walk away, across the parking lot, but the blond one stepped forward and grabbed my arm.

"Hey! I'm talking to you."

There's nothing helpful you can say at times like this, and if there had been, I was too scared to think of it. The other guy, brown-haired and shorter, came up and jabbed me in the stomach with two fingers. "You a draft dodger?" he said. "Scared to fight for your country?"

"Hippies make me puke," the blond one said thoughtfully.

They were drunk, for God's sake, and out on the town, and as excited in their way by the mass of people on the street above as I was. Which didn't make me feel any better when the brown-haired one punched me in the face.

I was lying on my back clutching my nose and waiting for the next bad thing to happen to me when I heard Willy say, "Don't do it." I'd heard him use his voice in more ways than I could count, but never before like that, never a ringing command that could turn you to stone.

I opened my eyes and found my two tormentors bracketing me, the blond one's foot still raised to kick me in the stomach. He lost his balance as I watched, and got the foot on the ground just in time to keep from falling over. They were both looking toward the river railing, so I did, too.

The parking lot didn't have any lights to reflect in his eyes. The green sparks there came from inside him. Nor was there any wind to lift and stir his hair like that. He stood very straight and tall, twenty feet from us, his hands held a little out from his sides like a gunfighter in a cowboy movie. Around his right hand, like a living glove, was a churning outline of golden fire. Bits of it dripped away like liquid from the ends of his fingers, evaporating before they hit the gravel. Like sparks from a sparkler.

I'm sure that's what my two friends told each other the next day—that he'd had a sparkler in his hand, and the liquor had made them see something more. That they'd been stupid to run away. But it wasn't a sparkler. And they weren't stupid. I heard them running across the parking lot; I watched Willy clench the fingers of his right hand and close his eyes tight, and saw the fire dim slowly and disappear. And I wished like hell that I could run away, too.

He crouched down beside me and pulled me up to sitting. "Your nose is bleeding."

"What are you?" I croaked.

The fire was still there, in his eyes. "None of your business," he said. He put his arm around me and hauled me to my feet. I'm not very heavy, but it still should have been hard work, because I didn't help. He was too slender to be so strong.

"What do you mean, none of my business? Jesus!"

He yanked me around to face him. When I looked at him, I saw wildness and temper and a fragile control over both. "I'm one of the Daoine Sidhe, Johnny-lad," he said, and his voice was harsh and colored by traces of some accent. "Does that help?"

"No," I said, but faintly. Because whatever that phrase meant, he was admitting that he was not what I was. That what I had seen had really been there.

"Try asking Steve. Or look it up, I don't care."

I shook my head. I'd forgotten my nose; a few drops of blood spattered from it and marked the front of his white shirt. I stood frozen with terror, waiting for his reaction.

It was laughter. "Earth and Air," he said when he caught his breath, "are we doing melodrama or farce out here? Come on, let's go lay you down and pack your face in ice."

There was considerable commotion when we came in the back door. Lisa got the ice and hovered over me while I told Steve about the two guys. I said Willy had chased them off; I didn't say how. Steve was outraged, and Lisa was solicitous, and it was all wasted on me. I lay on the floor with a cold nose and a brain full of rug fuzz, and let all of them do or say whatever they felt like.

Eventually I was alone in the back room, with the blank ceiling tiles to look at. Betsy Kaske was singing "Wild Women Don't Get the Blues." I roused from my self-indulgent stupor only once, when Steve passed on his way to the kitchen.

"Steve, what's a—" and I pronounced Daoine Sidhe, as best I could.

He repeated it, and it sounded more like what Willy had said. "Elves," he added.

"What?"

"Yeah. It's an Irish name for the elves."

"Oh, Christ," I said. When I didn't add to that, he went on into the kitchen.

I don't know what I believed. But after a while I realized that I hadn't seen Lisa go by in a long time. And she didn't know what I knew, or almost knew. So I crawled up off the floor and went looking for her.

Not in the front room, not in the kitchen, and if she was in the milling people who were still hanging out on State Street, I'd never find her anyway. I went out to the back steps, to see if she was in the parking lot.

Yes, sort of. They stood in the deep shadow where Orpheus's back wall joined the jutting flank of the next building. Her red-gold hair was a dim cascade of lighter color in the dark. The white streak in his was like a white bird, flying nowhere. And the pale skin of her face and arms, his pale face and white shirt, sorted out the rest of it for me. Lisa was so small and light-boned, he'd lifted her off her feet entirely. No work at all for him. Her arms were around his neck. One of his hands was closed over her shoulder—I could see his long fingers against her dark blouse—and the gesture was so intense, so hungry, that it seemed as if that one hand alone could consume her. I turned and went back into Orpheus, cold, frightened, and helpless.

Lisa didn't come back until a little before closing, several hours later. I know; I was keeping watch. She darted in the back door and snatched her shoulder bag from the kitchen. Her eyes were the only color in her face: gray, rimmed with red. "Lisa!" I called.

She stopped with her back to me. "What?"

I didn't know how to start. Or finish. "It's about Willy."

"Then I don't want to hear it."

"But—"

"John, it's none of your business. And it doesn't matter now, anyway."

She shot me one miserable, intolerable look before she darted out the back door and was gone. She could look like that and tell me it was none of my business?

I'd helped Steve clean up and lock up, and pretended that I was going home. But at three in the morning, I was sitting on the back steps, watching a newborn breeze ruffle a little heap of debris caught against the doorsill: a crushed paper cup, a bit of old newspaper, and one of the flyers for the march. When I looked up from it, Willy was standing at the bottom of the steps.

"I thought you'd be back tonight," I said.

"Maybe that's why I came back. Because you thought it so hard." He didn't smile, but he was relaxed and cheerful. After making music with him almost every day for a month, I could tell. He dropped loose-limbed onto the bottom step and stretched his legs out in front of him.

"So. Have you told her? What you are?"

He looked over his shoulder at me with a sort of stunned disbelief. "Do you mean Lisa? Of course not."

"Why not?" All my words sounded to me like little lead fishing weights hitting the water: plunk, plunk.

"Why should I? Either she'd believe me or she wouldn't. Either one is about equally tedious."

"Tedious."

He smiled, that wicked, charming, conspiratorial smile. "John, you can't think I care if Lisa believes in fairies."

"What *do* you care about?"

"John . . . ," he began, wary and a little irritable.

"Do you care about her?"

And for the second time, I saw it: his temper on a leash. "What the hell does it matter to you?" He leaned back on his elbows and exhaled loudly. "Oh, right. You want her for yourself. But you're too scared to do anything about it."

That hurt. I said, a little too quickly, "It matters to me that she's happy. I just want to know if she's going to be happy with you."

"No," he snapped. "And whether she's going to be happy *without* me is entirely her lookout. Rowan and Thorn, John, I'm tired of her. And if you're not careful, I'll be tired of you, too."

I looked down at his scornful face, and remembered Lisa's: pale, red-eyed. I described Willy Silver, aloud, with words my father had forbidden in his house.

He unfolded from the step, his eyes narrowed. "Explain to me, before I paint the back of the building with you. I've always been nice to you. Isn't that enough?" He said "nice" through his teeth.

"Why are you nice to me?"

"You're the only one who wants something important from me."

"Music?"

"Of course, music."

The rug fuzz had been blown from my head by his anger and mine. "Is that why you sing that way?"

"What the devil is wrong with the way I sing?"

"Nothing. Except you don't sound as if any of the songs ever happened to you."

"Of course they haven't." He was turning stiff and cold, withdrawing. That seemed worse than when he was threatening me.

The flyer for the protest march still fluttered in the doorway. I grabbed it and held it out. "See her?" I asked, jabbing a finger at the picture of the woman kneeling over the student's body. "Maybe she knew that guy. Maybe she didn't. But she cares that he's dead. And I look at this picture, and *I* care about *her.* And all those people who marched past you in the street tonight? They did it because they care about a lot of people that they're never even going to see."

He looked fascinated and horrified at once. "Don't you all suffer enough as it is?"

"Huh?"

"Why would you take someone else's suffering on yourself?"

I didn't know how to answer that. I said finally, "We take on each other's happiness, too."

He shook his head, slowly. He was gathering the pieces of himself together, putting all his emotional armor back on. "This is too strange even for me. And among my people, I'm notoriously fond of strange things." He turned and walked away, as if I'd ceased to exist.

"What about tonight?" I said. He'd taken about a half-dozen steps. "Why did you bother to scare off those guys who were beating me up?"

He stopped. After a long moment he half-turned, and looked at me, wild-eyed and . . . frightened? Then he went on, stiffly, across the parking lot, and disappeared into the dark.

The next night, when I came in, Willy's guitar and fiddle were gone. But Steve said he hadn't seen him.

Lisa was clearing tables at closing, her hair falling across her face and hiding it. From behind that veil, she said, "I think you should give up. He's not coming."

I jumped. "Was I that obvious?"

"Yeah." She swept the hair back and showed a wry little smile. "You looked just like me."

"I feel lousy," I told her. "I helped drive him away, I think."

She sat down next to me. "I wanted to jump off the bridge last night. But the whole time I was saying, 'Then he'll be sorry, the rat.' "

"He wouldn't have been."

"Nope, not a bit," she said.

"But I would have."

She raised her gray cat-eyes to my face. "I'm not going to fall in love with you, John."

"I know. It's okay. I still would have been sorry if you jumped off the bridge."

"Me, too," Lisa said. "Hey, let's make a pact. We won't talk about The Rat to anybody but each other."

"Why?"

"Well . . ." She frowned at the empty lighted space of the stage. "I don't think anybody else would understand."

So we shared each other's suffering, as he put it. And maybe that's why we wouldn't have called it that.

I did see him again, though.

State Street had been gentrified, and Orpheus, the building, even the parking lot, had fallen to a downtown mall where there was no place for shabbiness or magic—any of the kinds of magic that were made that Fourth of July. These things happen in twice seven long years. But there are lots more places like that, if you care to look.

I was playing at the Greenbriar Bluegrass Festival in Pocahontas County, West Virginia. Or rather, my band was. A columnist in *Folk Roots* magazine described us so:

Bird That Whistles drives traditional bluegrass fans crazy. They have the right instrumentation, the right licks—and they're likely to apply them to Glenn Miller's "In the Mood," or The Who's "Magic Bus." If you go to see them, leave your preconceptions at home.

I was sitting in the cookhouse tent that served as the musicians' green room, drinking coffee and watching the chaos that is thirty-some traditional musicians all tuning and talking and eating at once. Then I saw, over the heads, a raven's-wing black one with a white streak.

In a few moments, he stood in front of me. He didn't look five minutes older than he had at Orpheus. He wasn't nervous, exactly, but he wasn't at ease, either.

"Hi," I said. My voice was steady, for a miracle. "How'd you find me?"

"With this," he answered, smiling a little. He held out an article clipped from a Richmond, Virginia, paper. It was about the festival, and the photo was of Bird That Whistles.

"I'm glad you did."

He glanced down suddenly. "I wanted you to know that I've been thinking over what you told me."

I knew what he was talking about. "All this time?"

Now it was the real thing, his appealing grin. "It's a damned big subject. But I thought you'd like to know . . . well, sometimes I understand it."

"Only sometimes?"

"Rowan and Thorn, John, have mercy! I'm a slow learner."

"The hell you are. Can you stick around? You could meet the band, do some tunes."

"I wish I could," he said, and I think he meant it.

"Hey, wait a minute." I pulled a paper napkin out of the holder on the table and rummaged in my banjo case for a pen.

"What's that?" he asked, as I wrote.

"My address. I'm living in Detroit now, for my sins. If you ever need anything—or even if you just want to jam—let me know, will you?" And I slid the napkin across the table to him.

He reached out, hesitated, traced the edges of the paper with one long, thin finger. "Why are you giving me this?"

I studied that bent black-and-white head, the green eyes half-veiled with his lids and following the motion of his finger. "You decide," I told him.

"All right," he said softly, "I will." If there wasn't something suspiciously like a quaver in his voice, then I've never heard one. He picked up the napkin. "I won't lose this," he said, with an odd intensity. He put out his right hand, and I shook it. Then he turned and pushed through the crowd. I saw his head at the door of the tent; then he was gone.

I stared at the top of the table for a long time, where the napkin had been, where his finger had traced. Then I took the banjo out of its case and put it into mountain minor tuning.

Author of The Left Hand of Darkness, The Dispossessed, *and the world-famous Earthsea trilogy, Ursula K. Le Guin is one of the most popular writers of fantasy and science fiction alive today. In recent years she has returned to the world of Earthsea for more stories and novels. "The Bones of the Earth" is one of those stories.*

The Bones of the Earth

URSULA K. LE GUIN

It was raining again, and the wizard of Re Albi was sorely tempted to make a weather spell, just a little, small spell, to send the rain on round the mountain. His bones ached. They ached for the sun to come out and shine through his flesh and dry them out. Of course he could say a pain spell, but all that would do was hide the ache for a while. There was no cure for what ailed him. Old bones need the sun. The wizard stood still in the doorway of his house, between the dark room and the rain-streaked open air, preventing himself from making a spell, and angry at himself for preventing himself and for having to be prevented.

He never swore—men of power do not swear, it is not safe—but he cleared his throat with a coughing growl, like a bear. A moment later a thunderclap rolled off the hidden upper slopes of Gont Mountain, echoing round from north to south, dying away in the cloud-filled forests.

A good sign, thunder, Dulse thought. It would stop raining soon. He pulled up his hood and went out into the rain to feed the chickens.

He checked the henhouse, finding three eggs. Red Bucca was setting. Her eggs were about due to hatch. The mites were bothering her, and she looked scruffy and jaded. He said a few words against mites, told himself to remember to clean out the nest box as soon as the chicks hatched, and went on to the poultry yard, where Brown Bucca and Gray and Leggings and Candor and the King huddled under the eaves making soft, shrewish remarks about rain.

"It'll stop by midday," the wizard told the chickens. He fed them and squelched back to the house with three warm eggs. When he was a child he had liked to walk in mud. He remembered enjoying the cool of it rising between his toes. He still liked to go barefoot, but no longer enjoyed mud; it was sticky stuff, and he disliked stooping to clean his feet before going into the house. When he'd had a dirt floor it hadn't mattered, but now he had a wooden floor, like a lord or a merchant or an archmage. To keep the cold and damp out of his bones. Not his own notion. Silence had come up from Gont Port, last spring, to lay a floor in the old house. They had had one of their arguments about it. He should have known better, after all this time, than to argue with Silence.

"I've walked on dirt for seventy-five years," Dulse had said. "A few more won't kill me!"

To which Silence of course made no reply, letting him hear what he had said and feel its foolishness thoroughly.

"Dirt's easier to keep clean," he said, knowing the struggle already lost. It was true that all you had to do with a good hard-packed clay floor was sweep it and now and then sprinkle it to keep the dust down. But it sounded silly all the same.

"Who's to lay this floor?" he said, now merely querulous.

Silence nodded, meaning himself.

The boy was in fact a workman of the first order, carpenter, cabinetmaker, stonelayer, roofer; he had proved that when he lived up here as Dulse's student, and his life with the rich folk of Gont Port had not softened his hands. He brought the boards from Sixth's mill in Re Albi, driving Gammer's ox team; he laid the floor and polished it the next day, while the old wizard was up at Bog Lake gathering simples. When Dulse came home there it was, shining like a dark lake itself. "Have to wash my feet every time I come in," he grumbled. He walked in gingerly. The wood was so smooth it seemed soft to the bare sole. "Satin," he said. "You didn't do all that in one day without a spell or two. A village hut with a palace floor. Well, it'll be a sight, come winter, to see the fire shine in that! Or do I have to get me a carpet now? A fleecefell, on a golden warp?"

Silence smiled. He was pleased with himself.

He had turned up on Dulse's doorstep a few years ago. Well, no, twenty years ago it must be, or twenty-five. A while ago now. He had been truly a boy then, long-legged, rough-haired, soft-faced. A set mouth, clear eyes. "What do you want?" the wizard had asked, knowing what he wanted, what they all wanted, and keeping his eyes from those clear eyes. He was a good teacher, the best on Gont, he knew that. But he was tired of teaching, didn't want another prentice underfoot. And he sensed danger.

"To learn," the boy whispered.

"Go to Roke," the wizard said. The boy wore shoes and a good leather vest. He could afford or earn ship's passage to the school.

"I've been there."

At that Dulse looked him over again. No cloak, no staff.

"Failed? Sent away? Ran away?"

The boy shook his head at each question. He shut his eyes; his mouth was already shut. He stood there, intensely gathered, suffering: drew breath: looked straight into the wizard's eyes.

"My mastery is here, on Gont," he said, still speaking hardly above a whisper. "My master is Heleth."

At that the wizard whose true name was Heleth stood as still as he did, looking back at him, till the boy's gaze dropped.

In silence Dulse sought the boy's name, and saw two things: a fir cone, and the rune of the Closed Mouth. Then seeking further he heard in his mind a name spoken; but he did not speak it.

"I'm tired of teaching and talking," he said. "I need silence. Is that enough for you?"

The boy nodded once.

"Then to me you are Silence," the wizard said. "You can sleep in the nook under the west window. There's an old pallet in the woodhouse. Air it. Don't bring mice in with it." And he stalked off towards the Overfell, angry with the boy for coming and with himself for giving in; but it was not anger that made his heart pound. Striding along—he could stride, then—with the sea wind pushing at him always from the left and the early sunlight on the sea out past the vast shadow of the mountain, he thought of the Mages of Roke, the masters of the art magic, the professors of mystery and power. "He was too much for 'em, was he? And he'll be too much for me," he thought, and smiled. He was a peaceful man, but he did not mind a bit of danger.

He stopped then and felt the dirt under his feet. He was barefoot, as usual. When he was a student on Roke, he had worn shoes. But he had come back home to Gont, to Re Albi, with his wizard's staff, and kicked his shoes off. He stood still and felt the dust and rock of the cliff-top path under his feet, and the cliffs under that, and the roots of the island in the dark under that. In the dark under the waters all islands touched and were one. So his teacher Ard had said, and so his teachers on Roke had said. But this was his island, his rock, his dirt. His wizardry grew out of it. "My mastery is here," the boy had said, but it went deeper than mastery. That, perhaps, was something Dulse could teach him: what went deeper than mastery. What he had learned here, on Gont, before he ever went to Roke.

And the boy must have a staff. Why had Nemmerle let him leave Roke without one, empty-handed as a prentice or a witch? Power like that shouldn't go wandering about unchanneled and unsignaled.

My teacher had no staff, Dulse thought, and at the same moment thought, The boy wants his staff from me. Gontish oak, from the hands of a Gontish wizard. Well, if he earns it I'll make him one. If he can keep his mouth closed. And I'll leave him my lore-books. If he can clean out a henhouse, and understand the Glosses of Danemer, and keep his mouth closed.

The new student cleaned out the henhouse and hoed the bean patch, learned the meaning of the Glosses of Danemer and the Arcana of the Enlades, and kept his mouth closed. He listened. He heard what Dulse said; sometimes he heard what Dulse thought. He did what Dulse wanted and what Dulse did not know he wanted. His gift was far beyond Dulse's guidance, yet he had been right to come to Re Albi, and they both knew it.

Dulse thought sometimes in those years about sons and fathers. He had quarreled with his own father, a sorcerer-prospector, over his choice of Ard as his teacher. His father had shouted that a student of Ard's was no son of his, had nursed his rage, died unforgiving.

Dulse had seen young men weep for joy at the birth of a first son. He had seen poor men pay witches a year's earnings for the promise of a healthy boy, and a rich man touch his gold-bedizened baby's face and whisper, adoring, "My immortality!" He had seen men beat their sons, bully and humiliate them, spite and thwart them, hating the death they saw in them. He had seen the answering hatred in the son's eyes, the threat, the pitiless contempt. And seeing it, Dulse knew why he had never sought reconciliation with his father.

He had seen a father and son work together from daybreak to sundown, the old man guiding a blind ox, the middle-aged man driving the iron-bladed plough, never a word spoken. As they started home the old man laid his hand a moment on the son's shoulder.

He had always remembered that. He remembered it now, when he looked across the hearth, winter evenings, at the dark face bent above a lore-book or a shirt that needed mending. The eyes cast down, the mouth closed, the spirit listening.

"Once in his lifetime, if he's lucky, a wizard finds somebody he can talk to." Nemmerle had said that to Dulse a night or two before Dulse left Roke, a year or two before Nemmerle was chosen Archmage. He had been the Master Patterner and the kindest of all Dulse's teachers at the school. "I think, if you stayed, Heleth, we could talk."

Dulse had been unable to answer at all for a while. Then, stammering, guilty at his ingratitude and incredulous at his obstinacy—"Master, I would stay, but my work is on Gont. I wish it was here, with you—"

"It's a rare gift, to know where you need to be, before you've been to all the places you don't need to be. Well, send me a student now and then. Roke needs Gontish wizardry. I think we're leaving things out, here, things worth knowing . . ."

Dulse had sent students on to the school, three or four of them, nice lads with a gift for this or that; but the one Nemmerle waited for had come and gone of his own will, and what they had thought of him on Roke Dulse did not know. And Silence, of course, did not say. It was evident that he had learned there in two or three years what some boys learned in six or seven and many never learned at all. To him it had been mere groundwork.

"Why didn't you come to me first?" Dulse had demanded. "And then go to Roke, to put a polish on it?"

"I didn't want to waste your time."

"Did Nemmerle know you were coming to work with me?"

Silence shook his head.

"If you'd deigned to tell him your intentions, he might have sent a message to me."

Silence looked stricken. "Was he your friend?"

Dulse paused. "He was my master. Would have been my friend, perhaps, if I'd stayed on Roke. Have wizards friends? No more than they have wives, or sons, I suppose . . . Once he said to me that in our trade it's a lucky man who finds someone to talk to . . . Keep that in mind. If you're lucky, one day you'll have to open your mouth."

Silence bowed his rough, thoughtful head.

"If it hasn't rusted shut," Dulse added.

"If you ask me to, I'll talk," the young man said, so earnest, so willing to deny his whole nature at Dulse's request that the wizard had to laugh.

"I asked you not to," he said. "And it's not my need I spoke of. I talk enough for two. Never mind. You'll know what to say when the time comes. That's the art, eh? What to say, and when to say it. And the rest is silence."

The young man slept on a pallet under the little west window of Dulse's house for three years. He learned wizardry, fed the chickens, milked the cow. He suggested, once, that Dulse keep goats. He had not said anything for a week or so, a cold, wet week of autumn. He said, "You might keep some goats."

Dulse had the big lore-book open on the table. He had been trying to reweave one of the Acastan Spells, much broken and made powerless by the Emanations of Fundaur centuries ago. He had just begun to get a sense of the missing word that might fill one of the gaps, he almost had it, and—"You might keep some goats," Silence said.

Dulse considered himself a wordy, impatient man with a short temper. The necessity of not swearing had been a burden to him in his youth, and for thirty years the imbecility of prentices, clients, cows, and chickens had tried him sorely. Prentices and clients were afraid of his tongue, though cows and chickens paid no attention to his outbursts. He had never been angry at Silence before. There was a very long pause.

"What for?"

Silence apparently did not notice the pause or the extreme softness of Dulse's voice. "Milk, cheese, roast kid, company," he said.

"Have you ever kept goats?" Dulse asked, in the same soft, polite voice.

Silence shook his head.

He was in fact a town boy, born in Gont Port. He had said nothing about himself, but Dulse had asked around a bit. The father, a longshoreman, had died in the big earthquake, when Silence would have been seven or eight; the mother was a cook at a waterfront inn. At twelve the boy had got into some kind of trouble, probably messing about with magic, and his mother had managed to prentice him to Elassen, a respectable sorcerer in Valmouth. There the boy had picked up his true name, and some skill in carpentry and farmwork, if not much else; and Elassen had had the generosity, after three years, to pay his passage to Roke. That was all Dulse knew about him.

"I dislike goat cheese," Dulse said.

Silence nodded, acceptant as always.

From time to time in the years since then, Dulse remembered how he hadn't lost his temper when Silence asked about keeping goats; and each time the memory gave him a quiet satisfaction, like that of finishing the last bite of a perfectly ripe pear.

After spending the next several days trying to recapture the missing word, he had set Silence to studying the Acastan Spells. Together they finally worked it out, a long toil. "Like ploughing with a blind ox," Dulse said.

Not long after that he gave Silence the staff he had made for him of Gontish oak.

And the Lord of Gont Port had tried once again to get Dulse to come down to do what needed doing in Gont Port, and Dulse had sent Silence down instead, and there he had stayed.

And Dulse was standing on his own doorstep, three eggs in his hand and the rain running cold down his back.

How long had he been standing here? Why was he standing here? He had been thinking about mud, about the floor, about Silence. Had he been out walking on the path above the Overfell? No, that was years ago, years ago, in the sunlight. It was raining. He had fed the chickens, and come back to the house with three eggs, they were still warm in his hand, silky brown lukewarm eggs, and the sound of thunder was still in his mind, the vibration of thunder was in his bones, in his feet. Thunder?

No. There had been a thunderclap, a while ago. This was not thunder. He had had this queer feeling and had not recognized it, back—when? long ago, back before all the days and years he had been thinking of. When, when had it been?—before the earthquake. Just before the earthquake. Just before a half mile of the coast at Essary slumped into the sea, and people died crushed in the ruins of their villages, and a great wave swamped the wharfs at Gont Port.

He stepped down from the doorstep onto the dirt so that he could feel the ground with the nerves of his soles, but the mud slimed and fouled any messages the dirt had for him. He set the eggs down on the doorstep, sat down beside them, cleaned his feet with rainwater from the pot by the step, wiped them dry with the rag that hung on the handle of the pot, rinsed and wrung out the rag and hung it on the handle of the pot, picked up the eggs, stood up slowly, and went into his house.

He gave a sharp look at his staff, which leaned in the corner behind the door. He put the eggs in the larder, ate an apple quickly because he was hungry, and took up his staff. It was yew, bound at the foot with copper, worn to satin at the grip. Nemmerle had given it to him.

"Stand!" he said to it in its language, and let go of it. It stood as if he had driven it into a socket.

"To the root," he said impatiently, in the Language of the Making. "To the root!"

He watched the staff that stood on the shinning floor. In a little while he saw it quiver very slightly, a shiver, a tremble.

"Ah, ah, ah," said the old wizard.

"What should I do?" he said aloud after a while.

The staff swayed, was still, shivered again.

"Enough of that, my dear," Dulse said, laying his hand on it. "Come now. No wonder I kept thinking about Silence. I should send for him . . . send to him . . . No. What did Ard say? Find the center, find the center. That's the question to ask. That's what to do . . ." As he muttered on to himself, routing out his heavy cloak, setting water to boil on the small fire he had lighted earlier, he wondered if he had always talked to himself, if he had talked all the time when Silence lived with him. No. It had become a habit after Silence left, he thought, with the bit of his mind that went on thinking the ordinary thoughts of life, while the rest of it made preparations for terror and destruction.

He hard-boiled the three new eggs and one already in the larder and put them into a pouch along with four apples and a bladder of resinated wine, in case he had to stay out all night. He shrugged arthritically into his heavy cloak, took up his staff, told the fire to go out, and left.

He no longer kept a cow. He stood looking into the poultry

yard, considering. The fox had been visiting the orchard lately. But the chickens would have to forage if he stayed away. They must take their chances, like everyone else. He opened their gate a little. Though the rain was no more than a misty drizzle now, they stayed hunched up under the henhouse eaves, disconsolate. The King had not crowed once this morning.

"Have you anything to tell me?" Dulse asked them.

Brown Bucca, his favorite, shook herself and said her name a few times. The others said nothing.

"Well, take care. I saw the fox on the full-moon night," Dulse said, and went on his way.

As he walked he thought; he thought hard; he recalled. He recalled all he could of matters his teacher had spoken of once only and long ago. Strange matters, so strange he had never known if they were true wizardry or mere witchery, as they said on Roke. Matters he certainly had never heard about on Roke, nor had he ever spoken about them there, maybe fearing the Masters would despise him for taking such things seriously, maybe knowing they would not understand them, because they were Gontish matters, truths of Gont. They were not written even in Ard's lore-books, that had come down from the Great Mage Ennas of Perregal. They were all word of mouth. They were home truths.

"If you need to read the Mountain," his teacher had told him, "go to the Dark Pond at the top of Semere's cow pasture. You can see the ways from there. You need to find the center. See where to go in."

"Go in?" the boy Dulse had whispered.

"What could you do from outside?"

Dulse was silent for a long time, and then said, "How?"

"Thus." And Ard's long arms stretched out and upward in the invocation of what Dulse would know later was a great spell of Transforming. Ard spoke the words of the spell awry, as teachers of wizardry must do lest the spell operate. Dulse knew the trick of hearing them aright and remembering them. When Ard was done, Dulse had repeated the words in his mind in silence, half-sketching the strange, awkward gestures that were part of them. All at once his hand stopped.

"But you can't undo this!" he said aloud.

Ard nodded. "It is irrevocable."

Dulse knew no transformation that was irrevocable, no spell that could not be unsaid, except the Word of Unbinding, which is spoken only once.

"But why—?"

"At need," Ard said.

Dulse knew better than to ask for explanation. The need to speak such a spell could not come often; the chance of his ever having to use it was very slight. He let the terrible spell sink down in his mind and be hidden and layered over with a thousand useful or beautiful or enlightening mageries and charms, all the lore and rules of Roke, all the wisdom of the books Ard had bequeathed him. Crude, monstrous, useless, it lay in the dark of his mind for sixty years, like the cornerstone of an earlier, forgotten house down in the cellar of a mansion full of lights and treasures and children.

The rain had ceased, though mist still hid the peak and shreds of cloud drifted through the high forests. Though not a tireless walker like Silence, who would have spent his life wandering in the forests of Gont Mountain if he could, Dulse had been born in Re Albi and knew the roads and ways around it as part of himself. He took the shortcut at Rissi's well and came out before midday on Semere's high pasture, a level step on the mountainside. A mile below it, all in sunlight now, the farm buildings stood in the lee of a hill across which a flock of sheep moved like a cloud-shadow. Gont Port and its bay were hidden under the steep, knotted hills that stood inland above the city.

Dulse wandered about a bit before he found what he took

to be the Dark Pond. It was small, half mud and reeds, with one vague, boggy path to the water, and no tracks on that but goat hoofs. The water was dark, though it lay out under the bright sky and far above the peat soils. Dulse followed the goat tracks, growling when his foot slipped in the mud and he wrenched his ankle to keep from falling. At the brink of the water he stood still. He stooped to rub his ankle. He listened.

It was absolutely silent.

No wind. No birdcall. No distant lowing or bleating or call of voice. As if all the island had gone still. Not a fly buzzed.

He looked at the dark water. It reflected nothing.

Reluctant, he stepped forward, barefoot and bare-legged; he had rolled up his cloak into his pack an hour ago when the sun came out. Reeds brushed his legs. The mud was soft and sucking under his feet, full of tangling reed-roots. He made no noise as he moved slowly out into the pool, and the circles of ripples from his movement were slight and small. It was shallow for a long way. Then his cautious foot felt no bottom, and he paused.

The water shivered. He felt it first on his thighs, a lapping like the tickling touch of fur; then he saw it, the trembling of the surface all over the pond. Not the round ripples he made, which had already died away, but a ruffling, a roughening, a shudder, again, and again.

"Where?" he whispered, and then said the word aloud in the language all things understand that have no other language.

There was the silence. Then a fish leapt from the black, shaking water, a white-gray fish the length of his hand, and as it leapt it cried out in a small, clear voice, in that same language, "Yaved!"

The old wizard stood there. He recollected all he knew of the names of Gont, brought all its slopes and cliffs and ravines into his mind, and in a minute he saw where Yaved was. It was the place where the ridges parted, just inland from Gont Port, deep in the knot of hills above the city. It was the place of the fault. An earthquake centered there could shake the city down, bring avalanche and tidal wave, close the cliffs of the bay together like hands clapping. Dulse shivered, shuddered all over like the water of the pool.

He turned and made for the shore, hasty, careless where he set his feet and not caring if he broke the silence by splashing and breathing hard. He slogged back up the path through the reeds till he reached dry ground and coarse grass, and heard the buzz of midges and crickets. He sat down then on the ground, hard, for his legs were shaking.

"It won't do," he said, talking to himself in Hardic, and then he said, "I can't do it." Then he said, "I can't do it by myself."

He was so distraught that when he made up his mind to call Silence he could not think of the opening of the spell, which he had known for sixty years; then when he thought he had it, he began to speak a Summoning instead, and the spell had begun to work before he realized what he was doing and stopped and undid it word by word.

He pulled up some grass and rubbed at the slimy mud on his feet and legs. It was not dry yet, and only smeared about on his skin. "I hate mud," he whispered. Then he snapped his jaws and stopped trying to clean his legs. "Dirt, dirt," he said, gently patting the ground he sat on. Then, very slow, very careful, he began to speak the spell of calling.

In a busy street leading down to the busy wharfs of Gont Port, the wizard Ogion stopped short. The ship's captain beside him walked on several steps and turned to see Ogion talking to the air.

"But I will come, master!" he said. And then after a pause, "How soon?" And after a longer pause, he told the air something in a language the ship's captain did not understand, and made a gesture that darkened the air about him for an instant.

"Captain," he said, "I'm sorry, I must wait to spell your sails. An earthquake is near. I must warn the city. Do you tell them down there, every ship that can sail make for the open sea. Clear out past the Armed Cliffs! Good luck to you." And he turned and ran back up the street, a tall, strong man with rough graying hair, running now like a stag.

Gont Port lies at the inner end of a long narrow bay between steep shores. Its entrance from the sea is between two great headlands, the Gates of the Port, the Armed Cliffs, not a hundred feet apart. The people of Gont Port are safe from sea-pirates. But their safety is their danger: the long bay follows a fault in the earth, and jaws that have opened may shut.

When he had done what he could to warn the city, and seen all the gate guards and port guards doing what they could to keep the few roads out from becoming choked and murderous with panicky people, Ogion shut himself into a room in the signal tower of the Port, locked the door, for everybody wanted him at once, and sent a sending to the Dark Pond in Semere's cow pasture up on the Mountain.

His old master was sitting in the grass near the pond, eating an apple. Bits of eggshell flecked the ground near his legs, which were caked with drying mud. When he looked up and saw Ogion's sending he smiled a wide, sweet smile. But he looked old. He had never looked so old. Ogion had not seen him for over a year, having been busy; he was always busy in Gont Port, doing the business of the lords and people, never a chance to walk in the forests on the mountainside or to come sit with Heleth in the little house at Re Albi and listen and be still. Heleth was an old man, near eighty now; and he was frightened. He smiled with joy to see Ogion, but he was frightened.

"I think what we have to do," he said without preamble, "is try to hold the fault from slipping much. You at the Gates and me at the inner end, in the Mountain. Working together, you know. We might be able to. I can feel it building up, can you?"

Ogion shook his head. He let his sending sit down in the grass near Heleth, though it did not bend the stems of the grass where it stepped or sat. "I've done nothing but set the city in a panic and send the ships out of the bay," he said. "What is it you feel? How do you feel it?"

They were technical questions, mage to mage. Heleth hesitated before answering.

"I learned about this from Ard," he said, and paused again.

He had never told Ogion anything about his first teacher, a sorcerer of no fame even in Gont, and perhaps of ill fame. Ogion knew only that Ard had never gone to Roke, had been trained on Perregal, and that some mystery or shame darkened the name. Though he was talkative, for a wizard, Heleth was silent as a stone about some things. And so Ogion, who respected silence, had never asked him about his teacher.

"It's not Roke magic," the old man said. His voice was dry, a little forced. "Nothing against the balance, though. Nothing sticky."

That had always been his word for evil doings, spells for gain, curses, black magic: "sticky stuff."

After a while, searching for words, he went on: "Dirt. Rocks. It's a dirty magic. Old. Very old. As old as Gont Island."

"The Old Powers?" Ogion murmured.

Heleth said, "I'm not sure."

"Will it control the earth itself?"

"More a matter of getting in with it, I think. Inside." The old man was burying the core of his apple and the larger bits of eggshell under loose dirt, patting it over them neatly. "Of course I know the words, but I'll have to learn what to do as I go. That's the trouble with the big spells, isn't it? You learn what you're doing while you do it. No chance to practice." He looked up. "Ah—there! You feel that?"

Ogion shook his head.

"Straining," Heleth said, his hand still absently, gently patting the dirt as one might pat a scared cow. "Quite soon now, I think. Can you hold the Gates open, my dear?"

"Tell me what you'll be doing—"

But Heleth was shaking his head: "No," he said. "No time. Not your kind of thing." He was more and more distracted by whatever it was he sensed in the earth or air, and through him Ogion too felt that gathering, intolerable tension.

They sat unspeaking. The crisis passed. Heleth relaxed a little and even smiled. "Very old stuff," he said, "what I'll be doing. I wish now I'd thought about it more. Passed it on to you. But it seemed a bit crude. Heavy-handed . . . She didn't say where she'd learned it. Here, of course . . . There are different kinds of knowledge, after all."

"She?"

"Ard. My teacher." Heleth looked up, his face unreadable, its expression possibly sly. "You didn't know that? No, I suppose I never mentioned it. I wonder what difference it made to her wizardry, her being a woman. Or to mine, my being a man . . . What matters, it seems to me, is whose house we live in. And who we let enter the house. This kind of thing—There! There again—"

His sudden tension and immobility, the strained face and inward look, were like those of a woman in labor when her womb contracts. That was Ogion's thought, even as he asked, "What did you mean, 'in the Mountain'?"

The spasm passed; Heleth answered, "Inside it. There at Yaved." He pointed to the knotted hills below them. "I'll go in, try to keep things from sliding around, eh? I'll find out how when I'm doing it, no doubt. I think you should be getting back to yourself. Things are tightening up." He stopped again, looking as if he were in intense pain, hunched and clenched. He struggled to stand up. Unthinking, Ogion held out his hand to help him.

"No use," said the old wizard, grinning, "you're only wind and sunlight. Now I'm going to be dirt and stone. You'd best go on. Farewell, Aihal. Keep the—keep the mouth open, for once, eh?"

Ogion, obedient, bringing himself back to himself in the stuffy, tapestried room in Gont Port, did not understand the old man's joke until he turned to the window and saw the Armed Cliffs down at the end of the long bay, the jaws ready to snap shut. "I will," he said, and set to it.

"What I have to do, you see," the old wizard said, still talking to Silence because it was a comfort to talk to him even if he was no longer there, "is get into the mountain, right inside. But not the way a sorcerer-prospector does, not just slipping about between things and looking and tasting. Deeper. All the way in. Not the veins, but the bones. So," and standing there alone in the high pasture, in the noon light, Heleth opened his arms wide in the gesture of invocation that opens all the greater spells; and he spoke.

Nothing happened as he said the words Ard had taught him, his old witch-teacher with her bitter mouth and her long, lean arms, the words spoken awry then, spoken truly now.

Nothing happened, and he had time to regret the sunlight and the sea wind, and to doubt the spell, and to doubt himself, before the earth rose up around him, dry, warm, and dark.

In there he knew he should hurry, that the bones of the earth ached to move, and that he must become them to guide them, but he could not hurry. There was on him the bewilderment of any transformation. He had in his day been fox, and bull, and dragonfly, and knew what it was to change being. But this was different, this slow enlargement. I am vastening, he thought.

He reached out towards Yaved, towards the ache, the suffering. As he came closer to it he felt a great strength flow into him from the west, as if Silence had taken him by the hand after all. Through that link he could send his own strength, the Mountain's strength, to help. I didn't tell him I wasn't coming back, he thought, his last words in Hardic, his last grief, for he was in the bones of the mountain now. He knew the arteries of fire, and the beat of the great heart. He knew what to do. It was in no tongue of man that he said, "Be quiet, be easy. There now, there. Hold fast. So, there. We can be easy."

And he was easy, he was still, he held fast, rock in rock and earth in earth in the fiery dark of the mountain.

It was their mage Ogion whom the people saw stand alone on the roof of the signal tower on the wharf, when the streets ran up and down in waves, the cobbles bursting out of them, and walls of clay brick puffed into dust, and the Armed Cliffs leaned together, groaning. It was Ogion they saw, his hands held out before him, straining, parting: and the cliffs parted with them, and stood straight, unmoved. The city shuddered and stood still. It was Ogion who stopped the earthquake. They saw it, they said it.

"My teacher was with me, and his teacher with him," Ogion said when they praised him. "I could hold the Gate open because he held the Mountain still." They praised his modesty and did not listen to him. Listening is a rare gift, and men will have their heroes.

When the city was in order again, and the ships had all come back, and the walls were being rebuilt, Ogion escaped from praise and went up into the hills above Gont Port. He found the queer little valley called Trimmer's Dell, the true name of which in the Language of the Making was Yaved, as Ogion's true name was Aihal. He walked about there all one day, as if seeking something. In the evening he lay down on the ground and talked to it. "You should have told me. I could have said good-bye," he said. He wept then, and his tears fell on the dry dirt among the grass stems and made little spots of mud, little sticky spots.

He slept there on the ground, with no pallet or blanket between him and the dirt. At sunrise he got up and walked by the high road over to Re Albi. He did not go into the village, but past it to the house that stood alone north of the other houses at the beginning of the Overfell. The door stood open.

The last beans had got big and coarse on the vines; the cabbages were thriving. Three hens came clucking and pecking around the dusty dooryard, a red, a brown, a white; a gray hen was setting her clutch in the henhouse. There were no chicks, and no sign of the cock, the King, Heleth had called him. The king is dead, Ogion thought. Maybe a chick is hatching even now to take his place. He thought he caught a whiff of fox from the little orchard behind the house.

He swept out the dust and leaves that had blown in the open doorway across the floor of polished wood. He set Heleth's mattress and blanket in the sun to air. "I'll stay here a while," he thought. "It's a good house." After a while he thought, "I might keep some goats."

Orson Scott Card is the Hugo and Nebula–winning author of Ender's Game, *quite possibly the most popular SF novel of the last twenty years. For many years, in the novels* Seventh Son, Red Prophet, *and their several sequels, Card has also been telling the magical tale of Alvin Maker as he comes of age in a nineteenth-century America that never was. "Hatrack River" is where Alvin's story began.*

Hatrack River

ORSON SCOTT CARD

Little Peggy was very careful with the eggs. She rooted her hand through the straw till her fingers bumped something hard and heavy. She gave no never mind to the chicken drips. After all, Mama never even crinkled her face to open up Cally's most spctackler diapers. Even when the chicken drips were wet and stringy and made her fingers stick together, little Peggy gave no never mind. She just pushed the straw apart, wrapped her hand around the egg, and lifted it out of the brood box. All this while standing tip-toe on a wobbly stool, reaching high above her head. Mama said she was too young for egging, but little Peggy showed her. Every day she felt in every brood box and brought in every egg, every single one, that's what she did.

Every one, she said in her mind, over and over: I got to reach into every one.

Then little Peggy looked back into the northeast corner, the darkest place in the whole coop, and there sat Bloody Mary in her brood box, looking like the devil's own bad dream, hatefulness shining out of her nasty eyes, saying Come here little girl and give me nips. I want nips of finger and nips of thumb and if you come real close and try to take my egg I'll get a nip of eye from you.

Most animals didn't have much heartfire, but Bloody Mary's was strong and made a poison smoke. Nobody else could see it, but little Peggy could. Bloody Mary dreamed of death for all folks, but most specially for a certain little girl five years old, and little Peggy had the marks on her fingers to prove it. At least one mark, anyway, and even if Papa said he couldn't see it, little Peggy remembered how she got it and nobody could blame her none if she sometimes forgot to reach under Bloody Mary who sat there like a bushwhacker waiting to kill the first folks that just tried to come by. Nobody'd get mad if she just sometimes forgot to look there.

I forgot forgot forgot. I looked in every brood box, every one, and if one got missed then I forgot forgot forgot.

Everybody knew Bloody Mary was a lowdown chicken and too mean to give any eggs that wasn't rotten anyway.

I forgot.

She got the egg basket inside before Mama even had the fire het, and Mama was so pleased she let little Peggy put the eggs one by one into the cold water. Then Mama put the pot on the hook and swung it right on over the fire. Boiling eggs you didn't have to wait for the fire to slack, you could do it smoke and all.

"Peg," said Papa.

That was Mama's name, but Papa didn't say it in his Mama voice. He said it in his little-Peggy-you're-in-dutch voice, and little Peggy knew she was completely found out, and so she turned right around and yelled what she'd been planning to say all along.

"I forgot, Papa!"

Mama turned and looked at little Peggy in surprise. Papa wasn't surprised though. He just raised an eyebrow. He was holding his hand behind his back. Little Peggy knew there was an egg in that hand. Bloody Mary's nasty egg.

"What did you forget, little Peggy?" asked Papa, talking soft.

Right that minute little Peggy reckoned she was the stupidest girl ever born on the face of the earth. Here she was denying before anybody accused her of anything.

But she wasn't going to give up, not right off like that. She couldn't stand to have them mad at her and she just wanted them to let her go away and live in England. So she put on her innocent face and said, "I don't know, Papa."

She figgered England was the best place to go live, 'cause England had a Lord Protector. From the look in Papa's eye, a Lord Protector was pretty much what she needed just now.

"What did you forget?" Papa asked again.

"Just say it and be done, Horace," said Mama. "If she's done wrong then she's done wrong."

"I forgot one time, Papa," said little Peggy. "She's a mean old chicken and she hates me."

Papa answered soft and slow. "One time," he said.

Then he took his hand from behind him. Only it wasn't no single egg he held, it was a whole basket. And that basket was filled with a clot of straw—most likely all the straw from Bloody Mary's box—and that straw was mashed together and glued tight with dried-up raw egg and shell bits, mixed up with about three or four chewed-up baby chicken bodies.

"Did you have to bring that in the house before breakfast, Horace?" said Mama.

"I don't know what makes me madder," said Horace. "What she done wrong or her studying up to lie about it."

"I didn't study and I didn't lie!" shouted little Peggy. Or anyways she meant to shout. What came out sounded espiciously like crying even though little Peggy had decided only yesterday that she was done with crying for the rest of her life.

"See?" said Mama. "She already feels bad."

"She feels bad being caught," said Horace. "You're too slack on her, Peg. She's got a lying spirit. I don't want my daughter growing up wicked. I'd rather see her dead like her baby sister before I see her grow up wicked."

Little Peggy saw Mama's heartfire flare up with memory, and in front of her eyes she could see a baby laid out pretty in a little box, and then another one only not so pretty 'cause it was the second baby Missy, the one what died of pox so nobody'd touch her but her own Mama, who was still so feeble from the pox herself that she couldn't do much. Little Peggy saw that scene, and she knew Papa had made a mistake to say what he said 'cause Mama's face went cold even though her heartfire was hot.

"That's the wickedest thing anybody ever said in my presence," said Mama. Then she took up the basket of corruption from the table and took it outside.

"Bloody Mary bites my hand," said little Peggy.

"We'll see what bites," said Papa. "For leaving the eggs I give you one whack, because I reckon that lunatic hen looks fearsome to a frog-size girl like you. But for telling lies I give you ten whacks."

Little Peggy cried in earnest at that news. Papa gave an honest count and full measure in everything, but most especially in whacks.

Papa took the hazel rod off the high shelf. He kept it up there ever since little Peggy put the old one in the fire and burnt it right up.

"I'd rather hear a thousand hard and bitter truths from you, Daughter, than one soft and easy lie," said he, and then he bent over and laid on with the rod across her thighs. Whick

whick whick, she counted every one, they stung her to the heart, each one of them, they were so full of anger. Worst of all she knew it was all unfair because his heartfire raged for a different cause altogether, and it always did. Papa's hate for wickedness always came from his most secret memory. Little Peggy didn't understand it all, because it was twisted up and confused and Papa didn't remember it right well himself. All little Peggy ever saw plain was that it was a lady and it wasn't Mama. Papa thought of that lady whenever something went wrong. When baby Missy died of nothing at all, and then the next baby also named Missy died of pox, and then the barn burnt down once, and a cow died, everything that went wrong made him think of that lady and he began to talk about how much he hated wickedness and at those times the hazel rod flew hard and sharp.

I'd rather hear a thousand hard and bitter truths, that's what he said, but little Peggy knew that there was one truth he didn't ever want to hear, and so she kept it to herself. She'd never shout it at him, even if it made him break the hazel rod, 'cause whenever she thought of saying aught about that lady, she kept picturing her father dead, and that was a thing she never hoped to see for real. Besides, the lady that haunted his heartfire, she didn't have no clothes on, and little Peggy knew that she'd be whipped for sure if she talked about people being naked.

So she took the whacks and cried till she could taste that her nose was running. Papa left the room right away, and Mama came back to fix up breakfast for the blacksmith and the visitors and the hands, but neither one said boo to her, just as if they didn't even notice. She cried even harder and louder for a minute, but it didn't help. Finally she picked up her Bugy from the sewing basket and walked all stiff-legged out to Oldpappy's cabin and woke him right up.

He listened to her story like he always did.

"I know about Bloody Mary," he said, "and I told your papa fifty times if I told him once, wring that chicken's neck and be done. She's a crazy bird. Every week or so she gets crazy and breaks all her own eggs, even the ones ready to hatch. Kills her own chicks. It's a lunatic what kills its own."

"Papa like to killed me," said little Peggy.

"I reckon if you can walk somewhat it ain't so bad altogether."

"I can't walk much."

"No, I can see you're nigh crippled forever," said Oldpappy. "But I tell you what, the way I see it your mama and your papa's mostly mad at each other. So why don't you just disappear for a couple of hours?"

"I wish I could turn into a bird and fly."

"Next best thing, though," said Pappy, "is to have a secret place where nobody knows to look for you. Do you have a place like that? No, don't tell me—it wrecks it if you tell even a single other person. You just go to that place for a while. As long as it's a safe place, not out in the woods where a Red might take your pretty hair, and not a high place where you might fall off, and not a tiny place where you might get stuck."

"It's big and it's low and it ain't in the woods," said little Peggy.

"Then you go there, Maggie."

Little Peggy made the face she always made when Oldpappy called her that. And she held up Bugy and in Bugy's squeaky high voice she said, "Her name is Peggy."

"You go there, *Piggy,* if you like that better—"

Little Peggy slapped Bugy right across Oldpappy's knee.

"Someday Bugy'll do that once too often and have a rupture and die," said Oldpappy.

But Bugy just danced right in his face and insisted, "Not piggy, *Peggy!*"

"That's right, Puggy, you go to that secret place and if anybody says, We got to go find that girl, I'll say, I know where she is and she'll come back when she's good and ready."

Little Peggy ran for the cabin door and then stopped and turned. "Oldpappy, you're the nicest grown-up in the whole world."

"Your papa has a different view of me, but that's all tied up with another hazel rod that I laid hand on much too often. Now run along."

She stopped again right before she closed the door. "You're the *only* nice grown-up!" She shouted it real loud, halfway hoping that they could hear it clear inside the house. Then she was gone, right across the garden, out past the cow pasture, up the hill into the woods, and along the path to the spring house.

They had one good wagon, these folks did, and two good horses pulling it. One might even suppose they was prosperous, considering they had six big boys, from mansize on down to twins that had wrestled each other into being a good deal stronger than their dozen years. Not to mention one big daughter and a whole passel of little girls. A big family. Right prosperous if you didn't know that not even a year ago they had owned a mill and lived in a big house on a streambank in west New Hampshire. Come down far in the world, they had, and this wagon was all they had left of everything. But they were hopeful, trekking west along the roads that crossed the Hio, heading for open land that was free for the taking. If you were a family with plenty of strong backs and clever hands, it'd be good land, too, as long as the weather was with them and the Reds didn't raid them and all the lawyers and bankers stayed in New England.

The father was a big man, a little run to fat, which was no surprise since millers mostly stood around all day. That softness in the belly wouldn't last a year on a deepwoods homestead. He didn't care much about that, anyway—he had no fear of hard work. What worried him today was his wife, Faith. It was her time for that baby, he knew it. Not that she'd ever talk about it direct. Women just don't speak about things like that with men. But he knew how big she was and how many months it had been. Besides, at the noon stop she murmured to him, "Alvin Miller, if there's a road house along this way, or even a little broke-down cabin, I reckon I could use a bit of rest." A man didn't have to be a philosopher to understand her. And after six sons and six daughters, he'd have to have the brains of a brick not to get the drift of how things stood with her.

So he sent the oldest boy, Vigor, to run ahead on the road and see the lay of the land.

You could tell they were from New England, cause the boy didn't take no gun. If there'd been a bushwhacker the young man never would've made it back, and the fact he came back with all his hair was proof no Red had spotted him—the French up Detroit way were paying for English scalps with liquor and if a Red saw a white man alone in the woods with no rifle he'd own that white man's scalp. So maybe a man could think that luck was with the family at last. But since these Yankees had no notion that the road wasn't safe, Alvin Miller didn't think for a minute of his good luck.

Vigor's word was of a road house three miles on. That was good news, except that between them and that road house was a river. Kind of a scrawny river, and the ford was shallow, but Alvin Miller had learned never to trust water. No matter how peaceful it looks, it'll reach and try to take you. He was halfway minded to tell Faith that they'd spend the night this side of the river, but she gave just the tiniest groan and at that moment he knew that there was no chance of that. Faith had borne him a dozen living children, but it was four years since the last one and a lot of women took it bad, having a baby so late. A lot of women died. A good road house meant women to help with the birthing, so they'd have to chance the river.

And Vigor did say the river wasn't much.

The air in the spring house was cool and heavy, dark and wet. Sometimes when little Peggy caught a nap here, she woke up gasping like as if the whole place was under water. She had dreams of water even when she wasn't here—that was one of the things that made some folks say she was a seeper instead of a torch. But when she dreamed outside, she always knew she was dreaming. Here the water was real.

Real in the drips that formed like sweat on the milkjars setting in the stream. Real in the cold damp clay of the spring house floor. Real in the swallowing sound of the stream as it hurried through the middle of the house.

Keeping it cool all summer long, cold water spilling right out of the hill and into this place, shaded all the way by trees so old the moon made a point of passing through their branches just to hear some good old tales. That was what little Peggy always came here for, even when Papa didn't hate her. Not the wetness of the air, she could do just fine without that. It was the way the fire went right out of her and she didn't have to be a torch. Didn't have to see into all the dark places where folks hid theirselfs.

From her they hid theirselfs as if it would do some good. Whatever they didn't like most about theirself they tried to tuck away in some dark corner but they didn't know how all them dark places burned in little Peggy's eyes. Even when she was so little that she spit out her corn mash 'cause she was still hoping for a suck, she knew all the stories that the folks around her kept all hid. She saw the bits of their past that they most wished they could bury, and she saw the bits of their future that they most feared.

And that was why she took to coming up here to the spring house. Here she didn't have to see those things. Not even the lady in Papa's memory. There was nothing here but the heavy wet dark cool air to quench the fire and dim the light so she could be—just for a few minutes in the day—a little five-year-old girl with a straw puppet named Bugy and not even have to *think* about any of them grown-up secrets.

I'm not wicked, she told herself. Again and again but it didn't work because she knew she was.

All right then, she said to herself, I *am* wicked. But I won't be wicked anymore. I'll tell the truth like Papa says, or I'll say nothing at all.

Even at five years old, little Peggy knew that if she kept that vow, she'd be better off saying nothing.

So she said nothing, not even to herself, just lay there on a mossy damp table with Bugy clenched tight enough to strangle in her fist.

Ching ching ching.

Little Peggy woke up and got mad for just a minute.

Ching ching ching.

Made her mad because nobody said to her, Little Peggy, you don't mind if we talk this young blacksmith feller into settling down here, do you?

Not at all, Papa, she would've said if they'd asked. She knew what it meant to have a smithy. It meant your village would thrive, and folks from other places would come, and when they came there'd be trade, and when there was trade then her father's big house could be a forest inn, and when there was a forest inn all the roads would kind of bend a little just to pass the place, if it wasn't too far out of the way—little Peggy knew all that, as sure as the children of farmers knew the rhythms of the farm. A road house by a smithy was a road house that would prosper. So she would've said, sure enough, let him stay, deed him land, brick his chimney, feed him free, let him have my bed so I have to double up with Cousin Peter who keeps trying to peek under my nightgown, I'll put up with all that—just as long as you don't put him near the spring house so that all the time, even when I want to be alone with the water, there's that whack thump hiss roar, noise all the time, and a fire burning up the sky to turn it black, and the smell of charcoal burning. It was enough to make a body wish to follow the stream right back into the mountain just to get some peace.

Of course the stream was the smart place to put the blacksmith. Except for water, he could've put his smithy anywheres at all. The iron came to him in the shipper's wagon clear from New Netherland, and the charcoal—well, there were plenty of farmers willing to trade charcoal for a good shoe. But water, that's what the smith needed that nobody'd bring him, so of course they put him right down the hill from the spring house where his ching ching ching could wake her up and put the fire back into her in the one place where she had used to be able to let it burn low and go almost to cold wet ash.

A roar of thunder.

She was at the door in a second. Had to see the lightning. Caught just the last shadow of the light but she knew that there'd be more. It wasn't much after noon, surely, or had she slept all day? What with all these blackbelly clouds she couldn't tell—it might as well be the last minutes of dusk. The air was all a-prickle with lightning just waiting to flash. She knew that feeling, knew it meant the lightning'd hit close.

She looked down to see if the blacksmith's stable was still full of horses. It was. The shoeing wasn't done, the road would turn to muck, and so the farmer with his two sons from out West Fork way was stuck here. Not a chance they'd head home in *this,* with lightning ready to put a fire in the woods, or knock a tree down on them, or maybe just smack them a good one and lay them all out dead in a circle like them five Quakers they still was talking about and here it happened back in '90 when the first white folks came to settle here. People talked still about the Circle of Five and all that, some people wondering if God up and smashed them flat so as to shut the Quakers up, seeing how nothing else ever could, while other people was wondering if God took them up into heaven like the first Lord Protector Oliver Cromwell who was smote by lightning at the age of ninety-seven and just disappeared.

No, that farmer and his big old boys'd stay another night. Little Peggy was an innkeeper's daughter, wasn't she? Papooses learnt to hunt, pickaninnies learnt to tote, farmer children learnt the weather, and an innkeeper's daughter learnt which folks would stay the night, even before they knew it right theirselfs.

Their horses were champing in the stable, snorting and warning each other about the storm. In every group of horses, little Peggy figgered, there must be one that's remarkable dumb, so all the others have to tell him what all's going on. Bad storm, they were saying. We're going to get a soaking, if the lightning don't smack us first. And the dumb one kept nickering and saying, What's the noise, what's that noise.

Then the sky just opened right up and dumped water on the earth. Stripped leaves right off the trees, it came down so hard. Came down so thick, too, that little Peggy didn't even see the smithy for a minute and she thought maybe it got washed right away into the stream. Oldpappy told her how that stream led right down to the Hatrack River, and the Hatrack poured right into the Hio, and the Hio shoved itself on through the woods to the Mizzippy, which went on down to the sea, and Oldpappy said how the sea drank so much water that it got indigestion and gave off the biggest old belches you ever heard, and what came up was clouds. Belches from the sea, and now the smithy would float all that way, get swallered up and belched out, and someday she'd just be minding her own business and some cloud would break up and plop that smithy down as neat as you please, old Makepeace Smith still ching ching chinging away.

Then the rain slacked off a mite and she looked down to see the smithy still there. But that wasn't what she saw at all. No, what she saw was sparks of fire way off in the forest, downstream toward the Hatrack, down where the ford was, only there wasn't a chance of taking the ford today, with this rain. Sparks, lots of sparks, and she knew every one of them was folks. She didn't hardly think of doing it anymore, she only had to see their heartfires and she was looking close. Maybe future, maybe past, all the visions lived together in the heartfire.

What she saw right now was the same in all their hearts. A wagon in the middle of the Hatrack, with the water rising and everything they owned in all the world in that wagon.

Little Peggy didn't talk much, but everybody knew she was a torch, so they listened whenever she spoke up about trouble. Specially this kind of trouble. Sure the settlements in these parts were pretty old now, a fair bit older than little Peggy herself, but they hadn't forgotten yet that anybody's wagon caught in a flood is everybody's loss.

She fair to flew down that grassy hill, jumping gopher holes and sliding the steep places, so it wasn't twenty seconds from seeing those far-off heartfires till she was speaking right up in the smithy's shop. That farmer from West Fork at first wanted to make her wait till he was done with telling stories about worse storms he'd seen. But Makepeace knew all about little Peggy. He just listened right up and then told those boys to saddle them horses, shoes or no shoes, there was folks caught in the Hatrack ford and there was no time for foolishness. Little Peggy didn't even get a chance to see them go—Makepeace had already sent her off to the big house to fetch her father and all the hands and visitors there. Wasn't a one of them who hadn't once put all they owned in the world into a wagon and dragged it west across the mountain roads and down into the forest. Wasn't a one of them who hadn't felt a river sucking at that wagon, wanting to steal it away. They all got right to it. That's the way it was then, you see. Folks noticed other people's trouble every bit as quick as if it was their own.

Vigor led the boys in trying to push the wagon, while Eleanor hawed the horses. Alvin Miller spent his time carrying the little girls one by one to safety on the far shore. The current was a devil clawing at him, whispering, "I'll have your babies, I'll have them all," but Alvin said no, with every muscle in his body as he strained shoreward he said no to that whisper, till his girls stood all bedraggled on the bank with rain streaming down their faces like the tears from all the grief in the world.

He would have carried Faith, too, baby in her belly and all, but she wouldn't budge. Just sat inside that wagon, bracing herself against the trunks and furniture as the wagon tipped and rocked. Lightning crashed and branches broke; one of them tore the canvas and the water poured into the wagon but Faith held on with white knuckles and her eyes staring out. Alvin knew from her eyes there wasn't a thing he could say to make her let go. There was only one way to get Faith and her unborn baby out of that river, and that was to get the wagon out.

"Horses can't get no purchase, Papa," Vigor shouted. "They're just stumbling and bound to break a leg."

"Well we can't pull out without the horses!"

"The horses are *something,* Papa. We leave 'em in here and we'll lose wagon and horses too!"

"Your mama won't leave that wagon."

And he saw understanding in Vigor's eyes. The *things* in the wagon weren't worth a risk of death to save them. But Mama was.

"Still," he said. "On shore the team could pull strong. Here in the water they can't do a thing."

"Set the boys to unhitching them. But first tie a line to a tree to hold that wagon!"

It wasn't two minutes before the twins Wastenot and Wantnot were on the shore making the rope fast to a stout tree. David and Measure made another line fast to the rig that held the horses, while Calm cut the strands that held them to the wagon. Good boys, doing their work just right, Vigor shouting directions while Alvin could only watch helpless at the back of the wagon, looking now at Faith who was trying not to have the baby, now at the Hatrack River that was trying to push them all down to hell.

Not much of a river, Vigor had said, but then the clouds came up and the rain came down and the Hatrack became something after all. Even so it looked passable when they got to it. The horses strode in strong, and Alvin was just saying to Calm, who had the reins, "Well, we made it not a minute to spare," when the river went insane. It doubled in speed and strength all in a moment, and the horses got panicky and lost direction and started pulling against each other. The boys all hopped into the river and tried to lead them to shore but by then the wagon's momentum had been lost and the wheels were mired up and stuck fast. Almost as if the river knew they were coming and saved up its worst fury till they were already in it and couldn't get away.

"Look out! Look out!" screamed Measure from the shore.

Alvin looked upstream to see what devilment the river had

in mind, and there was a whole tree floating down the river, endwise like a battering ram, the root end pointed at the center of the wagon, straight at the place where Faith was sitting, her baby on the verge of birth. Alvin couldn't think of anything to do, couldn't think at all, just screamed his wife's name with all his strength. Maybe in his heart he thought that by holding her name on his lips he could keep her alive, but there was no hope of that, no hope at all.

Except that Vigor didn't know there was no hope. Vigor leapt out when the tree was no more than a rod away, his body falling against it just above the root. The momentum of his leap turned it a little, then rolled it over, rolled it and turned it away from the wagon. Of course Vigor rolled with it, pulled right under the water—but it worked, the root end of the tree missed the wagon entirely, and the shaft of the trunk struck it a sidewise blow.

The tree bounded across the stream and smashed up against a boulder on the bank. Alvin was five rods off, but in his memory from then on, he always saw it like as if he'd been right there. The tree crashing into the boulder, and Vigor between them. Just a split second that lasted a lifetime, Vigor's eyes wide with surprise, blood already leaping out of his mouth, spattering out onto the tree that killed him. Then the Hatrack River swept the tree out into the current. Vigor slipped under the water, all except his arm, all tangled in the roots, which stuck up into the air for all the world like a neighbor waving good-bye after a visit.

Alvin was so intent on watching his dying son that he didn't even notice what was happening to his own self. The blow from the tree was enough to dislodge the mired wheels, and the current picked up the wagon, carried it downstream, Alvin clinging to the tailgate, Faith weeping inside, Eleanor screaming her lungs out from the driver's seat, and the boys on the bank shouting something. Shouting, "Hold! Hold! Hold!"

The rope held, one end tied to a strong tree, the other end tied to the wagon, it held. The river couldn't tumble the wagon downstream; instead it swung the wagon to shore the way a boy swings a rock on a string, and when it came to a shuddering stop it was right against the bank, the front end facing upstream.

"It held!" cried the boys.

"Thank God!" shouted Eleanor.

"The baby's coming," whispered Faith.

But Alvin, all he could hear was the single faint cry that had been the last sound from the throat of his firstborn son, all he could see was the way his boy clung to the tree as it rolled and rolled in the water, and all he could say was a single word, a single command. "Live," he murmured. Vigor had always obeyed him before. Hard worker, willing companion, more a friend or brother than a son. But this time he knew his son would disobey. Still he whispered it. "Live."

"Are we safe?" said Faith, her voice trembling.

Alvin turned to face her, tried to strike the grief from his face. No sense her knowing the price that Vigor paid to save her and the baby. Time enough to learn of that after the baby was born. "Can you climb out of the wagon?"

"What's wrong?" asked Faith, looking at his face.

"I took a fright. Tree could have killed us. Can you climb out, now that we're up against the bank?"

Eleanor leaned in from the front of the wagon. "David and Calm are on the bank, they can help you up. The rope's holding, Mama, but who can say how long?"

"Go on, Mother, just a step," said Alvin. "We'll do better with the wagon if we know you're safe on shore."

"The baby's coming," said Faith.

"Better on shore than here," said Alvin sharply. "Go *now.*"

Faith stood up, clambered awkwardly to the front. Alvin climbed through the wagon behind her, to help her if she should stumble. Even he could see how her belly had dropped. The baby must be grabbing for air already.

On the bank it wasn't just David and Calm, now. There were strangers, big men, and several horses. Even one small wagon, and that was a welcome sight. Alvin had no notion who these men were, or how they knew to come and help, but there wasn't a moment to waste on introductions. "You men! Is there a midwife in the road house?"

"Goody Guester does with birthing," said a man. A big man, with arms like oxlegs. A blacksmith, surely.

"Can you take my wife in that wagon? There's not a moment to spare." Alvin knew it was a shameful thing, for men to speak so openly of birthing, right in front of the woman who was set to bear. But Faith was no fool—she knew what mattered most, and getting her to a bed and a competent midwife was more important than pussyfooting around about it.

David and Calm were careful as they helped their mother toward the waiting wagon. Faith was staggering with pain. Women in labor shouldn't have to step from a wagon seat up onto a riverbank, that was sure. Eleanor was right behind her, taking charge as if she wasn't younger than all the boys except the twins. "Measure! Get the girls together. They're riding in the wagon with us. You too, Wastenot and Wantnot! I know you can help the big boys but I need you to watch the girls while I'm with Mother." Eleanor was never one to be trifled with, and the gravity of the situation was such that they didn't even call her Eleanor of Aquitaine as they obeyed. Even the little girls mostly gave over their squabbling and got right in.

Eleanor paused a moment on the bank and looked back to where her father stood on the wagon seat. She glanced downstream, then looked back at him. Alvin understood the question, and he shook his head no. Faith was not to know of Vigor's sacrifice. Tears came unwelcome to Alvin's eyes, but not to Eleanor's. Eleanor was only fourteen, but when she didn't want to cry, she didn't cry.

Wastenot hawed the horse and the little wagon lurched forward, Faith wincing as the girls patted her and the rain poured. Faith's gaze was somber as a cow's, and as mindless, looking back at her husband, back at the river. At times like birthing, Alvin thought, a woman becomes a beast, slack-minded as her body takes over and does its work. How else could she bear the pain? As if the soul of the earth possessed her the way it owns the souls of animals, making her part of the life of the whole world, unhitching her from family, from husband, from all the reins of the human race, leading her into the valley of ripeness and harvest and reaping and bloody death.

"She'll be safe now," the blacksmith said. "And we have horses here to pull your wagon out."

"It's slacking off," said Measure. "The rain is less, and the current's not so strong."

"As soon as your wife stepped ashore, it eased up," said the farmer-looking feller. "The rain's dying, that's sure."

"You took the worst of it in the water," said the blacksmith. "But you're all right now. Get hold of yourself, man, there's work to do."

Only then did Alvin come to himself enough to realize that he was crying. Work to do, that's right, get hold of yourself, Alvin Miller. You're no weakling, to bawl like a baby. Other men have lost a dozen children and still live their lives. You've had twelve, and Vigor lived to be a man, though he never did get to marry and have children of his own. Maybe Alvin had to weep because Vigor died so nobly; maybe he cried because it was so sudden.

David touched the blacksmith's arm. "Leave him be for a minute," he said softly. "Our oldest brother was carried off not ten minutes back. He got tangled in a tree floating down."

"It wasn't no *tangle,*" Alvin said sharply. "He jumped that tree and saved our wagon, and your mother inside it! That river paid him back, that's what it did, it punished him."

Calm spoke quietly to the local men. "It run up against that boulder there." They all looked. There was a smear of blood on the rock.

"The Hatrack has a mean streak in it," said the blacksmith, "but I never seen this river so riled up before. I'm sorry about your boy. There's a slow, flat place downstream where he's bound to fetch up. Everything the river catches ends up there. When the storm lets up, we can go down and bring back the—bring him back."

Alvin wiped his eyes on his sleeve, but since his sleeve was soaking wet it didn't do much good. "Give me a minute more and I can pull my weight," said Alvin.

They hitched two more horses and the four beasts had no trouble pulling the wagon out against the much weakened current. By the time the wagon was set to rights again on the road, the sun was even breaking through.

"Wouldn't you know," said the blacksmith. "If you ever don't like the weather hereabouts, you just set a spell, cause it'll change."

"Not this one," said Alvin. "This storm was laid in wait for us."

The blacksmith put an arm across Alvin's shoulder, and spoke real gentle. "No offense, mister, but that's crazy talk."

Alvin shrugged him off. "That storm and that river wanted us."

"Papa," said David, "you're tired and grieving. Best be still till we get to the road house and see how Mama is."

"My baby is a boy," said Papa. "You'll see. He would have been the seventh son of a seventh son."

That got their attention, right enough, that blacksmith and the other men as well. Everybody knew a seventh son had certain gifts, but the seventh son of a seventh son was about as powerful a birth as you could have.

"That makes a difference," said the blacksmith. "He'd have been a born douser, sure, and water hates that." The others nodded sagely.

"The water had its way," said Alvin. "Had its way, and all done. It would've killed Faith and the baby, if it could. But since it couldn't, why, it killed my boy Vigor. And now when the baby comes, he'll be the sixth son, cause I'll only have five living."

"Some says it makes no difference if the first six be alive or not," said a farmer.

Alvin said nothing, but he knew it made all the difference. He had thought this baby would be a miracle child, but the river had taken care of that. If water don't stop you one way, it stops you another. He shouldn't have hoped for a miracle child. The cost was too high. All his eyes could see, all the way home, was Vigor dangling in the grasp of the roots, tumbling through the current like a leaf caught up in a dust devil, with the blood seeping from his mouth to slake the murderous thirst of the Hatrack.

Little Peggy stood in the window, looking out into the storm. She could see all those heartfires, especially one, one so bright it was like the sun when she looked at it. But there was a blackness all around them. No, not even black—a nothingness, like a part of the universe God hadn't finished making, and it swept around those lights as if to tear them from each other, sweep them away, swallow them up. Little Peggy knew what that nothingness was. Those times when her eyes saw the hot yellow heartfires, there were three other colors, too. The rich dark orange of the earth. The thin gray color of the air. And the deep black emptiness of water. It was the water that tore at them now. The river, only she had never seen it so black, so strong, so terrible. The heartfires were so tiny in the night.

"What do you see, child?" asked Oldpappy.

"The river's going to carry them away," said little Peggy.

"I hope not."

Little Peggy began to cry.

"There, child," said Oldpappy. "It ain't always such a grand thing to see afar off like that, is it."

She shook her head.

"But maybe it won't happen as bad as you think."

Just at that moment, she saw one of the heartfires break away and tumble off into the dark. "Oh!" she cried out, reaching as if her hand could snatch the light and put it back. But of course she couldn't. Her vision was long and clear, but her reach was short.

"Are they lost?" asked Oldpappy.

"One," whispered little Peggy.

"Haven't Makepeace and the others got there yet?"

"Just now," she said. "The rope held. They're safe now."

Oldpappy didn't ask her how she knew, or what she saw. Just patted her shoulder. "Because you told them. Remember that, Margaret. One was lost, but if you hadn't seen and sent help, they might all have died."

She shook her head. "I should've seen them sooner, Oldpappy, but I fell asleep."

"And you blame yourself?" asked Oldpappy.

"I should've let Bloody Mary nip me, and then Father wouldn't've been mad, and then I wouldn't've been in the spring house, and then I wouldn't've been asleep, and then I would've sent help in time—"

"We can all make daisy chains of blame like that, Maggie. It don't mean a thing."

But she knew it meant something. You don't blame blind

people 'cause they don't warn you you're about to step on a snake—but you sure blame somebody with eyes who doesn't say a word about it. She knew her duty ever since she first realized that other folks couldn't see all that she could see. God gave her special eyes, so she'd better see and give warning, or the devil would take her soul. The devil or the deep black sea.

"Don't mean a thing," Oldpappy murmured. Then, like he just been poked in the behind with a ramrod, he went all straight and said, "Spring house! Spring house, of course." He pulled her close. "Listen to me, little Peggy. It wasn't none of your fault, and that's the truth. The same water that runs in the Hatrack flows in the spring house brook, it's all the same water, all through the world. The same water that wanted them dead, it knew you could give warning and send help. So it sang to you and sent you off to sleep."

It made a kind of sense to her, it sure did. "How can that be, Oldpappy?"

"Oh, that's just in the nature of it. The whole universe is made of only four kinds of stuff, little Peggy, and each one wants to have its own way." Peggy thought of the four colors that she saw when the heartfires glowed, and she knew what all four were even as Oldpappy named them. "Fire makes things hot and bright and uses them up. Air makes things cool and sneaks in everywhere. Earth makes things solid and sturdy, so they'll last. But water, it tears things down, it falls from the sky and carries off everything it can, carries it off and down to the sea. If the water had its way, the whole world would be smooth, just a big ocean with nothing out of the water's reach. All dead and smooth. That's why you slept. The water wants to tear down these strangers, whoever they are, tear them down and kill them. It's a miracle you woke up at all."

"The blacksmith's hammer woke me," said little Peggy.

"That's it, then, you see? The blacksmith was working with iron, the hardest earth, and with a fierce blast of air from the bellows, and with a fire so hot it burns the grass outside the chimney. The water couldn't touch him to keep him still."

Little Peggy could hardly believe it, but it must be so. The blacksmith had drawn her from a watery sleep. The smith had *helped* her. Why, it was enough to make you laugh, to know the blacksmith was her friend this time.

There was shouting on the porch downstairs, and doors opened and closed. "Some folks is here already," said Oldpappy.

Little Peggy saw the heartfires downstairs, and found the one with the strongest fear and pain. "It's their mama," said little Peggy. "She's got a baby coming."

"Well, if that ain't the luck of it. Lose one, and here already is a baby to replace death with life." Oldpappy shambled on out to go downstairs and help.

Little Peggy, though, she just stood there, looking at what she saw in the distance. That lost heartfire wasn't lost at all, and that was sure. She could see it burning away far off, despite how the darkness of the river tried to cover it. He wasn't dead, just carried off, and maybe somebody could help him. She ran out then, passed Oldpappy all in a rush, clattered down the stairs.

Mama caught her by the arm as she was running into the great room. "There's a birthing," Mama said, "and we need you."

"But Mama, the one that went downriver, he's still alive!"

"Peggy, we got no time for—"

Two boys with the same face pushed their way into the conversation. "The one downriver!" cried one.

"Still alive!" cried another.

"How do you know!"

"He can't be!"

They spoke so all on top of each other that Mama had to hush them up just to hear them. "It was Vigor, our big brother, he got swept away—"

"Well he's alive," said little Peggy, "but the river's got him."

The twins looked to Mama for confirmation. "She know what she's talking about, Goody Guester?"

Mama nodded, and the boys raced for the door, shouting, "He's alive! He's still alive!"

"Are you sure?" asked Mama fiercely. "It's a cruel thing, to put hope in their hearts like that, if it ain't so."

Mama's flashing eyes made little Peggy afraid, and she couldn't think what to say.

By then, though, Oldpappy had come up from behind. "Now Peg," he said, "how would she know one was taken by the river, lessun she saw?"

"I know," said Mama. "But this woman's been holding off birth too long, and I got a care for the baby, so come on now, little Peggy, I need you to tell me what you see."

She led little Peggy into the bedroom off the kitchen, the place where Papa and Mama slept whenever there were visitors. The woman lay on the bed, holding tight to the hand of a tall girl with deep and solemn eyes. Little Peggy didn't know their faces, but she recognized their fires, especially the mother's pain and fear.

"Someone was shouting," whispered the mother.

"Hush now," said Mama.

"About him still alive."

The solemn girl raised her eyebrows, looked at Mama. "Is that so, Goody Guester?"

"My daughter is a torch. That's why I brung her here in this room. To see the baby."

"Did she see my boy? Is he alive?"

"I thought you didn't tell her, Eleanor," said Mama.

The solemn girl shook her head.

"Saw from the wagon. Is he alive?"

"Tell her, Margaret," said Mama.

Little Peggy turned and looked for his heartfire. There were no walls when it came to this kind of seeing. His flame was still there, though she knew it was afar off. This time, though, she drew near in the way she had, took a close look. "He's in the water. He's all tangled in the roots."

"Vigor!" cried the mother on the bed.

"The river wants him. The river says, Die, die."

Mama touched the woman's arm. "The twins have gone off to tell the others. There'll be a search party."

"In the dark!" whispered the woman scornfully.

Little Peggy spoke again. "He's saying a prayer, I think. He's saying—seventh son."

"Seventh son," whispered Eleanor.

"What does that mean?" asked Mama.

"If this baby's a boy," said Eleanor, "and he's born while Vigor's still alive, then he's the seventh son of a seventh son, and all of them alive."

Mama gasped. "No wonder the river—" she said. No need to finish the thought. Instead she took little Peggy's hands and led her to the woman on the bed. "Look at this baby, and see what you see."

Little Peggy had done this before, of course. It was the chief use they had for torches, to have them look at an unborn baby just at the birthing time. Partly to see how it lay in the womb, but also because sometimes a torch could see who the baby was, what it would be, could tell stories of times to come. Even before she touched the woman's belly, she could see the baby's heartfire. It was the one that she had seen before, that burned so hot and bright that it was like the sun and the moon, to compare it to the mother's fire. "It's a boy," she said.

"Then let me bear this baby," said the mother. "Let him breathe while Vigor still breathes!"

"How's the baby set?" asked Mama.

"Just right," said little Peggy.

"Head first? Facedown?"

Little Peggy nodded.

"Then why won't it come?" demanded Mama.

"She's been telling him not to," said Little Peggy, looking at the mother.

"In the wagon," the mother said. "He was coming, and I did a beseeching."

"Well, you should have told me right off," said Mama sharply. "Speck me to help you and you don't even tell me he's got a beseeching on him. You, girl!"

Several young ones were standing near the wall, wide-eyed, and they didn't know which one she meant.

"Any of you, I need that iron key from the ring on the wall."

The biggest of them took it clumsily from the hook and brought it, ring and all. Mama dangled the large ring and the key over the mother's belly, chanting softly.

"Here's the circle, open wide,
Here's the key to get outside,
Earth be iron, flame be fair,
Fall from water into air."

The mother cried out in sudden agony. Mama tossed away the key, cast back the sheet, lifted the woman's knees, and ordered little Peggy fiercely to *see.*

Little Peggy touched the woman's womb. The boy's mind was empty, except for a feeling of pressure and gathering cold as he emerged into the air. But the very emptiness of his mind let her see things that would never be clearly visible again. The billion billion paths of his life lay open before him, waiting for his first choices, for the first changes in the world around him to eliminate a million futures every second. The future was there in everyone, a flickering shadow that was never visible behind the thoughts of the present moment; but here, for a few precious moments, little Peggy could see them clearly.

And what she saw was death down every path. Drowning, drowning, every path of his future led this child to a watery death.

"Why do you hate him so!" cried little Peggy.

"What?" demanded Eleanor.

"Hush," said Mama. "Let her see what she sees."

Inside the unborn child, the dark blot of water that surrounded his heartfire seemed so terribly strong that little Peggy was afraid he would be swallowed up.

"Get him out to breathe!" shouted little Peggy.

Mama reached in, even though it tore the mother something dreadful, and hooked the baby by the neck with strong fingers, drawing him out.

In that moment, the dark water retreated inside the child's mind, and just before the first breath came, little Peggy saw ten million deaths by water disappear. Now, for the first time, there were some paths open, some paths leading to a dazzling future. And all the paths that did not end in early death had one thing in common. On all those paths, little Peggy saw herself doing one simple thing.

So she did that thing. She took her hands from the slackening belly and ducked under her mother's arm. The baby's head had just emerged, and it was still covered with a bloody caul, a scrap of the sac of soft skin in which he had floated in his mother's womb.

His mouth was open, sucking inward on the caul, but it didn't break, and he couldn't breathe.

Little Peggy did what she had seen herself do in the baby's future. She reached out, took the caul from under the baby's chin, and pulled it away from his face. It came whole, in one moist piece, and in the moment it came away, the baby's mouth cleared, he sucked in a great breath, and then gave that mewling cry that birthing mothers hear as the song of life.

Little Peggy folded the caul, her mind still full of the visions she had seen down the pathways of this baby's life. She did not know yet what the visions meant, but they made such clear pictures in her mind that she knew she would never forget them. They made her afraid, because so much would depend on her, and how she used the birth caul that was still warm in her hands.

"A boy," said Mama.

"Is he," whispered the mother. "Seventh son?"

Mama was tying the cord, so she couldn't spare a glance at little Peggy. "Look," she whispered.

Little Peggy looked for the single heartfire on the distant river. "Yes," she said, for the heartfire was still burning.

Even as she watched, it flickered, died.

"Now he's gone," said little Peggy.

The woman on the bed wept bitterly, her birth-wracked body shuddering.

"Grieving at the baby's birth," said Mama. "It's a dreadful thing."

"Hush," whispered Eleanor to her mother. "Be joyous, or it'll darken the baby all his life!"

"Vigor," murmured the woman.

"Better nothing at all than tears," said Mama. She held out the crying baby, and Eleanor took it in competent arms—she had cradled many a babe before, it was plain. Mama went to the table in the corner and took the scarf that had been blacked in the wool, so it was night-colored clear through. She dragged it slowly across the weeping woman's face, saying, "Sleep, Mother, sleep."

When the cloth came away, the weeping was done, and the woman slept, her strength spent.

"Take the baby from the room," said Mama.

"Don't he need to start his sucking?" asked Eleanor.

"She'll never nurse this babe," said Mama. "Not unless you want him to suck hate."

"She can't hate him," said Eleanor. "It ain't his fault."

"I reckon her milk don't know that," said Mama. "That right, little Peggy? What teat did the baby suck?"

"His mama's," said little Peggy.

Mama looked sharp at her. "You sure of that?"

She nodded.

"Well, then, we'll bring the baby in when she wakes up. He doesn't need to eat anything for the first night, anyway." So Eleanor carried the baby out into the great room, where the fire burned to dry the men, who stopped trading stories about rains and floods worse than this one long enough to look at the baby and admire.

Inside the room, though, Mama took little Peggy by the chin and stared hard into her eyes. "You tell me the truth, Margaret. It's a serious thing, for a baby to suck on its mama and drink up hate."

"She won't hate him, Mama," said little Peggy.

"What did you see?"

Little Peggy would have answered, but she didn't know the words to tell most of the things she saw. So she looked at the floor. She could tell from Mama's quick draw of breath that she was ripe for a tongue-lashing. But Mama waited, and then her hand came soft, stroking across little Peggy's cheek. "Ah, child, what a day you've had. The baby might have died, except you told me to pull it out. You even reached in and opened up its mouth—that's what you did, isn't it?"

Little Peggy nodded.

"Enough for a little girl, enough for one day." Mama turned to the other girls, the ones in wet dresses, leaning against the wall. "And you, too, you've had enough of a day. Come out of here, let your mama sleep, come out and get dry by the fire. I'll start a supper for you, I will."

But Oldpappy was already in the kitchen, fussing around, and refused to hear of Mama doing a thing. Soon enough she was out with the baby, shooing the men away so she could rock it to sleep, letting it suck her finger.

Little Peggy figured after a while that she wouldn't be missed, and so she snuck up the stairs to the attic ladder, and up the ladder into the lightless, musty space. The spiders didn't bother her much, and the cats mostly kept the mice away, so she wasn't afraid. She crawled right to her secret hiding place and took out the carven box that Oldpappy had given her, the one he said his own papa brought from Ulster when he came to the colonies. It was full of the precious scraps of childhood—stones, strings, buttons—but now she knew that these were nothing compared to the work before her all the rest of her life. She dumped them right out, and blew into the box to clear away dust. Then she laid the folded caul inside and closed the lid.

She knew that in the future she would open that box a dozen times. That it would call to her, wake her from her sleep, tear her from her friends, and steal from her all her dreams. All because a baby boy downstairs had no future at all, except a death from the dark water, excepting if she used that caul to keep him safe, the way it once protected him in the womb.

For a moment she was angry, to have her own life so changed. Worse than the blacksmith coming, it was, worse than Papa and the hazel wand he whupped her with, worse than Mama when her eyes were angry. Everything would be different forever and it wasn't fair. Just for a baby she never invited, never asked to come here, what did she care about any old baby?

She reached out and opened the box, planning to take the

caul and cast it into a dark corner of the attic. But even in the darkness, she could see a place where it was darker still: near her heartfire, where the emptiness of the deep black river was all set to make a murderer out of her.

Not me, she said to the water. You ain't part of me.

Yes I am, whispered the water. I'm all through you, and you'd dry up and die without me.

You ain't the boss of me, anyway, she retorted.

She closed the lid on the box and skidded her way down the ladder. Papa always said that she'd get splinters in her butt doing that. This time he was right. It stung something fierce, so she walked kind of sideways into the kitchen where Oldpappy was. Sure enough, he stopped his cooking long enough to pry the splinters out.

"My eyes ain't sharp enough for this, Maggie," he complained.

"You got the eyes of an eagle. Papa says so."

Oldpappy chuckled. "Does he now."

"What's for dinner?"

"Oh, you'll like this dinner, Maggie."

Little Peggy wrinkled up her nose. "Smells like chicken."

"That's right."

"I don't like chicken soup."

"Not just soup, Maggie. This one's a-roasting, except the neck and wings."

"I hate *roast* chicken, too."

"Does your Oldpappy ever lie to you?"

"Nope."

"Then you best believe me when I tell you this is one chicken dinner that'll make you *glad*. Can't you think of any way that a partickler chicken dinner could make you glad?"

Little Peggy thought and thought, and then she smiled. "Bloody Mary?"

Oldpappy winked. "I always said that was a hen born to make gravy."

Little Peggy hugged him so tight that he made choking sounds, and then they laughed and laughed.

Later that night, long after little Peggy was in bed, they brought Vigor's body home, and Papa and Makepeace set to making a box for him. Alvin Miller hardly looked alive, even when Eleanor showed him the baby. Until she said, "That torch girl. She says that this baby is the seventh son of a seventh son."

Alvin looked around for someone to tell him if it was true.

"Oh, you can trust her," said Mama.

Tears came fresh to Alvin's eyes. "That boy hung on," he said. "There in the water, he hung on long enough."

"He knowed what store you set by that," said Eleanor.

Then Alvin reached for the baby, held him tight, looked down into his eyes. "Nobody named him yet, did they?" he asked.

"Course not," said Eleanor. "Mama named all the other boys, but you always said the seventh son'd have—"

"My own name. Alvin. Seventh son of a seventh son, with the same name as his father. Alvin Junior." He looked around him, then turned to face toward the river, way off in the nighttime forest. "Hear that, you Hatrack River? His name is Alvin, and you didn't kill him after all."

Soon they brought in the box, and laid out Vigor's body with candles, to stand for the fire of life that had left him. Alvin held up the baby, over the coffin. "Look on your brother," he whispered to the infant.

"That baby can't see nothing yet, Papa," said David.

"That ain't so, David," said Alvin. "He don't *know* what he's seeing, but his eyes can see. And when he gets old enough to hear the story of his birth, I'm going to tell him that his own eyes saw his brother Vigor, who gave his life for this baby's sake."

It was two weeks before Faith was well enough to travel. But Alvin saw to it that he and his boys worked hard for their keep. They cleared a good spot of land, chopped the winter's firewood, set some charcoal heaps for Makepeace Smith, and widened the road. They also felled four big trees and made a strong bridge across the Hatrack River, a covered bridge so that even in a rainstorm people could cross that river without a drop of water touching them.

Vigor's grave was the third one there, beside little Peggy's two dead sisters. The family paid respects and prayed there on the morning that they left. Then they got in their wagon and rode off westward, "But we leave a part of ourselves here always," said Faith, and Alvin nodded.

Little Peggy watched them go, then ran up into the attic, opened the box, and held little Alvin's caul in her hand. No danger, for now at least. Safe for now. She put the caul away and closed the lid. You better be something, baby Alvin, she said, or else you caused a powerful lot of trouble for nothing.